Praise for the novels of Sara Ackerman

"*The Lieutenant's Nurse* illuminates the attack on Pearl Harbor with a riveting drama told from a unique perspective. Sara Ackerman brings a time and place to vivid life, putting a human and heroic face on events that changed history. I savored every page!"
—Susan Wiggs, #1 *New York Times* bestselling author

"Set against the backdrop of the attack on Pearl Harbor, *The Lieutenant's Nurse* is an emotional and heartfelt tale of love and courage. Depicting a dramatic period in history, Ackerman's richly detailed and evocative writing transports the reader, bringing Hawaii to life."
—Chanel Cleeton, *USA TODAY* bestselling author of *Next Year in Havana*

"With the wit and richness of a Beatriz Williams novel, *The Lieutenant's Nurse* weaves a tale of love and courage. Bittersweet and suspenseful, it offers readers a firsthand, female perspective of the harrowing days surrounding Pearl Harbor, honoring both the complexities of war and resilience of the human spirit."
—Amanda Skenandore, author of *Between Earth and Sky*

"Ackerman writes about WWII Hawaii with vivid detail, wit, and a sense of place evocative of Kristin Hannah. She re-examines history with a nuanced and immersive narrative that is impossible to put down. Simply put, *The Lieutenant's Nurse* is a fantastic and enthralling read."
—Emily Strelow, author of *The Wild Birds*

"A dramatic saga of motherhood, loss and the possibility of renewal.... With a sensitive touch and an instinct for authenticity, Ackerman depicts the fraught nature of wartime relationships...[and] mixes romance, suspense and history into a bittersweet story of cinematic proportions."
—*BookPage* on *Island of Sweet Pies and Soldiers*

"A close-up look at how wart[................................]p of women living on Hawaii in 1[..................................]t.... [Violet's] journey overcoming [....................................]lship, family, and romance is a story[.............................]
—[.............................] *Soldiers*

"Strong female friendships and an unusual World War II home front setting add to this debut novel's appeal for historical fiction fans."
—*Library Journal* on *Island of Sweet Pies and Soldiers*

Also by Sara Ackerman

Island of Sweet Pies and Soldiers

Look for Sara Ackerman's next novel
available soon from MIRA Books.

SARA ACKERMAN

THE
LIEUTENANT'S
NURSE

mira

mira

Recycling programs for this product may not exist in your area.

ISBN-13: 978-0-7783-0791-4

The Lieutenant's Nurse

Copyright © 2019 by Sara Ackerman

For questions and comments about the quality of this book, please contact us at CustomerService@Harlequin.com.

BookClubbish.com

Printed in U.S.A.

This book is for my father, Douglas Ackerman

A swimmer with feet like fins, a craftsman of the highest order,
a surfer, a gifted cookie maker, an architect and an early pioneer
of the tiny house, a rebel, a naturalist, a hiker of tall mountains,
a comedian, a rascal, a skilled *palapa* builder, a musician, a traveler,
a birdhouse maker, a pancake and waffle magician, a hopeless
romantic, a visionary, an adventurer, a true child of Hawaii
and a beloved friend to so many, myself included.
He was and always will be my biggest fan.

THE
LIEUTENANT'S
NURSE

In war, truth is the first casualty.

—AESCHYLUS

A PECULIAR MESSAGE

November 22

Achtung! Warning! *Alerte!* We hope you'll never have to spend a long winter's night in an air-raid shelter, but we were just thinking...it's only common sense to be prepared. If you're not too busy between now and Christmas, why not sit down and plan a list of the things you'll want to have on hand...and though it's no time, really, to be thinking of what's fashionable we bet that most of your friends will remember to include those intriguing dice and chips which make Chicago's favorite game: THE DEADLY DOUBLE.

—MYSTERIOUS ADVERTISEMENT IN THE *NEW YORKER* MAGAZINE, TWO WEEKS BEFORE THE AIR RAID ON PEARL HARBOR.

BANZAI!

November 26

The men understand nothing. The leaves have changed from green to red and the wind has turned icy. Something big is afoot and they are told there is a good chance they will not be coming back. They are given warm winter clothing for the journey. The sky is dark, the sun still below the horizon. The ships *Akagi, Kaga, Shōkaku, Zuikaku, Hiryū* and *Sōryū* lead the way, battering through the whitecaps and wild seas. Anticipation is something they can taste on the wind. Once they leave the Kurile Islands, north of Japan, the fleet will head north, into the vast and blue Pacific. Strict radio silence is ordered. *Banzai!* they shout as they say goodbye to their homeland.

No one knows how this will end.

ROUGH SEAS

November 28

The sea was dark green and angry, not the lazy blue that her imagination had conjured up. Eva was well versed in lakes, but here in San Francisco, the air was thick with salt and the tang of dead fish. Toward the horizon, storm clouds blacked out the sky. She wrapped her scarf tighter around her neck as wind whipped her hair in every direction. Cold lodged into her bones, as she had little extra padding to keep her warm. Nevertheless, people crammed all along the edges of the ship, throwing serpentine and waving madly at the crowd along the pier.

After the ship had let out two long horn blasts, guests began to file off, stuffed full after the bon voyage festivities. She had meandered around before departure, watching pounds of cheese balls, pigs in a blanket and pâté disappear into people's mouths, and startling at champagne corks being fired off. As she had stood off to the side gaping at the decadence, one of the stewards proudly told her that it was not unusual to go through five hundred bottles on sailing day.

"Good Lord!" she'd said.

Eva had had champagne all of once in her life—the day she'd graduated from nursing school.

She leaned against the cold steel railing, overcome with the realization that she was leaving the continent for a tiny speck of an island thousands of miles away. She searched the throngs of people for any familiar faces, and was thankful to see none. A tall figure pushing against the debarking guests on the gangplank caught her eye. Dressed in a blue service uniform, the man stood out not only because of his height, but the look on his face. While everyone else was gay and merry, his jaw was clenched and his expression set in stone. What would he have to worry about? Eva tried to keep abreast of news and knew that tensions were rising around the world, but being stationed on a tiny island in the Pacific would certainly have its perks. Being in a whole separate hemisphere from the Germans and their U-boats, for one. But also isolated by thousands of miles of ocean and protected by much of the Pacific Fleet. Eva tried to look away, but her gaze was fixed on the powerful way he moved. Something about being in uniform, too, gave him an air of gravity. There weren't too many soldiers in the backwoods of Michigan. The man ducked onto the ship and then he was gone.

Couples and families and an athletic team of boisterous young men grouped around her. Most everybody was attached to someone else, and she wished Ruby could be here with her. This was just the kind of thing her younger sister would have loved, obsessed as she was with fashion and the latest trends. Ruby never met a piece of material she didn't want to nip and tuck and whip into some unique article of clothing. Her sister was the one meant to be in San Francisco or New York or traveling the globe. *You left her,* said a gnawing voice inside. But she'd had no choice. As soon as she settled in her room, she would write her a postcard.

In the colorful brochures, Eva had noted how well dressed the passengers were. But nothing could have prepared her for the real thing. These women seemed another breed altogether. Pencil-thin skirts and blazers, with rows of pearls around their necks and corsages made from gardenias and baby's breath pinned to their lapels. Hair twisted and piled and coiffed into updos. Eva owned exactly two fancy dresses and she was saving those for dinners, and her hair, which she had gone through the effort to pin curl set, was quickly blowing out.

After another fifteen minutes, three long blasts of the horn sounded, the massive anchor pulled up and Matson's grandest luxury liner, the *Lurline*, backed away. Four o'clock sharp. The amount of black smoke pouring from the two stacks on board was enough to require a gas mask. No one had mentioned *that* in the brochure. She moved upwind as best she could. People ran alongside the ship as though not quite ready to say goodbye. Even though she didn't know anyone, Eva waved a dingy white handkerchief to the crowd below.

She had been imagining this moment for so long, and now that it was finally here, she felt a tightening in her chest. Hawaii was about as far away as you could get from Michigan, which was precisely why she had joined the Army Nurse Corps. But not long after she'd made her decision to go, Ruby had come down with fever, headache, back pain. And then the paralysis. The fear was something she had no defense against. *Polio*. A word that ruined lives. Ruby had been admitted to the hospital the next day, and Eva departed two weeks later, feeling like she'd been split in two. Ruby had stabilized, but whether she would walk again still remained to be seen.

It was easy to get caught up in the guilt, but Eva ordered herself to enjoy the journey as best she could. Focus on what lay ahead. Warm lagoons and coconut trees. A fresh start, where no one knew who she was. And of course, Billy would meet her at the dock. It had been so long since she'd seen him, half of her felt weak-kneed at the thought, and the other was worried that he wasn't the same Billy she had fallen for. His last few letters had been brief and businesslike, not his usual pressed flowers and professions of love.

If anyone was concerned at all about the storm they would soon be sailing into, it didn't show. This was not the California she had been promised—sunny skies and smooth water. Instead, fog obscured much of the Golden Gate Bridge as they passed underneath. They weren't even in the open seas yet and the ship swayed from side to side.

Pretty soon, raindrops began to fall and people took cover on the long side deck. Eva found an empty chair and sat back, watching the city grow smaller and smaller and disappear in the clouds. *Goodbye, America.*

A steward came around offering warm tea, which she gladly accepted.

"Will the weather be worsening?" she asked, thinking about all the ship skeletons at the bottoms of the Great Lakes.

"Hard to tell, but not to worry. This ship could sail right through a hurricane with barely a wobble."

"So we won't have to worry about seasickness?" she asked.

He laughed. "I wish I could say that was the case. You never know who will be immune and who won't. But most people gain their sea legs in a day or two."

She sipped her tea and watched a toddler in a ruffled dress zigzagging across the deck like a drunk sailor. The mother had a glass of champagne in one hand and a teddy bear in the other. On the chairs next to her, some of the college athletic team were huddled up under blankets. Tall, gangly boys on the cusp of manhood. From their chatter, she found out they were football players from Oregon and California off on a trip to play the University of Hawaii. Eva caught herself staring. She hadn't been to a football game in ages. Not since summertime, when life was still moving in a whole different direction.

With no chance for a sunset and night falling early, she made her way back to her stateroom on D deck—"Dog Deck," as it was called—passing by many folks who looked green in the face. At several points along the way, she commanded herself to breathe and keep an eye on the horizon. But that became difficult once inside the walls and heading downstairs. The stale air didn't help. When she opened the door to her room, there was a woman curled on the second bed, groaning.

"Heavens, are you all right?" Eva asked, rushing to her side.

"Do you think they could turn around? I need to get off immediately."

Eva fought back a laugh. "Not likely, but they say by morning, the sickness usually wears off." The trash can was pulled up next to the bed. She did her best not to look inside, as though seasickness might be contagious. "I'm Eva. What's your name?"

A long pause. "Jo." It came out like *ruff*, almost like a dog's bark.

Jo was man-size, with wrists the size of tree branches and a dockworker's shoulders. To lift her would be impossible, and Eva hoped for a fast recovery. Assessing people based on how hard they'd be to move was a built-in habit, formed after years helping her father set a broken leg or turn over an invalid with bedsores. Being small, she'd made up for it with ingenuity and leverage.

Eva set a glass of water on the bedside table. "I'm going to get set up here, but let me know if you need anything. I'm a nurse," she said, as if that mattered right now.

Jo moaned.

The windowless room was small but not cramped, with enough room for two twin beds and two small bureaus. An ornate gold mirror with lamps, and a blue patterned rug made for lovely accents. She peeked into the bathroom, which was shared with another cabin, and admired the black-and-white tile floor and porcelain tub. Even cabin class on the *Lurline* was fancier than what she was accustomed to.

While she unpacked, the ship's swaying seemed to grow even more pronounced. On the bureau, she noticed her dining assignment card: Eva Cassidy, Second Seating in the Waikiki Dining Room. It was going to take a while to adjust to a new last name. Jo Holstad was meant to be seated next to her. That would not likely happen.

All of Eva's clothes fit nicely in the drawers, and she hung her two dresses. She also set a small framed photograph of Ruby—holding an armful of ducklings and smiling as though she had just won the lottery—on a built-in shelf next to her bed. She hurried to freshen up and get topside into the open air, regardless of her seating time. She would sit on the deck and wait if she had to, this time armed with a warm sweater and a blanket.

"Do you want to come up for dinner? Fresh air would do wonders for you," Eva said, already knowing the answer.

"I'm going to die on this ship, one way or another," Jo said.

"Oh, nonsense, you just feel that way now."

The poor woman did look about as miserable as one could be. Perspiration matted her hair to her forehead and her mouth hung slack with a stripe of dried spit off to the side. Suddenly, the ship listed sharply and Ruby's picture, a comb and a perfume bottle flew onto the floor. Eva steadied herself against the wall.

"See? We should have never set sail," Jo said.

Eva had to admit that all this rocking was unnerving. "I trust they know what they're doing. If it were dangerous, we would have waited a few days."

Jo looked up at her with big brown eyes. "I sure as hell hope so."

★ ★ ★

Up top, Eva was almost thankful for the darkness. Probably better not to see the fury of the seas. The whole upper section of the ship had turned into a ghost town, and she strolled around to stretch out her legs. Surely she was not the only person immune to seasickness. At the edge of the main deck, frigid rain blasted in, so she turned around and explored the areas that she had missed earlier due to her late arrival.

She found several men playing cards in the smoking room. She poked her head in, but wasn't fond of smoke and moved on. Down the hall, she came across an empty ballroom with polished wooden floors and a gilded ceiling. There was also a main lounge decorated with palm-print fabric, a library with wall-to-wall books, an elegant bar room, and a writing room complete with dainty tables and big leather chairs. The *Lurline* was a floating palace, but it felt eerie without many people to fill the space.

Every so often the ship would list or plunge and Eva had to reach out to steady herself. Perhaps she should have worn sandals instead of heels, but she had wanted to make a good first impression. In the dining room, there were only two tables with people—out of seven-hundred-odd passengers. One was full, seated with a mixture of men and women; the other was half-full of men only. All eyes were on her when she entered the room. Should she wave? Say something? Her cheeks burned. She would have turned around and left, but felt silly, so she kept on going, reading the table numbers along the way. She found hers halfway across the room. It would be an awkward dinner at best, dining alone.

"Miss," one of the men called. "Why don't you join us? We have plenty of seats."

When she neared the table, she realized it was the captain

himself who had invited her over. "It would be a lovely honor to sit with you, sir," she said.

An older man stood and pulled out a chair. "Please," he said.

"Thank you, this may not be my seating time, but since everyone else is under, I thought I would check."

"This may be it for the night—count yourself among the fortunate few," the man said.

Captain Brinck, two seats away, leaned over and winked. "Charles Darwin once said, if it weren't for seasickness, the whole world would be sailors."

She laughed. "This is my first time on the ocean, so I'm not sure why I'm spared."

"Heredity—or luck," said the man next to her. "I'm Dr. John Wallace, by the way."

She tensed. Just her luck to have a doctor at the table, but his name was unfamiliar to her and she was certain she had never seen his face before.

"Eva...Cassidy. Pleased to meet you." She caught herself just in time.

The other men introduced themselves. Two were army, Mr. Balder ran a sugarcane plantation, Tommy Woods worked in hotels, and the last, a man called Ogden, told her he was headed to Australia to find a wife as his eyes dropped down to her chest. She made a mental note to stay away from that one.

Eva was impressed at how well the dishes stayed in place despite the motion. "Isn't it risky to have the glassware out?"

"It's heavier than the usual stuff, but there is always the chance in seas like these," Captain Brinck said.

"When will it calm?" she asked.

"In another day or two, it should improve. November tends to be this way. When we near Hawaii, it'll be much warmer, but the seas can still be huge."

"Well, my poor roommate looks half-dead. I worry about her," she said.

He shrugged. "I sure wish I had a say in the weather."

In the center of the table, plates were heaped with lobster tails, steak, French-fried potatoes, glazed carrots and peas. There were also various food items she couldn't identify. Back at home, they stuck to simple. It was all they could afford.

The men continued their conversations about the war in Europe and the recent sinking of a British battleship by a U-boat. One of her nurse friends had recently left for England and had been terrified to bits of crossing the Atlantic.

A deep voice behind her said, "My table is empty over there. Mind if I join you?"

She spun to see the navy man she'd seen on the gangplank. Up close, and from this vantage point, he looked seven feet tall.

"Please," everyone said.

The man seemed to be deciding between the two empty seats at the table. Eva was sure he was going to choose the one away from her, which was fine, because she wanted to learn more about Dr. Wallace, but he sat next to her. He was still in uniform and smelled faintly of Old Spice.

"Lieutenant Clark Spencer," he said to the group, and then to her, "Impressive to see a lady out and about in these seas."

"Dr. Wallace here blames it on luck," she said.

His stony face softened. "If that's the case, I hope some of it rubs off on me, on all of us, Miss…"

"Cassidy. Eva." She was getting better at the name thing.

He looked vaguely familiar, and for a moment she wondered if they had met before. But there was nothing vague about him. Intensity lifted off him in waves. With wavy brown hair and a dark five o'clock shadow, the lieutenant had the build of a football player with a baritone voice. She suddenly felt self-conscious, which was ridiculous because she had a man waiting in Honolulu.

The plantation manager spoke up. "You stationed at Pearl?"

"More or less," the lieutenant said.

"What's the latest with the Japs?"

Eva had never seen an actual Japanese person, but she'd heard that Hawaii was full of them. She also knew that *Jap* was not a friendly term, especially now with tense relations and whispers of war. In fact, her state representative back home had gone as far as suggesting that ten thousand Japanese in Hawaii be held hostage to make sure Japan didn't do anything rash. It seemed extreme and rather un-American, but what did she know?

"I'm not at liberty to say much, other than what you hear in the press. And if you've been keeping track of that, you know negotiations are questionable with Tokyo."

The captain lowered his voice. "Just between us, those submarines of theirs make me nervous. I heard they got a bunch from the Germans."

Eva sat up. "Submarines where?"

"In the ocean," Ogden said with a smug look on his face.

She shot him a glance. "No doubt, but where in the ocean?"

One of the army men said, "Rest assured the Japanese would never bother with Hawaii or the US mainland. They know they'd be crushed."

Being tucked away in Michigan, all war talk had seemed so remote. About distant lands and faraway oceans, involving nameless people who had no bearing on her own life. Here, she felt like she was in the front row, listening to people who knew what was happening from experience. It both frightened and exhilarated her.

Eva looked to Lieutenant Spencer for reassurance. "Is that true?"

He stiffened. "The Japanese are proud and complicated people," was all he said.

"And?"

"And no comment."

She felt shortchanged. But he seemed like the kind of man who couldn't be budged once he'd made up his mind. Like her father's mule, who had an uncanny ability to turn into a statue when he wasn't in the mood to work. But the result was that Eva wanted to know even more.

Lieutenant Spencer turned his attention to his plate. So much food she had never seen in her life, and after a week on the train with little physical activity, her body felt sluggish. Not only that, but the past two months of nerves and worry had whittled her away to half her normal size, so much so that Mr. Lingle at the drugstore hadn't even recognized her the last time she'd gone in. Her appetite hadn't returned, but she piled her plate with carrots and peas and rice anyway. Might as well taste what was supposedly a diet staple in Hawaii. The men continued debating what the Japanese had up their sleeves, which was strange because all along, she'd been far more concerned about the Germans. You could tell just by looking at pictures of Adolph Hitler that the man was evil.

"So, Dr. Wallace, what takes you to Hawaii?" she asked.

"I'll be giving a course on traumatic surgery at Queen's Hospital."

"Sounds fascinating."

He chuckled. "Not the reaction I get from most women. A brutal but necessary field."

Eva hesitated opening herself up for questioning, but figured she might as well practice. "I'm a nurse, and my father was a doctor, so I have reason to be interested."

Wallace cocked his head to the side and looked down his beak-like nose at her very seriously. She braced herself, and was surprised when he said, "My best anesthetist in France was a woman. Agnes Brodie. God knows we need more women in the field."

"Why, thank you, sir. I wish everyone felt that way."

He swirled the ice in his glass. "Sharp as my best scalpel, she was. And able to keep her wits with bombs whistling and exploding around us. I just pray your skills won't be needed for anything other than peacetime affairs."

"I've committed to a year at Tripler, so we'll see what happens after that."

Ogden cleared his throat and piped up. "I'd still take a man over a woman doc any day. Women are meant to wear dresses, not pants."

Eva was well versed in doctors with this same sentiment, and it still drove her crazy. She had the molten urge to stick her finger in his chest and tell him to kindly find the gangplank, but she knew better than to engage. Instead, she asked, "And what is your profession, Mr. Ogden?"

"Businessman, ma'am."

"What sort of business?"

The table had grown quiet around them.

"A little of this and a little of that. And, anyway, what I do is not relevant to this conversation. We were talking about medicine."

Lieutenant Spencer was suddenly paying attention. "Is this a big convention of docs in Hawaii?" he asked Wallace.

Eva was relieved for the distraction and turned her attention to the doctor.

"From all over. Civilian and military. The US is gearing up for something big out there in the Pacific, you can be sure of that, but where and when, who knows," Wallace said.

She was going to have to get herself invited to the lecture, though with hundreds of doctors, there was a chance she would run into someone who recognized her.

Lieutenant Spencer lowered his voice. "It may happen sooner than later, keep that in mind."

"Say, what exactly is your role in the navy, Lieutenant?" she asked, unsettled by his words.

"Communications," he said curtly.

Wallace raised an eyebrow.

"What sort of communications?" Eva said.

Lieutenant Spencer paused a beat too long and Wallace answered for him. "The kind we don't talk about, I'm guessing."

The man seemed more reserved than the other servicemen at the table, as though cut from a different cloth. The way his hair was slightly longer, his suit less stiff. Eva was new to the army, having signed on less than a month ago. For someone not accustomed to the military, all the ranks and unique lingo baffled her. She was still trying to figure out the difference between a lieutenant and a sergeant and a captain. As a nurse, she was considered a second lieutenant. *Lieutenant Cassidy.* That would take some getting used to.

"I'm a linguist. We'll leave it at that," Lieutenant Spencer said.

"You speak German?" she asked.

"Japanese."

"How does a fella like you end up speaking Japanese?" she wanted to know.

Suddenly, the bow of the ship climbed, and Eva's chair felt like it might tilt over backward. Lieutenant Spencer's arm shot out behind her, his hand twice the size of her scapula. A small surge of nausea threatened but she willed her stomach to behave. Unattended glasses rolled around and several crashed to the ground. A moment later, it felt like the bottom of the ocean had pulled away from under them and the enormous ship plunged. She checked Captain Brinck's face for signs of concern; it was pinched into a grimace, but she couldn't be sure if it was for the plate of lobster in danger of sliding off the table, or for the *Lurline* herself.

A moment later, he wiped his chin with a napkin and excused himself. "No cause for concern. I've seen worse, but I should probably get going back to the bridge."

Wallace turned to her. "At least we don't have icebergs to worry about out here."

"You can steer around an iceberg. I'm not sure about a hurricane," she said, feeling slightly panicky.

On the train ride to San Francisco, as they traversed the country, the Pacific Ocean had been big on her mind, and putting as much distance between her and Michigan as possible. She had pictured herself lounging on a deck chair, soaking in the warmth and admiring the blue waters and sunshine. Bellboys would be delivering pineapple juice when the sun grew too hot. Whales would be spouting. All of it would help erase the nightmare of the past months. And maybe along the way, her appetite would return.

Another rise and fall, and the plates all slid a few inches one way and then another. This had not been in her plans.

Her stomach swirled and she decided to call it a night. "I think I'll head to my room now. Good night, gentlemen." She nodded to Wallace and smiled at Lieutenant Spencer, who saluted her.

"Ma'am," he said.

She moved away unsteadily, hoping to God she could sleep in these conditions. But what did it matter if the ship ended up going down.

MOSCOW MULES

On the way out the door, it felt as though Eva was walking downhill, then by the time she passed the ballroom, uphill. If only she could go out on deck and watch the horizon to help gain her bearings. Sleeping in these conditions would be a challenge. Sleep in general was a challenge. And then there was Jo and her wretched state. Perhaps Eva should find some soda to bring back to their cabin. Instead of passing by the bar, she stepped inside.

The dark paneled room was empty but for two men tucked away in a leathery booth. A wall full of bottles looked like an accident waiting to happen. On closer inspection, she saw a small wire strapping them in place. She approached and sat down, hoping the bartender would appear soon. Sitting at a fancy bar by herself was not her usual custom and she felt very out of her league. She waited a few more minutes and was about to leave when the bartender returned with a crate full of limes.

He set a floral coaster on the polished wood in front of her. "What can I get you, ma'am?"

She was about to ask for a can of soda water when someone interrupted. "How about a Moscow mule, and one for me, too," a deep voice next to her said.

Eva nearly choked when she saw who it was and gave thanks for the dim lighting, or Lieutenant Spencer might have seen the blush spreading across her cheeks.

"A Moscow mule?" she said. Where did people come up with these names?

"Something to settle the stomach, with a little kick." He grinned like he knew a secret and if she were lucky, he just might share it with her.

"Mind if I join you?" he asked somewhat tentatively.

Under normal circumstances, having a drink alone with a naval officer might be seen as improper, but these were not normal circumstances. Life had been flipped on its side, and she no longer knew where home was. Still, she almost declined. But his smile was so earnest and real, with a one-sided dimple that she couldn't refuse. Plus, the bartender was already pouring and mixing.

"I get the feeling you won't take no for an answer," she said.

He laughed. When sitting down, he put enough space between them that another person might have been able to squeeze in. She suddenly noticed he wore a wedding band, and yet something about him had given her the impression he wasn't married. Maybe it was how she had caught him watching her throughout dinner, or the swagger in his walk that said, *Hey, look at me.* But it worked out perfectly that he was married; that way things wouldn't get awkward between them.

Why was she even paying attention to these details? Habit, she told herself. Being twenty-four and unwed sometimes made her feel like an old crone, and she was a keen observer of other folks around her and their status. Billy wanted to marry; he had made that much clear. But with the recent turn of events and her sudden enlistment in the army, marriage was the farthest thing from her mind. Nor were army nurses allowed to marry. So that solved that for the time being.

"So why were you back in America, Lieutenant?" she said.

"Call me Clark, ma'am."

Despite his easy smile, he was fiddling with his napkin.

"If you don't call me ma'am, I won't call you lieutenant, how's that?"

He nodded. "Deal. Eva. And I was on a brief work trip. Nothing too exciting."

"Eva" came out with a light Southern twang.

"Where are you originally from, Clark?" she asked.

"How about you tell me? Can't you guess from my accent?"

She felt like she was being tested. "Give me a few minutes, then, and I will."

He reminded Eva of her father, who was always requiring her to answer her own questions and solve her own problems. *Questions can more often than not be answered by the mind asking them*, he liked to say. In his opinion, much of the world's failures were due to people not paying attention and to simple lack of imagination.

The bartender set down two copper mugs with lime slices on the sides. The pungent smell of ginger wafted up. It made perfect sense to use it for seasickness. Anytime she and her father visited patients with stomach ailments, ginger ale and soda crackers were their initial treatment.

Clark raised his mug. "To fair winds and following seas… and new acquaintances."

"To all that, cheers," she said, clinking her mug with his.

She watched him take a gulp, his eyes widening. "Phew, our buddy here at the bar has a heavy hand."

The first sip burned her nostrils and she tried to remain ladylike while her whole mouth puckered. "What *is* this? It tastes like firewater."

"Vodka, ginger brew and lime."

He held his *i* in *lime*. Not thick enough for Georgia or

Mississippi. Maybe the Carolinas. She wanted to get him talking to be sure.

"So again, how did you learn to speak Japanese?" she asked.

"I spent some years in Tokyo."

"Well, that's different. Was this through the navy?"

"Yes, ma'am."

She held her nose and took another sip, ignoring his continued use of *ma'am*.

"They sent a handful of us boys over to learn Japanese. They figured it couldn't hurt to be able to communicate. Whether they are our friends or enemies, we need people who know the language. My boss was one of the first there. He has a story about a bunch of Japanese seamen visiting San Francisco, and he and a few guys had the honor of showing them around. It turned out they spoke perfect English, and some of them French, too. But none of the Americans knew a lick of Japanese. A few years down the line, he and another guy were sent off. We went later."

We.

"What was it like?" she said.

"Hot as the devil in the summer, I'll tell you that. And Tokyo is crowded. But the mountains are about as beautiful as can be. I stayed in a place called Karuizawa, which is an active volcano. The hills are green and rolling, with waterfalls and views of snowy peaks. I fell in love with it, actually. The people, too. At least some of them."

"I've never met one," she said, feeling the alcohol go straight to her head.

"One what?"

"A Japanese person."

A wide grin spread across his face and he chuckled. "Like I said earlier, the ones I knew were hardworking and orderly and efficient and generous. Once you had their trust, they'd give you the shirt off their own backs. For them, honor was everything."

"How long did it take you to learn?"

"We were lucky. We had the best teacher over there. He didn't waste time with textbooks, but took us to see American silent films with an interpreter telling us what was going on. He was a genius and within a few months we were conversing. It took a lot longer to learn to read and write. But that was all we did there. Learn."

It all sounded so exotic and daring. And he brushed it off as though it was nothing, but she had a hunch that learning Japanese was not as easy as it sounded. Having to learn a whole new set of characters that looked like hieroglyphics. That would be something else.

She turned toward him. "Say something in Japanese to me."

He stared into his glass as though he might not have heard, then said, *"Eva-san ga kokoni itekurete ureshiiyo. Motto isshoni sugoshitaina."*

His voice sounded like it came from deeper in his chest, spouting out pure gibberish. But his look and tone said otherwise. Like he had spoken a sermon, or given a vow. Whatever it was, she was impressed.

"What does that mean?"

"What did it sound like it meant?"

There he went again, challenging her. "Determining a regional accent is a far easier job than understanding Japanese. I have no idea whatsoever."

"Most of communication is nonverbal. Did you know that?" he said.

He had a way of looking directly into her, as though he was trying to get to the bottom of who Eva was. It was disarming. And appealing.

"I have no idea what you said, but you did sound serious.

Perhaps you were telling me some top secret piece of information? Something you shouldn't be sharing," she said.

His eye twinkled. "Very perceptive, Miss Cassidy."

An emphasis on the *miss*. She had better bring up Billy.

"So, tell me," she said.

"I was just commenting on what a beautiful day it was, and
our good fortune at sailing on this ship."

She laughed, unconvinced. "The day was horrid!"

"Storms are beautiful in their own way, don't you think?"

He had a point. But this particular storm had very bad timing. "They can be. But I am not going to Hawaii for storms."

"What are you going for?" he said.

As far as the army was concerned, she was simply a nurse
looking to serve her country, not a woman running from her
own life. "My orders are for Tripler Hospital at Pearl Harbor,
so I'm going there to work, but of course I hear it's the love-
liest place on earth."

"I overheard you saying you're a nurse."

"I am."

"What kind of nursing do you do?" he said.

An odd question, since most people just left it at *nurse*.
"Well, a little of this, and a bit of that."

"Sounds mysterious."

"I've done everything from wiping a baby's bottom to helping amputate a leg," she said.

He squinted at her. "They let a woman do that?"

Her body went rigid. "You don't think it's something
women can handle?"

"I don't recall actually saying that."

"No, but the implication was there: I could hear it in your
tone," she said.

He tapped his glass to hers. "You're observant, aren't you?
And I admit, there may be that assumption, but mainly be-

cause it's all I've known, not because I think it's beyond the scope of a woman's capabilities."

By now the effects of the Moscow mule had taken hold, causing an uptick in boldness. "I would like to go on record as saying we are better at handling *it*."

"And why is that?"

"Because women are natural nurturers. At least most of us are. We know how to put the patient at ease, willing to hold a hand or whisper comforting words. It helps them heal. And that is a step most men are woefully unprepared for. Especially in a tough case."

Her father had seen this in her from an early age, and this was partly why he began dragging her with him for visits whenever she wasn't in school. And sometimes even when she was, he would show up on the steps of the schoolhouse, which was a stone's throw away from their cabin. She knew the particular knock of his boots against the wooden planks. *I need to borrow Evelyn again*, he would say.

Clark looked amused. "I won't argue with that. Boys out there on the battlefield all shot up, some of them are just crying for their mothers."

All Quiet on the Western Front had been ingrained in her mind as a teenage girl. Blood-soaked uniforms, missing limbs, watching friends die. The bitter agony. "It's not something I hope to ever see."

"You and me both," he said.

He went quiet for a minute, swirling his mug around and staring at the bottles on the wall. Such a handsome and engaging man. His wife was a fortunate woman. Eva noticed the square angles of his face, and how the dark stubble on his jaw almost seemed to be painted on. She got the strange urge to reach out and touch it, and felt her cheeks heat up.

"I'm going to guess South Carolina," she said, shaking off the thought.

He raised an eyebrow. "Getting warm."

"North?"

"Bingo."

The bartender came by. "Care for another cocktail?"

She realized then that she would be willing to sit there half the night and keep on talking, or even more so, listening. To learn more about world affairs and Hawaii and subjects like nonverbal communication. He knew so much. But she didn't want to give the wrong impression. Not only that, but one more drink would do her in.

"That's it for me. I'm feeling the effects of the day," she said.

Clark escorted her toward the staircase leading down to their rooms. Walking side by side, the top of her head barely reached his chin. The ship still swayed, and every so often, she had to reach out for the wall to keep her balance.

"It's been a pleasure," he said, when it finally came time to part.

That same fluttery feeling overcame her again. "Thank you for the company, Lieutenant."

"Will I see you again?" he asked, looking far more serious than he ought to.

"This ship is big, but not that big. I think you will."

As much as she wanted to see more of him, she got the sense that spending time with Lieutenant Clark would be a risky endeavor, married or not. One she might not walk away from unscathed.

"Oyasuminasai, Kanojyo," he said.

"Excuse me?"

"Good night, Eva."

EAST WIND, RAIN

From: Tokyo.

To: Washington.

19 November 1941 Circular #2353

Regarding the broadcast of a special message in an emergency.

In case of emergency (danger of cutting off our diplomatic relations), and the cutting off of international communications, the following warnings will be added in the middle of the daily Japanese-language shortwave news broadcast.

(1) In case of a Japan-US relations in danger: HIGASHI NO KAZEAME.*

(2) Japan-USSR relations: KITANOKAZE KUMORI.**

(3) Japan-British relations: NISHI NO KAZE HARE.***

This signal will be given in the middle and at the end as a weather forecast and each sentence will be repeated twice. When this is heard, please destroy all

code papers, etc. This is as yet to be a completely secret
arrangement.

Forward as urgent intelligence.
25432
JD-1: 6875
(Y) Navy Trans. 11-28-41 (S-TT)
*East wind, rain.
**North wind, cloudy.
***West wind, clear.

> —*A message that was intercepted and decoded from Tokyo to
> the Japanese embassy in Washington, picked up in Singapore
> by the British, and transmitted to US Asiatic Fleet HQ, and
> on to commanders at Fourteenth Naval District (Hawaii) and
> Sixteenth Naval District.*

WAR CHESS

November 29

Negotiations with Japan appear to be terminated to all practical purposes with only the barest possibilities that the Japanese government might come back and offer to continue. Japanese future action unpredictable but hostile action possible at any moment. If hostilities cannot, repeat, not be avoided the United States desires that Japan commit the first overt act.

—*Chief of Naval Operations Harold Stark copies Chief of Staff George Marshall's message in a cable to his admirals.*

LADY LUCK

Eva awoke to the painful sounds of retching. A lamp was already lit and she checked her watch. Eight o'clock! A rare occasion of sleeping in. Poor Jo had a brief respite of sleep, and now was beginning her day in a most unfortunate way. Being tucked away in the bowels of the *Lurline* with no windows did not help matters.

"I'm going to get you better if it's the last thing I do. Get dressed, and put on a sweater," Eva said.

Jo sighed and shook her head. "I can't."

"You can and you will. Now, sit up."

If Jo was surprised at Eva's bossiness, she didn't show it. Instead, she lugged herself up, staggered to the bathroom and spit up in the sink. She slammed the door behind her. Eva heard the faucet turn on, and a few minutes later Jo came out with her short hair smoothed down and tamed with a headband. Spiderwebs of red laced her eyes, and her face glistened milky.

"You need fresh air, to start with," said Eva.

"But I can't—"

"I will carry the wastebasket for you. Come on," Eva said, picking up the metal trash bin, as if that would do much good.

The ship still lurched about, causing the occasional loss of balance. The worst thing was you never knew which direction it was coming from. Jo had managed to slip on a plaid dress and wrap herself in a threadbare gray sweater. She wouldn't win any fashion awards, but there were plenty more days for that, unlikely as it might be.

On the way up, Jo had to stop several times to catch her breath, but they made it topside and followed a hallway astern. A handy flyer on the bureau had listed ship terms, and Eva studied it the night before as she tried to fall asleep. A fathom was six feet, while the fo'castle, the seamen's quarters. And of course *port* was left, *starboard* right. Sleep had eventually come, though fitfully and littered with thoughts of Ruby.

Wind whipped along the decks and rain pelted sideways. Eva found a seat for Jo, handed her the wastebasket and said, "Hang on, I'll be back soon. In the meantime, watch the horizon and inhale as much of this salt air as you can." Jo looked shocked but was too weak to object.

The hallways were still empty, but there were signs of recovery with small groups in the lounge and more tables full in the dining room. Eva scanned for signs of anyone she recognized from last night, but the only familiar faces were those of the football team. The bar was closed, so she flagged down a bellboy and ordered several ginger brews and packets of soda crackers, and took them back to Jo.

"I knew Hawaii would not be good for me," Jo said, still green.

"Drink this." Eva handed her a bottle.

Jo obeyed. Leaning her head back against the wall in between sips, she nevertheless managed to get the whole thing down, followed by several soda crackers.

Eva added, "Once you get there, you can stay ashore all you want. Where are you from anyway?"

Jo, it turned out, was born in Ohio, lived in North Dakota

and worked as a schoolteacher. She had been recruited in the middle of winter. A smart ploy on the part of the recruiters. Who wouldn't be lured by the promise of year-round summers where you could lounge in a hammock under a palm tree three hundred and fifty days a year?

"Why did you sign up if you knew it would be bad for you?" Eva asked.

"Because I was sick to death of being frozen, and our schoolhouse closed down. But at the time I didn't factor in my temperament. It sounded romantic and warm."

Jo looked as though she might retch again, but instead she let out an enormous belch. Eva pretended to look out at the ocean as a few heads turned their way.

"What's wrong with your temperament?" Eva said.

"I have weak nerves."

"It would seem to me that picking up and moving halfway across the world requires a certain amount of courage."

"I hadn't much choice," Jo said, chewing another cracker and looking as though she might cry. "And now I'll be stuck there because I will not be able to survive another crossing. That is a dreadful fact."

"You might surprise yourself. I've seen people survive much worse," Eva said.

Here she was, taking care of others. It made her feel useful and important and good. If there was anything she knew about herself, it was that she was born to help others. If only she were a little better at helping herself. Eva rounded up a blanket and left Jo on a covered deck chair to soak in the blustery Pacific air.

The halls were still sparsely filled, but there seemed to now be twice as many people milling about as last night. Most of the passengers would still be reeling in their beds. The breakfast buffet was more elaborate than dinner had been, with

plates of strawberries, pineapple and banana with silver bowls
of shredded coconut. Tiers of cinnamon buns, pecan snails and
twisted doughnuts. Pancakes and waffles and tropical syrup.
You could even choose your own omelet, made to order. What
happened to plain old steak and eggs?

There was an extra seat at the football players' table, and
Eva took it. She wasn't in the mood for any more talk of war
or medicine. Each one of the boys had enough food on their
plates to each feed an elephant. She surprised herself by being
able to eat half a cinnamon bun and a banana, but that was
all her stomach would allow in.

Clark was nowhere to be seen, and as much as she fought
it, a small sting of disappointment arose. But what did she really know about the man, other than he was navy and spoke
Japanese? And was dashing as all get-out. She couldn't quite
shake him from her mind.

After eating, she spent the rest of the morning exploring
the cavernous ship, getting the lay of the place; she admired
colorful South Pacific artwork with native women adorned
in flowers holding platters of fruit, rooms with gilded ceilings
and full of real-looking fake plants. You could walk for hours
and never cross the same path, it seemed. That a thing of such
size floated was beyond her ability to comprehend. She finally
settled in the library, where several others were posted up in
oversize leather chairs, faces hidden by books. Lucky for them.

While others had attended the elaborate bon voyage par-
ties yesterday, Eva had been tied up in a bookstore picking
out medical texts to read on the way over. Instead of reading
about Lassie or Philip Marlowe, she would be busy memorizing *The American Pocket Medical Dictionary* and soaking in the
latest journal articles on anesthesia.

On a nearby shelf, Matson postcards with various oceangoing motifs were stacked high. Eva picked one out with a Pacific islander riding a wave on a long plank. She sat down to write.

Dear Ruby,

Today is our second day out and the seas are wild. No one is up and around because of seasickness, but I am miraculously fine. Fate has her reasons, none of which we know. I am sticking to my promise and trying to enjoy myself, but I miss you terribly. There are lots of interesting characters aboard, from football players to doctors, and even a soldier who speaks Japanese, but I still wish you were here. You would love it, especially the fashion! I will write more when the seas settle and I can keep my pen straight.

Your friend,
Eva
PS I hope you are enjoying the candy I left with you.

That evening, Eva chose her sapphire velvet dress for its warmth, even though it was old and now gaped where it should have hugged. She pinned her hair on the sides with beaded bobby pins. The humid weather was giving it a mind of its own, but she eventually managed to tame the unruliness. Her mother's only pearl brooch matched nicely, so she stuck that on, too. When all was said and done, she just might be able to fit in. It felt like the *Lurline* and everyone on it had been immune to the Depression, and hardships had skipped this whole neck of the woods.

The storm was easing by now, still blustery and cool, but the seas were calming down. Jo dressed for dinner, too. "I may make it through this after all, thanks to you," Jo said with her first real smile of the trip.

"The whole world can seem hopeless when you're under the weather. Sickness does that to a person."

Their table was full of singles and couples, with a pair of twin sisters heading back to Australia, a merchant by the name of Donny Honk from Los Angeles, an Englishman, two ladies from Chicago decked to the nines, and Mr. Ogden, who seemed extraordinarily cheered by his good fortune. He couldn't tear his eyes off the twins, who were blonde and lovely. Frankly, Eva couldn't blame him. Everybody was lamenting over their past twenty-four hours—*my head was in the toilet, I would just as soon cut off my own leg as go through that again*—and excited for the trip to really get going. Eva ordered the breast of chicken with wild rice, glacé pineapple and truffle sauce, but was only able to pick at it. Try as she might, her stomach was just not interested.

Donny, who had traveled on the *Lurline* before, went on and on about the midnight snack. "Don't be fooled by the word *snack*, just you wait."

Jo had a laugh like a lonely donkey, but at least she was in good spirits, as the whole room seemed to be. Latecomers filed in, and Eva admired the outfits, much like she was watching a fashion show—something she had never done before. Gingham and floral and satin. Many of the women were in strapless dresses in bold pinks and oranges or wore plunging necklines, making her feel like a prude. Eva found herself intrigued by the twins' Australian accents, with the vowels all mixed up and drawn out, and every sentence sounding like a question. It made them sound sweet and highly feminine. Sasha and Bree were their names.

"Where are you ladies returning from?" Eva asked, just wanting to hear the sound of their voices.

"New York—"

"And San Francisco—"

"We're joining up with the Australian Army Nursing Service, and our father wanted us to see a bit of America before we head off overseas. 'Travel is a girl's best friend' is his motto."

Eva would not have pegged the two as nurses, but imagined that any wounded soldier would be happy to have either one looking over him. "Fellow nurses, I had no idea. Where will you be going?"

"Somewhere in the Mediterranean, maybe Egypt or Palestine," Bree said.

"And if we can see the great Pyramids, all the better."

"Why, those are dangerous places. Are you afraid?" Eva asked.

Bree waved her fork. "We want to do our bit. Have you seen 'em in the papers? Those poor blokes deserve all the help they can get."

"Very noble of you, ladies," Eva said, impressed.

The thought of volunteering overseas, in the thick of the war, had never crossed her mind. Hawaii had seemed remote enough and a far safer choice. Would she have the nerve if it came down to it?

Sasha leaned into Bree and they touched heads. "As long as we get to be together, we can handle anything."

Eva knew the feeling.

Halfway through dinner, the twins both caught sight of someone and began waving their napkins in the air. "Lieutenant! Hello, Lieutenant. Over here!"

Eva didn't want to turn around, but sure enough, Clark showed up a moment later.

"Good evening, ladies, you're looking lovely," he said to the twins, who were in matching sleeveless dresses, one lime green and one powder blue.

"Sit with us at bingo, will you?" they begged.

He scanned the table and stopped when his gaze found Eva.
A thin smile and subtle nod was all he gave.

"I have previous arrangements, but will see what I can
do," he said.

"Well, a little lady luck is always nice, so do find us," Bree
said.

He cleared his throat. "That it is. Enjoy your meal."

And he was off. The twins turned to each other, whisper-
ing. Eva thought she heard the words *share him*. Eva's neck
heated up and she turned her attention to the tangy pineapple
sauce on her plate.

All through dinner, she was preoccupied with the notion of
Clark with one of the twins. But hadn't he said he had other
arrangements for bingo? Perhaps his wife was on board and
confined to her room with seasickness. But surely he would
have mentioned that. There was plenty of talk about sailors, especially those fresh from sea, and how they flocked to
Chinatown for weekends of boozing and womanizing. Clark
didn't seem that type, but one never knew. And at most, for
Eva, he was simply a welcome distraction from worrying over
Ruby every spare moment, or fretting that someone at Pearl
Harbor would recognize her and she would lose her job and
be court-martialed.

Dessert was baked Alaska—a core of ice cream with walnut
sponge cake and torched meringue. Jo polished off the half of
Eva's that she couldn't finish, and several petits fours to boot.
"Making up for lost time," she said with cream on her chin.

Jo was also adamant about playing bingo. Eva had mixed
feelings. It sounded pleasant enough, but the open air was
calling to her and she felt like walking several laps around the
ship before sitting in another enclosed room.

"I'm going for a stroll. How about I see you in a half hour
in the card room?" she said.

The rise and fall of the swells were reduced to easy rocking, enough to lull, but not enough to induce nausea. Clusters of people gathered to smoke, play cards and compare seasickness stories, and mothers with dark circles under their eyes stood on the decks while their young children ran back and forth like chickens just released from their cage. On the side deck, Eva enjoyed a damp and thick wind, which smelled briny and foreign to her. Nothing like the scent of parched earth she was accustomed to.

To say the last ten years back home had been difficult was an understatement of great proportions. Empty wallets, sparse food, people around them losing homes, farms, everything. One family Eva and her father would visit had set up a system where Monday was John's day to eat, Tuesday was Mary's. Along with medicine, she and her father would bring them eggs and greens he sent Ruby out to forage for.

Eva's thoughts went to her father, as they often did. What would he think of her running off to Hawaii? At least Billy was there. *He's good stock and he can take care of you. Women are meant to be married, Evelyn.* Her father had been a difficult man to please. *Evelyn, what do these symptoms say to you?* When Eva would answer, usually correctly, his response would be, *Yes, but… Yes, but what about the swollen tongue? Yes, but what about the pain in the lower back?* Anytime someone said "Yes, but" to her, her stomach twisted. And yet Eva and Ruby had meant everything to him. He loved them with the fierceness of the noonday sun. And that had only doubled once their mother died.

Every so often, wafts of smoke blew through, and Eva moved to the front deck to be upwind of the smokestack. The rain had stopped and her wool sweater was pulled tight around her. Up in the sky, the clouds had parted, exposing a small patch of stars.

From out of the dark next to her came a voice. "Did you make a wish?"

She must have jumped three feet in the air before clutching the railing to stabilize herself. "Horsefeathers, Lieutenant, I could have fallen overboard."

"Just you wait until the weather clears. There is no place like the middle of the ocean to view the stars. Far away from city lights, no trees or mountains in the way. It never gets old," he said, moving in beside her and looking up.

"How long have you been in Hawaii?" she asked.

"Six months."

"How long will you be stationed there?"

"Until they send me someplace else, I guess. I thought I'd be in Japan longer, but they shipped us out. It all depends on what happens over there in Tokyo and in Europe," he said.

She was dying to ask more, but didn't want to seem nosy. "How about your family?"

"The folks are still in North Carolina and I have a brother overseas in Britain and another working on a ranch in Montana," he said.

What about your wife? she wanted to ask, instead coming out with, "Do you miss them?"

Even when she had been away at school, home was only a day away by train. The ache for Ruby seemed to grow with each mile of ocean crossed. It would be at least a year before she would see her sister again. And knowing that she was sick and scared only magnified the feeling tenfold.

"You get used to it. At first I went home at every opportunity, but then I was stationed in China and the Philippines and Japan. I got real good at writing letters."

All the places he'd been. She felt boring in comparison.

"That writing room on deck is something else. They've thought of everything and more on this ship," she said.

Her words were carried off by the wind, and he inched closer, nearly brushing her shoulder. They were both leaning over the railing, looking into the swirling seas. She held her breath. What was wrong with her?

He nodded. "A far cry from a destroyer or a transport."

"How come you're traveling on a civilian ship?" she asked.

"I'm needed back in Honolulu and the timing worked better with the *Lurline*. I'm not complaining one bit, though," he said.

She could feel his gaze, intensity boring through the skin on the side of her face.

"So, if you had to suggest one thing for me to do when I arrive, or one place to see, what would it be?" she said, turning to meet his eyes, which were trained on her.

He thought for a few moments. "Everyone loves Waikiki Beach, but I would say take a drive or even the train out north and see the swells along the coast near a town called Haleiwa. Right offshore, they're as tall as buildings and the beach goes on for miles. There's shells and big white chunky sand and the sun sets right into the ocean." He cut himself off but looked like he wanted to say something else.

"Sounds dreamy," she said, using one of Ruby's favorite terms. Her little sister read like the dickens and was full of catchy phrases. Eva had absorbed many of them just by being in close proximity.

"It's a long ride, but well worth it. Out of the hustle and bustle."

"For a girl who's never even seen the ocean before, everything over there is going to seem magical, even the so-called hustle and bustle."

Clark cleared his throat and his face stiffened. "Look, I'm not sure what your situation is, but if you need a tour guide, I can drive you out there one weekend, or anywhere else for that matter."

She found herself wanting nothing more than to be driven around the island with this man. Was it possible to keep him as a friend? He and Billy would probably get on well, maybe they even knew each other. And maybe she and his wife could become friends. Wait, that was ridiculous, it wasn't how things worked.

"What a lovely offer—"

She was about to ask him about his wife when loud voices floated up behind them and a couple of young men from the football team showed up. "Lieutenant Spencer, we're waiting on you. Bingo's getting underway."

Clark looked at his watch. "The time got away from me," he said.

"I can see why," said one of the players, and Eva felt the blood rush to her cheeks.

Clark touched her wrist. "Can we continue this conversation another time?"

"Of course. I promised Jo I would join her in there anyway."

"Sit with us," he said.

It sounded like an order. One she would be pleased to obey.

Speaking of hustle and bustle, the card room was swarming with people. Eva had never been keen to throw her money away, but a few games wouldn't hurt. Jo was already seated with Donny and there were no seats around them, so Eva ended up purchasing bingo cards with Clark and sitting to his left. There were five long tables set up with enough room for at least twenty-five seats. Each one was nearly full. More than food, it turned out, people liked a good game.

"It should be a nice kitty," Clark said, raising his voice to be heard over the chatter.

"Back at home, you'd win a goat if you were lucky," she said.

He laughed. "Get out of here."

"I'm serious. People played in the town hall but no one had any money to put in, so each week, a new person would offer up a prize. One week my father came home with a baby goat. Another time, a bucketful of bullfrogs."

"What did you do with them?"

"We took them down to a creek the next day and let 'em loose. Dad said that since they ate mosquitos, and mosquitos cause disease, then you could never have too many bullfrogs in the neighborhood," she said.

"There won't be any goats or bullfrogs tonight. More like crisp bills."

In the bright lights she noticed for the first time a large brown fleck in his right iris—which was sky blue—and smile lines fanning out from his eyes. She guessed him to be about thirty, give or take.

Up onstage, the announcer rattled off numbers he pulled from a box. "*B*-7, *O*-5, *N*-10." She had none of those on her card, but Clark's was quickly filling with chips. The young football players were cheering and laughing and jabbing each other.

"Can you guess which one is the quarterback?" he asked.

She knew enough about football to know that quarterbacks had to be quick-witted. She surveyed the bunch. After ruling out the bulky ones, she decided on a tall fellow with dark hair and a calm demeanor.

"Him?" She nodded his way.

"Impressive."

She shrugged. "I'm willing to bet that you were a quarterback, too, weren't you?"

His smile answered her question. "We could use someone

like you in our operation. Nuances are important and not everyone has the knack."

"There must be something you can tell me about your work?" she said.

He bent toward her ear like he was going to spill a secret. *"Natsu no kusa, nokori subete heishi no yume no uchi."*

"You don't say?"

I-8 was called and Clark put another chip on his card.

"Can you guess what it means?" he said.

"In case you've forgotten, I have never even met a Japanese person." She thought about his tone. Soft, almost flowery. "I'll wager you weren't telling me about your job, though."

"Righto. It was a type of Japanese short poem. Haiku they're called. Like hauntingly beautiful fragments of the world."

"What did this one say?" she asked.

"Summer grasses, all that remains of soldiers' dreams."

The simple truth of the words hit smack in the center of her chest. So much so that she could feel the weight of all those lost dreams. Men bleeding into the fields.

"Why, it's genius," she said.

He nodded. "The simplicity of it."

"All very nice, but it still doesn't answer my question of what you do, Lieutenant."

"That's for another time," he said with a slight shake of his head. "And, boy, do I wish things were different right now."

"What's that supposed to mean?" she asked.

"G-9," boomed the man on the microphone.

"Bingo!" the quarterback yelled, jumping up and running toward the man in the suit pulling numbers.

Eva watched him run up and caught sight of the Australian twins at the table behind them. She was more relieved than she should have been that Clark had not joined the two women. Ogden was sitting with them as well as the plantation manager and two other men.

"A nice purse of twenty-five dollars!" called the man up front.

They had purchased five cards each, and the next few games went along without Eva even getting close. Each time someone yelled "Bingo," she deflated like someone had just let all of her air out. She could see why the game was addictive. And being here surrounded by velvet curtains was a far cry from the goats and bullfrogs of Hollowcreek. On the last card, Eva needed only B-4, and Clark B-9. The man pulling numbers was dillydallying and telling dumb jokes. "He—Why didn't you answer my letter? She—I didn't get it. He—You didn't get it? She—No, and besides, I didn't like some of the things you said in it."

"Come on, man, call it," Clark said.

"B…"

Clark reached down and squeezed her hand, seemingly without even a second thought. The warmth ran right through her, sending her insides into a frenzy.

"…4."

It took her a moment to register that she had won. Clark nudged her, then held up her arm and called out. "Over here, bingo!"

The announcer bellowed, "Another happy customer going to Honolulu with some extra lettuce." When she reached the stage, he asked her what she would be spending it on.

Eva turned to the room and froze. "Um, well…" She caught sight of Clark watching her, his presence reassuring, and regained her wits. *Send it to my sister*—which is what she would probably end up doing—sounded so boring, so she improvised. "Maybe take a train ride out to the north side of the island, and buy some pineapple along the way."

"And who will be the lucky companion?" he said, shoving the microphone in her face.

Talk about being put on the spot. She hemmed and hawed before finally saying, "That remains to be seen."

DANGEROUS SEAS

The ships feel like they may break apart and sink into the abyss. Such is winter in the North Pacific. Heaving, bucking seas toss them about like toy boats. Refueling is almost impossible, with hoses whipping loose in the wind and oiling the decks. The men tie straw rope to their shoes. Several men are swept overboard. Lost.

They survive on rice balls, radishes and pickled plums, wrapped in seaweed. Some say they are going to attack Dutch Harbor in Alaska, but others know better. Japan would not dare to spark a war with America and Britain. The one on board who does know where they are going has been told that if they are spotted before December 6, return home. Spotted on the sixth, the decision is his. Spotted after the sixth, proceed. He is constantly on edge. A fleet of twenty-eight ships is hard to hide.

A BOLD STATEMENT

November 30

JAPAN MAY STRIKE OVER WEEKEND!

—*Headline of the* Honolulu Advertiser *newspaper, also on
the front of* Hilo Tribune-Herald.

THE GAME

Overnight, the seas went from crashing and windswept to a flat blue field as far as the eye could see. Eva and Jo stood on deck with the sun at their backs, staring at the new landscape before them. Loads more people were coming out of the woodwork and gawking at the placid water.

"This is the ocean I've been imagining all these weeks," Eva said.

Jo tossed a coin in. "I didn't get a chance to do this when we left. A toll for Neptune for safe passage," she said.

Eva tossed one, too. "Storms or submarines, I'm not sure which is worse."

"I know which is worse. Submarines," Jo said.

After breakfast, the two went back to their room to dress for sunbathing. Where once Eva's stomach had been shapely, now it was flat enough to see her hip bones protrude. She didn't like how she looked. But if Eva felt self-conscious in her bathing suit, Jo looked downright uncomfortable. She filled it out like one of the football players would have and waited until she was sitting on the lounge chair before taking off her dress. Four seconds after they sat down, Bree and Sasha joined them.

"Love your cozzie!" Bree said.

"Cozzie?" Eva asked.

"Your swimming suit, silly."

Ruby had picked the suit up at a secondhand store. A red-and-white polka-dotted number that Eva felt ridiculous in. She had sent Ruby to a nearby town with a small shopping list, not wanting anyone to get wind of her plans. If people asked how Eva was or where she had gone, Ruby was to tell them, *She's gone south to work at an orphanage.* If pressed, Ruby would say, *In a town called Clayton.* There were no less than twenty Claytons in the country.

Sasha finished her sentence. "You're cute as a pixie in it."

One look at the twins' suits and Eva felt like a real prude. Strapless, bright yellow floral and cut high on the thigh. Nor were they small breasted, in fact they oozed out above the material like fresh-cooked bread. Somehow, they got away with it. Maybe it was the roasting heat and being in the middle of the ocean that caused all modesty to dissolve into the thick air. Both women had golden skin with freckles, and Eva envied their plush figures.

They had come early to secure a spot on the back deck near the pool, which the crew had covered with purple and white flower petals. A ball *thwacked* on a deck above them, where two couples were playing tennis. A handful of men and women played shuffleboard across the way. The women wore only bathing suits, fortunately all with straps.

Sasha sipped from a pink drink with a miniature umbrella in it. "You were lucky last night at bingo. We were one away every game."

"And you were sitting next to Lieutenant Spencer, to boot. How did you fix that?" Bree said.

Eva felt herself tense up. "I ran into him and the boys on the way in, and Jo here hadn't saved me a seat," she said.

"I wasn't sure if you were coming or not," Jo protested.

"We met Clark back home in Oz, when we were just wee things," Bree said.

That got Eva's interest. "Oh?"

"He passed through when he was stationed in the Philippines," Bree informed her. "Our father is the mayor in Sydney, you see. All the Yanks pass through our home when down under. Anyone who is anyone."

"Ah," was all Eva could manage to say, itching to inquire about his wife.

"Clark was the one that all the girls were swooning over," Sasha said.

"He's married now, though, it appears," Eva said, trying to sound neutral.

Bree lowered her voice. "We were wondering about that. It's been years since we've seen him and we lost touch. But we noticed the ring."

"And we are working on gathering intelligence on him," Sasha said.

Eva laughed.

"Maybe it's none of our bizzo, but he seemed to be paying you a lot of attention last night," Bree said, cocking her head sideways and meeting Eva's gaze squarely.

All these funny Australian words, Eva had to guess at their meaning. Jo was facedown in a book called *The Spanish Bride*, and offered up no help.

"He was just being a gentleman. I've noticed that on the boat, people are more friendly and outgoing. And, anyway, I have a man in Honolulu."

Bree peered over her sunglasses. "Do tell."

It was hard to determine whether the twins were feeling her out because of their own interest in Clark, or just being girls.

"His name is Billy. He's navy, too. Our fathers knew each

other from medical school, and we met a year and a half ago, just before he was transferred to Hawaii."

"Are you engaged?" Bree said.

"He wants to marry, but as a nurse in the army, I have to remain single. And what's the rush anyway?" Eva said.

"Oh, I like you already!" Bree said, clapping her hands together. "Sasha and I have each been proposed to several times but we aren't ready to be tied down, plus who knows what will happen when we go overseas."

Sasha added, "Having a husband at this age would be a real drag."

Eva laughed. "You two are something else. My sister, Ruby, would love you."

Just then, Clark and the young quarterback, whose name Eva had learned was Buddy, walked across the deck carrying tennis rackets. Clark looked over and held up his racket to them, but made no move to come say hello. Sasha and Bree wiggled in their seats and waved back. Eva smiled.

Sasha fanned herself with a coaster. "Now, there's a match I'd like to watch. Wait until you see him without a shirt on, you're liable to overheat."

"Clark is one man I might consider packing it up for," Bree said.

Eva was caught between enjoying the lightness of the conversation and feeling like she was guarding a secret. She shook her head at the absurdity of it because her innocent attraction to Clark was perfectly natural and apparently catching. Having been holed up in the hospital with bedridden patients all day, a reaction like this was bound to happen. But what about that dimple? And the way Clark looked at her as though she was the only woman on the ship.

"Say, why don't we go watch the match?" Sasha said.

White lines were painted on the slatted wooden deck to

make a tennis court. Smaller than customary, it was tucked in next to the smokestack. As they were unable to tear Jo away from her book, the three women moved to a small table nearby. A few minutes later a steward came over.

"I'll have another strawberry lemonade with a splash of vodka, please," Sasha said.

Bree raised her hand. "Make that two."

It wasn't even noon yet.

"Nothing for me," Eva said.

"Bring her one of these, too," Sasha said to the steward.

"But—"

"Live it up, lovey, how often do you get to be aboard a ship like this? And from the sounds of it, once you get to Honolulu, it'll be all work. When at sea…"

"Do as the seamen do," Bree said.

They both giggled.

Men around them were dressed in Hawaiian-print shirts bright as lemons and tangerines straight off the tree, and women wore bathing suits of the same fabric. That combined with the salty air and sun-splashed skies gave her a real taste of where they were headed. If only she could feel as carefree as all these people around her seemed to be.

Clark was tall enough that he could almost stand midcourt and reach his arm out to hit the ball anywhere it landed without taking a step. Buddy proved a worthy opponent and within the first five minutes, both men were dripping in sweat, their shirts plastered to their backs. Eva was so riveted by the match that she sipped her drink empty before realizing it.

The next thing she knew, Clark was standing in front of the table. "Doubles, anyone?" he asked.

Was he speaking to her? A little fuzzy headed, she turned around to check who he might be addressing. But when she looked back, he was still there, staring straight at her.

Bree sprang up. "I'm in."

"I am fine just watching, but thank you," Eva said.

"My wrist has been acting up, it doesn't like all that cold weather," Sasha said. Then to Eva, "Go on, get out there."

Bree slipped on a white skirt and strolled over to the steward in charge, who handed her two more rackets. If table tennis counted as experience, Eva had a chance, if not, she would make a big fool of herself in front of the crowd.

"I can't play in just my suit," she said.

Sasha handed her a scrunched-up piece of material. "Wear this."

The material turned out to be an eyelet skirt that would have been long enough for a toddler, but it was better than nothing.

"The two of us against them two?" Bree said, sidling up to Clark.

"Which one of you has more experience?" he said.

Eva wasn't sure if she should volunteer that she had never played. "Certainly not me."

"How about we partner up, then?" he said.

Why did he look even more handsome in his civvies?

"I don't think you want me," she said.

The edges of his mouth curled up. "You're wrong there, ma'am."

A flush ran from the top of her head to her toes, warm and tingly. She was stuck looking up at him, unable to turn away or respond or even think.

Bree latched onto him anyway. "But I asked first. Come on, Lieutenant."

Clark let himself be led off, and Buddy stepped closer. "Do you prefer backhand or forehand?" he asked.

"It shouldn't make much difference."

She was still stuck on *you're wrong there, ma'am.*

Buddy took the left side, and offered a few tips. To warm up, they rallied. Eva's first ball went clear over the railing, probably to be swallowed by some poor fish. The racket was so springy! The alcohol didn't help, either, running through her underfed frame.

"Less swing, keep your wrist firm," Buddy advised.

Too hard, into the net, directly at Bree's face. This wasn't going well. "I'm afraid I won't be much of a partner," she said.

"Relax and have fun, you'll get it," Clark said from across the net.

They lost the first game sorely. Bree and Clark played well together and Eva felt a stab of jealousy. Her accuracy improved slightly during the next game, and what she lacked in experience, she made up for in speed. Smallness had its perks. Buddy seemed to be everywhere at once, too, as though he had springs in his shoes. Pretty soon, they were holding off Bree and Clark.

Bree hit every shot to Eva, while Clark hit every ball to Buddy.

"You can hit to me, too, you know. I won't break," she called.

Before the last game, Buddy called a huddle. "Let them make the mistakes, just get it over. We can do this."

As best she could, Eva followed his orders, concentrating on hitting the ball smack in the middle of the court, not at either Clark or Bree, and not going for a kill. She had to regularly tug her skirt down over her suit, but other than that, her focus was pure. They were neck and neck at game point, a small crowd had gathered and Buddy hit the ball short. She was sure they were going to win, but Clark's long arms not only got to the ball, he smacked it full force—into her cheek. Flesh, bone and ball. The impact stunned her and she dropped to the ground with her hand over her face. The metallic taste of blood filled her mouth.

She's bleeding! Are you okay? Nice shot, Lieutenant. Get a towel!

Pinched and nervous faces hovered over her. Bree, Buddy, Sasha. "Looks like her skin split neatly on the bone," someone said.

Where was Clark? He was the one responsible and he had vanished when it mattered most. A few moments later, he pushed through with Dr. Wallace by his side.

"That must have been some hit. Nothing a few stitches can't fix, though. Head wounds bleed," Wallace said.

Eva felt as though someone had held a glowing fire poker to her cheek. Sasha knelt in front of her and dabbed her face with a towel. When it came away scarlet, the first wave of dizziness struck. Her vision narrowed.

"Is she going to faint?" Clark asked, himself looking porcelain.

Why was everyone talking as though she wasn't there? "I'm not dead, people."

And that was the last she remembered.

THE TROUBLE WITH TOMMY LEMON

September 21, 1941

The first thing Eva noticed were his shaky hands. Dr. Brown's breath smelled faintly of alcohol, too, as if he'd decided on a glass of whiskey instead of coffee this morning. It was also time for him to pluck his nose hairs, but that was irrelevant. The fluorescent lights lit up more than just the cold steel table of the operating room.

"There you are, Evelyn." Dr. Brown glared at her for a moment, then pointed to the boy's face and right side of his ribs. "He came in last night after wrapping his mother's car around a lamppost. Lacerations and a swollen abdomen, possible internal bleeding. They wanted to wait until morning to see if the swelling went down."

The swelling had not gone down, in fact he looked six months pregnant. His blood pressure was elevated and breathing seemed distressed. One look at the boy's pale face and she could tell he was in bad shape. She felt his hands. Cold and clammy. His pulse was thready.

"Was he conscious?" Evelyn asked.

Brown nodded. "He was frantic, raving on about how his father was going to kill him."

Wait a minute, the boy looked familiar. "He looks like Tommy Lemon," she said.

"That's because he *is* Tommy Lemon," Brown huffed.

The mayor's son. Local football star. Every girl's dream. One of those people who were too lucky to die.

"Did he complain of pain on the right side or left?" she asked.

"Both." Brown looked worried. "He was in shock last night, but then stabilized. See those bruises? I'm worried about lacerations to his liver or spleen, he's possibly bleeding out. I want you to set up the IV for surgery. His folks went out to grab some breakfast, but we can't wait for their permission."

Evelyn felt her stomach clench. Making suggestions to Dr. Brown was a losing proposition, and yet she had to say something. An IV meant sodium thiopental, and sodium thiopental meant putting the patient at risk. "Have you considered using ether?" she asked as politely as possible.

He bellowed back, "We're using sodium thiopental."

"But—"

Just then, a young new nurse walked in and headed for the closet. "Excuse me, I need to grab a few extra sheets," she mumbled.

Dr. Brown kept his furious eyes on Evelyn. He had a unique way of wiping away all her confidence with one burning glare and reducing her to a mute and dumb schoolgirl. The way her knees were shaking, you could have heard them knocking together three rooms down the hallway. Her father would have told her to grow some whiskers.

"But, Doctor, he's still in shock. Look at his color, feel his pulse," she forced herself to say.

He towered nearly a foot over her and she often felt he used his height as an intimidation factor. It worked. "I asked you to set up the IV," he said, this time with the coolness of ice.

She couldn't bear to look him in the eye and instead looked at Tommy Lemon's chalky face when she managed to say in barely a whisper, "I believe that ether is the best choice right now."

Brown's nostrils flared. Having worked with him for the past six months, Evelyn recognized the signs. He was about to go into one of his rants. "Are you telling me what to do, Nurse?"

She *was* telling him. "Of course not, but at the Mayo Clinic, we almost lost several patients that were already in shock. The sodium thiopental sends them into cardiovascular collapse—"

"Does this look like the Mayo Clinic? Get him prepped."

Tommy Lemon was running out of time and Evelyn was losing the battle with Dr. Brown. Was she missing something? Maybe Brown was right and she should let it go. But a gnawing hunch told her to keep on pressing.

"But—"

His face turned beefsteak tomato red. "Don't ever suggest that you know better than me. Do you understand?"

Evelyn prepped Tommy Lemon for the IV, rubbing his limp arm with antiseptic and alcohol and feeling for a usable vein. His vital signs were deteriorating rapidly and she didn't want to delay any longer. A heavy sensation threatened to drag her to the ground. Dr. Brown left the room for a minute and came back in all scrubbed up with another nurse in tow.

"You can be excused, Nurse," he said.

She froze.

"At least let me help, you certainly could use an extra set of hands," she pleaded.

He ignored her. "I understand that they need help in the Woods Wing. Tell them I sent you."

The Woods Wing was Infectious Disease. They didn't have

much use for an anesthetist. Which was precisely why he was sending her there.

Evelyn glanced at the other woman in hopes of a little nursish solidarity. This one was new and only offered a weak smile as if to say, *You're on your own with this one, sorry.*

"Start off with the lowest dose and pray for the best," Evelyn said to her, as she walked out the door.

There was nothing else she could do. Dr. Brown was legendary. He *was* Hollowcreek General Hospital.

A BUMP IN THE NIGHT

November 30

Clark stood at the door feeling awful. Sunflowers would be little consolation for a blast to the face, but they were all he had. He knocked twice. When no one answered, he knocked harder. Then the door swung open. Eva stood there, wide-eyed, looking beautiful despite her gash and swollen eye. If he hadn't known better, he'd have thought someone false cracked her.

"Clark, what a surprise," she said.

He pulled the flowers from behind his back. "You deserved roses, but all I could find were these. I'm so sorry—"

At first he thought she was going to turn him away, but she waved him off like it was nothing. "Would you like to come in? I was about to apply another pack of ice before going up to dinner."

Big Jo was apparently out, and he was glad for it.

"Can I help in any way?" he asked, standing in the middle of the room, unsure of where to sit.

She smiled and then winced. "You can keep me company, tell me more stories about Hawaii or Japan or wherever, as long as they don't involve tennis. Jo has not been back since morning, and I don't know whether to be concerned or pleased," she said.

Clark sat on the only chair. He wondered how much she remembered about getting to the sick bay, and how he had half walked, half carried her down there, worried she might pass out again. Her skin was smooth as cream and she smelled like violet or lavender or one of those purple flowers his mother loved so much.

She sat back on the bed, leaning into a pile of pillows to prop her up and held a small packet of ice wrapped in cloth to her cheek. "I'm usually not squeamish about blood, unless it's mine, then all bets are off," she said.

There *had* been a boatload of blood. Enough that he'd had to take a few deep breaths to steady himself. Being in the navy didn't necessarily cure one of squeamishness. A weakness he was not proud of.

"You're one up on me, then," he said. "I don't do well with blood in general."

"Being a doctor's daughter made me immune, or so I thought. I've never actually had stitches myself or any type of surgery," she said, closing her eyes and sinking back.

"I imagine it's different when you, or someone you care about, is hurt," he said, thinking of Beth. He tried to shut the memory out of his mind but it was always there, just beneath the surface. A gash in his soul that would never heal. "Dr. Wallace must be a skilled surgeon, because those stitches look like they were done by a Singer machine."

At the mention of Wallace, she perked up. "Lucky me. What are the odds there was a trauma surgeon on deck? He's someone I'd like to learn from and he seems more reasonable than many doctors I know. I do anes—" She stopped midsentence and looked flustered, then changed course. "I'm going to try to attend his lectures in Honolulu."

He contemplated asking what she'd meant, but got the

feeling she didn't want to talk about it. "*Lucky* may not be the word I'd have chosen," he said.

She brightened, trying to maintain a straight face. "Please don't make me laugh, and not lucky you hit me, lucky for Wallace being on hand."

"After last night's bingo, I get the feeling that luck follows you around on a leash," he said.

"You're wrong there," she said in a flat voice.

She did look awfully thin. Her cheekbones were more pronounced than they should have been. Her collarbones, too. He was all too familiar with the haunting ravages of hardships and loss, and got a feeling she was, as well. You could see it in the hollows of her eyes and the sharp angles of her face. Maybe that was what was drawing him to her almost like an invisible force.

Watching the way she kept switching arms to hold the ice on her cheek, Clark finally had to intervene. He scooted the chair to the side of her bed. "Let me hold that for you."

For a moment, he thought she would refuse, but her arm flopped down. He took the cloth from her hand and touched it to her cheek.

She closed her eyes again and sighed. "Thank you."

A pool of purple was forming under her eye, just below where her lashes hit. What an asinine maneuver. He blamed it on his reflexes. And his stupid drive to win. But no game was worth splitting a woman's cheek open.

"I feel like such a louse. How can I make it up to you?" he said.

Eva must have been thinking hard, because she took her sweet time in answering. "How about teaching me a few phrases in Japanese? If Hawaii is full of Japanese people, it might help me to know a little," she said, raising an eyebrow his way.

Despite himself, he'd been thinking more along the lines of dinner in Waikiki or taking a drive to the Pali Lookout, but he sensed a hesitance on her part. Just a whisper, but there.

"You got it," he said.

God, why was he so easy all of a sudden?

Dinner was spent discussing war theories again. The army guys were certain Japan was going to go for the Dutch East Indies for their oil, while the plantation manager said no, it would be the British stronghold of Singapore. The general public only knew what they read in the papers or heard on the radio. Enough to raise alarm, but what Clark knew was even more troubling. The recent change in naval call signs, the withdrawal of all Japanese merchant vessels from Western Hemisphere waters, hell, there were possibly even carriers in the Mandate Islands. Yet the scuttlebutt going around was all the same. *Japan would never attack us. The US is too big and too powerful.*

Back at Pearl, all the guys in the Dungeon were edgy. The Japanese were backed into a corner and Admiral Yamamoto was a reckless firebrand, according to Clark's boss, Ford. Smart as the dickens, too. In fact, Ford had recently put his crew on a twenty-four-hour schedule, manning the place seven days a week, working to decode, translate and track enemy messages.

The trouble was, Clark could never talk to anyone about this. A lonely business, but one he was built for. He loved all of it—the Japanese language, the codes, the camaraderie built on a mountainous challenge with sky-high stakes.

Bored with the chitter chatter, he kept searching the room for a thin, dark-haired woman with arched eyebrows. Eva had said she might or might not come up, as she'd had a mild head-ache when he'd left her. A loud racket from the ballroom reminded him that the band was warming up, and he wandered through the lounge and the bar and the card room, ending up at the same spot on the deck he'd found her last night. The railing was unoccupied, but the sky was stamped full of stars.

It took him a little time to locate the North Star, and from there, his eyes traced the constellations that he recognized. *Big Dipper, Scorpio, Orion.* A funny thing that the night sky looked the same here as it did in Japan, but was all twisted around from Australia. He would have been able to stay out here all night, just staring up and listening to the waves below.

"You weren't lying," said a voice right next to him.

A small yell escaped before he could help himself. "Geez, woman, you got me good. I guess you owed me one."

She looked pleased with herself. "This sky really is something else."

"I was just trying to chart a line to Honolulu, see where we're headed."

"You can do that?"

"If you hold your hand out at arm's length, you can measure degrees that way. All three hundred and sixty of them," he told her. "That one there is Polaris, the North Star."

"I see a gazillion."

He leaned nearer and pointed. "See the Big Dipper? If you draw a line down from the two stars that make the top of its bowl, you will always end up at Polaris. In Hawaii, it's about twenty degrees off the horizon, which is like your hand stretched wide like you're waving." He demonstrated. "Three fingers is about five degrees, and your pinky is one."

"If mine is one, yours must be three or four degrees," she said.

"It's relational, though, because our arms are different lengths."

She glanced up at him with wide eyes. "How do you know so much?"

"The navy. We need to be prepared in case our navigation goes out, or we're lost at sea," he said.

"It doesn't sound like you spend much time at sea, though," she said.

"Not anymore."

He had a strong urge to explain to her what he did in detail. About the Japanese Flag Officers Code that they were racing to crack, and the smoky basement that he worked out of, full of nutty characters and IBM machines. When he had first arrived on Oahu and walked through what looked like a broom-closet door, down the sixteen steps and into the murky walls of COM14, it was like stepping into a pool hall. One filled with burn bags of cryptologic worksheets. It had taken him a while to get used to the smoke, and just when he had, they figured out that all they'd had to do was open the fresh-air intake.

He snapped himself out of the memory, much preferring to be where he was now. "So about those language lessons, is there anything particular you want to learn to say?"

"Greetings, everyday kinds of things, I guess?"

"*Konnichiwa* and *ohayou gozaimasu* are greetings."

She laughed. "Say it again, more slowly."

"*Kon-ni-chi-wa.*"

"We had Latin in school, but this sounds *so* different."

"It's not a Romance language, so not only are you starting from scratch, but you have to change the way you think to really speak and understand it," he said.

"The foreignness of it is appealing, but I'm not sure my tongue is designed for such words," she said.

"Last I checked, all humans had the same kind of tongues. And brains and hearts, for that matter," he said.

A faint smile crossed her face. "You make a good point, I

often feel the same. It's a shame that not everyone can see it that way."

He was about to give his best shot at a reply when she asked, "What made you join the navy, Clark?"

He usually gave the same response—*they recruited me*—but felt the need to give her more. "I did well in school, and with my background in physics I was recruited, but it turned out to be my ease with language that sent me overseas and got me into the intel. I was never the guy who wanted to be out in the trenches blowing people up. I wanted to be the guy who could figure out what was coming down the pipes and prevent attacks on American soil."

A burst of wind flicked at her hair. "Do you think there will be an attack on American soil?"

He wished he could say no, but that would make him a liar. "I sure hope not, but you never know. In the Dungeon, we work on staying one step ahead of the Japanese."

"The Dungeon?"

"Where I work."

"Sounds mysterious," she said.

"Just a smoky room filled with a bunch of eccentric men."

"I have to admit when I left home, I had so much on my mind that the last thing I was thinking about was us going to war," she said.

If that was the case, there must have been trouble. Talk of war was rampant. He was dying to know more about her, but afraid to push.

"War may happen sooner than we all think," he said.

The words slipped out. She deserved to know.

Eva's whole body wilted. "Well, then, shall we set up a time for tomorrow? In the lounge?" she asked.

"How about one o'clock?" Clark said, at the same time

hearing footsteps behind them on the deck. He half turned his head.

"Excuse me, are you Lieutenant Spencer?" a man in a white uniform asked.

"That's me."

Old enough to be his father, with piercing blue eyes, the man said, "Sir, the captain suggested I might have a word with you. I'm Hank Wilson, second radio officer, sir."

"What is it?" Clark said.

Wilson nodded toward Eva. "It's a private matter, if you don't mind."

"Can it wait until morning?" Clark said, annoyed at the intrusion, but he'd just about scared her off anyway with his talk of war. Dumb move.

"No, sir, it can't."

"Give me a minute, please," he said to Eva, who looked on the verge of tearing up. He led Wilson to the far back railing, beyond earshot and where their voices would be lost over the Pacific. "What's this about?"

"I've been picking up signals on the lower marine radio frequency that I thought you might want to hear."

Clark felt his chest constrict. "What kind of signals?"

"Japanese signals. Why don't you come with me and see for yourself? It's highly unusual."

Wilson had piqued his interest enough to drag him away from Eva, which might have been a good thing, otherwise he sensed he might do something stupid. Like put his arm around her waist. Or accidentally lean over and kiss her. Any fool knew that the eve of a war was not the time to start something with a woman. And on top of that, these were unexpected feelings. Since Beth, his heart had been closed down. For years now, the sight of a beautiful woman had stirred nothing in him. And then along came Eva. Wrong time, wrong place and yet here he was acting like a love-struck teenager.

Something had to give.

The radio room was high up on the bridge deck, full of dials and receivers. Clark was impressed at the modern equipment and comfort of the space. Wilson slumped down in the chair and put on a set of headphones, leaving Clark standing there waiting.

A few minutes later, he peeled the headphones off. "Dang, this is getting stranger and stranger. I'll be glad to get your take on it."

"What do we have?" Clark said.

"The Japs are just blasting away using call letters JOS and JCS and other Japanese-based stations. Nor are they using any deception of signal detection. It's all in code, but they've been going at it for a good hour now. The damnedest part of it is the repeat-back is being acknowledged verbatim," Wilson said.

Certainly odd. "Repeat-back from where? Can you tell?"

Wilson rubbed his eyes with his leathery fists. "Some of the signals are good enough that we got a general bearing. I can't be sure, but the majority of them are coming from a northwest-by-west area. Which, from here, means north or west of Honolulu. Nothing but ocean out there."

Surely he had to be wrong. "Hold on, are you saying the repeat-back is from ships?"

"Possibly, sir," Wilson said.

The bitter cold of the room, coupled with this new bit of information, caused a shiver to run from the base of his spine through to his heels. Everyone knew something was coming, but Japanese ships near Honolulu would be impossible. Someone would have had a run-in with them by now.

"Here's the thing," Wilson said. "In my thirty years of

crossing the Pacific, I've never heard JCS Yokohama Japan before 2100 hours. We can't be picking up signals sent during daylight hours from Japanese homeland right now. It's impossible."

Clark needed to know more. "Show me the DF."

Wilson walked him to a toaster-size box. "A huff-duff, impressive," Clark said.

"Matson likes to be on top of the game. These ships aren't cheap."

"You think the repeat-backs are for crafts with smaller antennas?" Clark said.

"Or submarines."

They took turns listening to signals, and Clark wished he had Hal or Mike, his crypto buddies, there to give their take on things. At least Wilson seemed to know his stuff. A younger, less experienced man would never have picked up that these could only be repeat-backs.

During Wilson's turn listening, he kept scratching his head, mumbling to himself, and then finally took off the earphones and looked Clark in the eye. "If anyone should ask me, I'd say it's the Japs' mobilization battle order."

"There has to be a reasonable explanation," Clark said, though his gut was telling him Wilson might be right.

"What other explanation can there be?"

"I don't know but it doesn't add up," Clark said.

"We're running out of time. Should we tell the captain to radio Pearl Harbor?"

"What does the captain know?" Clark asked.

"Just that I was picking up confusing radio signals. I was purposefully vague."

"Good. There's no way we can send a message without the Japanese picking it right up. We'll have to wait until we're in Honolulu."

Wilson was chewing his lip. "I don't like this one bit."

"Neither do I."

If the Japanese fleet was north or west of Honolulu, who knew where else they might be?

AN UNUSUAL OCCURENCE

December 1

At promptly 0000 hours all radio call signs of the Japanese naval forces afloat are suddenly changed. This is the second time in thirty days they have done so. The last time was November 1. The Japanese ordinarily do not change their call signs until they have been in use for at least six months.

OFF TO THE RACES

When Eva was thirteen, she had gone with her father to treat a woman who supposedly had been kicked by a horse. When they arrived, the husband did all the talking and hovered around the bed like a nervous Nellie. At first, Eva had been shocked at what a vicious horse they'd had because it had kicked her under both eyes, in the shoulder, thigh and in her abdomen, leaving ghastly purple, green and yellow marks.

You might want to consider giving your horse away, she had said to the woman, before her father shot her a menacing look.

Then the horrible truth dawned on her.

The bruise under her eye wasn't quite as black as the woman's had been, but it was bad enough. A plum color that seeped into her face, blending in with the fresh sunburn on her cheeks. The wound had been stuck to her pillow when she first woke, but she managed to break free without causing any more damage.

She spent more time than usual fussing with her hair and makeup, and put on a pair of slacks and an emerald blouse that brought out the green in her eyes. She suddenly wished she had more clothes to choose from. Despite the bruise and swelling, she felt clearheaded, ready to get upstairs and force-feed herself and hopefully run into Clark. She was now more determined than ever to put on a few pounds and plump up.

There was also the question of what had been so important last night that the radio officer sought out Clark to talk radio something or other. Clark's words about war were now stamped in her mind.

As soon as she entered the dining room, heads turned. Word of her injury and fainting had probably spread around the ship like a bad case of smallpox.

"Eva, over here!"

At the far left of the room, Sasha and Bree were both waving her over. She wasn't quite in the mood for small talk, but went to join them anyway. Something about their accents was so cheery, and it was refreshing to be around happy people for a change.

"All things considered you're looking bright," Sasha said.

"Thank you, I think I'm going to live."

Bree laughed. "You had us worried yesterday, all splayed out on the deck like a rag doll."

"One good thing about fainting is that all self-consciousness goes out the window," she said, forcing a smile on one side of her face. Heavens, had she been exposed for half the deck to see? In that skirt, too!

Sasha leaned in and hushed her voice. "You know, Clark seems pretty buttoned up. But yesterday I thought he might have a fit when he hit you."

Bree took a sip of an orange drink in a champagne glass. "You ask me, he has a thing for you."

Eva shrugged it off. "I'm sure he just felt responsible. Anyone would have done the same."

"And the flowers?" Sasha said.

How could they possibly know about the flowers?

"An apology."

"Or an excuse to get into your room?" Bree said.

"He's married, you guys, remember?"

Eva took a big bite of her strawberry waffle so she wouldn't have to discuss this anymore. After the incident back home, she was wary of people overly interested in her business. Too many run-ins with ladies like Thelma and Mable Duffy, the two spinster sisters who owned the general store and were always spreading rumors the way other people spread birdseed on a summer's day. You couldn't kill a fly without them knowing. In fact, before the newspapers got wind of the Hollowcreek General Hospital story, Thelma and Mable were already eyeing Eva like she was a murderer.

Sasha continued, "I would mention your boy in Honolulu, so Clark doesn't get his heart broken."

"I have a feeling the wife is no longer in the picture," said Bree, nodding.

"Why would he be wearing a ring, then?" Eva asked.

"You should ask him," the twins said in unison.

Maybe she would, when the timing was right. And speaking of timing, every time Eva had thought to bring up Billy with Clark, something had gotten in the way. Really, she meant to. The truth of the matter was, Clark was on her mind an awful lot. At least half the time. Maybe more, if she was 100 percent honest.

Out on the veranda, with the hot Pacific sun beating down, a crowd had gathered for a day at the races. Of all the absurd things aboard this vessel, a felt racetrack had been laid out with six wooden horses and riders, about a foot tall. Hollering men were lined up several rows thick, and ladies lounged in chairs sipping on tall blue and pink drinks.

"What a spectacle," Eva said to Bree.

"Come on, let's place a bet."

All this gambling was not her way, but with her bingo winnings, Eva had a few dollars to spare.

"How does it work?" she asked.

Sasha pointed to a man in a white blazer. "When he throws the dice, one represents the horse, the other, how many spaces the horse moves forward."

Bree went and grabbed race cards and handed her one. There were six races, including the Pacific Coast Steeplechase, the Missouri Thoroughbred Mile and the Hawaii Handicap, with horses called Vacation Time, Hula Lassie, Aloha Malihini, Little Brown Gal, Orchid Lei and Kamaaina. Tickets were fifty cents to place a bet.

"Do you know what *kamaaina* means?" Eva asked, wondering how to pronounce the funny-looking word.

"You need lessons in Hawaiian, and fast. It's what they call a person born and raised in Hawaii."

"Or how about *malihini*?"

She was likely butchering that one, too.

"Someone new to Hawaii."

"I think I'll get a ticket for that one. Aloha Malihini."

All the hooting and hollering was contagious, and Eva found herself rooting for Golden Gait in the first race, who Bree had picked. But Sunset Strip won out in the end. She hadn't imagined wooden horse racing could be so fun, and, boy, people took it seriously. Her race was the fourth race, and when she looked at her watch, she realized that one o'clock was rapidly approaching. Clark had left in such a hurry last night that they hadn't solidified their plans, but she wanted to show up just in case. Show Boat took the next race, with a narrow lead over Blue Grass.

At about three minutes to one, she told Bree, "I have to go."

Bree frowned. "What about your ticket?"

"You take it."

"Where on earth do you have to be?"

"I made plans."

A look of knowing. "With who?"

"Lieutenant Spencer promised to teach me a little Japanese as repayment for the tennis ball." She hoped she wasn't as transparent as she felt. For there was a certain amount of giddiness at the idea of sitting with him alone in the lounge.

Bree just shook her head.

The lounge was empty. Which made sense, considering the shocking blue of the sky and that half the ship was at the horse races. Clark probably had other matters to attend to, but Eva sat down and waited anyway. Being outside in the sun insulted the slice on her face and she was feeling a bit moody. Homesickness seemed a whole lot worse when you knew you might not be going back. Life had up and flipped 180 degrees, and it filled her with a dense longing. For the familiar sound of creek water running over rocks, the copse of pine trees on her favorite trail, the delight of Ruby's laughter.

Meeting Clark in this state was probably not a good idea, and she stood to leave.

At that same moment, he appeared next to her chair. *"Konnichiwa,"* he said. Then, seeing her face, he asked, "Are you all right?"

Her skin stretched when she smiled, but she made an effort. "Yes, I'm fine. *Konnichiwa* to you, too." The words sounded silly coming from her mouth. Learning Japanese. What had she been thinking?

"Sorry to keep you waiting, but I got sidetracked with a bit of work," he said.

"Anything to do with last night?" she asked.

He didn't answer, instead pulled up another lounge chair. His eyes looked bleary and his shirt was wrinkled.

"You look lovely in green, have I mentioned that?" he said instead.

"Oh, I forgot, you're not supposed to talk about it."

"He just wanted a second opinion."

Eva had been numb as of late, but ever since hearing the captain mention submarines that first night at dinner, and now Clark's mention of war, thoughts of Japanese torpedoes were surfacing more than they should. "Are there submarines nearby?"

"Nothing to concern yourself about," he said.

He looked toward the carpet, as if it were suddenly the most interesting thing aboard the ship.

"Would you be able to tell me if there were?" she asked.

His face grew serious and he met her gaze. "If I thought you were in immediate danger, I would tell you."

They sat there, neither one looking away, for more than a few seconds. He swallowed hard. She tapped her foot. Hawaiian steel guitar music played in the background. And the danger was not from any submarine.

While he was teaching her basic words like *onegaishimasu* and *hai* and *arigatou* in Japanese—"please," "yes" and "thank you"—she was having a hard time concentrating on anything other than his well-formed arms as he scribbled out words, and how the corners of his mouth curled up when he laughed. He was patient, too, and happy to repeat things over and over again. A quality she admired in people, and one she was short on herself.

"Are you sure you don't want to go see the horse races? They're a riot," she said, feeling bad for keeping him from the action.

"I've been back and forth a few times on this ship, so I don't feel like I'm missing anything. It's nice to have some downtime, too, since we've been working overtime lately," he said, leaning back and eyeing her. "I don't mean to pry, but you seemed so sad when I walked up. Did something happen?"

His tenderness touched her. And yet to bring up Ruby and life back home would be pulling a whole netful of troubles on board this ship. But he seemed so earnest in his wanting to know that she gave in.

"It's my little sister, Ruby. She came down with polio earlier this month and I feel awful for leaving her behind. I'm her one and only. The thing was, I had already committed to the army and we need the money for her treatment."

At her words, he leaned closer. Enough so she could smell mint on his breath. "What about your folks?"

"They've both passed on."

That was another bundle of woes to leave for another time.

"Will Ruby recover?"

"You never know. In some, the paralysis clears up all the way, while others end up like the president with mostly useless limbs."

She pictured Ruby lying there in that cold hospital bed with her legs like two fallen branches in the snow, a look of terror pressed onto her face. *I will get better, won't I, Evelyn? Tell me I will.* The truth was, only God knew. A sob formed under Eva's ribs and she tried to hold it all in.

Clark surprised her by volunteering, "I know what it's like to have to leave someone."

Eva felt her lungs constrict at the hollow tone his voice suddenly took on. She had a feeling that whatever he was going to tell her had broken him at one time.

He paused for a moment before continuing. "My wife, Beth, was pregnant when we lived in Japan. Orders had me go to China for a couple of weeks. She was having a difficult pregnancy. I tried to get out of it, but they said I was needed."

He fiddled with a string on his shirt, as though remembering. "She died before I could get back."

His words burned a hole right through her. When Bree and Sasha had mentioned they had a feeling he was no longer married, this was not what she had expected. She touched his hand, but would have rather wrapped her arms around him and siphoned out the hurt.

What could she say? "Oh, Clark..."

"They live inside you, you know?"

"I do know. But that...that is devastating."

He seemed to want to get it off his chest. "For the first year, I moved around like a man with no soul. Just a body going through motions of eating, sleeping, working. What keeps a person going after something like that is a mystery to me."

Something she had witnessed over the years, to be sure. "People say it's God, but I like to think we each have our own fire burning deep inside of us, one that's almost impossible to extinguish," Eva said.

"Self-preservation, maybe?"

"Yes, but even more profound."

"Could be. I am slowly coming around," he said.

"How long had you been together?"

"Four years. We met back home and I brought her over there to Japan a year later. She hated being so far from her family, and so when she became pregnant, she struggled with it even more. Japan was not where she wanted to raise our child. But what could I do?"

"That must have been a tough position to be in," Eva said.

"You can say that again, and then when I had to go to China. I feel like it was all my fault."

Eva knew that feeling. "Blaming is a waste of time. Nobody knows what the future holds, and of course if you had, you would have done things differently."

"But I knew she was miserable."

"We can only be responsible for ourselves," Eva said, while thinking how ironic it was that here she was, dishing out advice she herself couldn't even follow.

She felt pinned to the chair, the way Clark was looking at her. How did Japanese lessons turn into something like this? A mingling of wounds. And yet she felt all the better for it.

He sighed. "Time is really the only thing that has helped."

"Give yourself credit for being resilient, not everyone is, you know. From the outside looking in, I'd say you've done well for yourself—you have important work, you are personable and make friends easily, and I've seen you enjoying yourself aboard this ship," she said, leaving out the charming and magnetic part.

"I guess you're right."

Her mind went to Ruby. "You seem like a fighter. And you know, if there's one thing about my sister, she is, too. As much as I worry, I also have a feeling that she'll be fine no matter what. She's the kind of person who turns a tragedy upside down and makes it into a blessing."

"My kind of gal," he said.

"You would love her. Everyone does."

She wanted him to meet Ruby one day. But would she even see him again after arriving in Honolulu? It seemed unlikely.

"I plan on bringing her out here next year," she said.

Clark got quiet. There was a vein above his left temple throbbing with blood. She sensed he wanted to ask her something, but instead he excused himself and said he'd be right back. In the time that he was gone, she sank back in the rattan chair, closed her eyes and pictured Billy. Had Billy ever made her feel like this?

The first time they had met had been a surprise encounter, planned and orchestrated by her father. For someone who spent his whole life putting people back together, her father's interest in guns seemed a strange fascination. But he held the belief that the better prepared one was, the less likely trouble was to come knocking. And all that time out in the sticks tending to patients required him to leave his family alone frequently. So he made sure Evelyn and Ruby could load and fire and clean their weapons like any good sharpshooter. At the ripe old age of eight.

On that first day with Billy, Evelyn had been home over the Christmas weekend when her father asked if she wouldn't mind packing a picnic lunch for his old doctor friend Herman and him, as they had planned a morning of target practice down by the creek.

"And if you don't mind, I'd like to show you off a bit," he had told her.

She laughed. "Show me off?"

"I told him you could shoot an apple from two hundred yards away."

"Why waste a good apple?"

His face grew stern, but he had a twinkle in his eye. "Haven't you learned to do as you're told, my dear?"

Evelyn replied, "Not yet."

He chuckled. "That's my girl."

As it turned out, Herman was not alone that morning. As the sun played hide-and-seek behind the bare trees, spilling light through the cracks, he showed up at the door with his son, Billy. Evelyn was the first one there to greet them, and she felt as though she had swallowed a toad when introductions were made. She knew right away what her father was up to. Both men removed their hats, and Billy did a once-over and then did not take his eyes from hers.

"A pleasure to meet you, Evelyn. My father told me you were brilliant, but he failed to mention beautiful, too," he said.

Evelyn went fiery-hot pink in the cheeks. The nerve of her father to catch her off guard like this. "I assure you, the pleasure is mine, sirs."

It didn't take long before she knew all about him, too. Between both fathers, neither Billy nor Evelyn could get a word out edgewise. *Billy was at the top of his class at the Naval Academy. Evelyn studied at the Mayo Clinic. Billy has an assignment at Pearl Harbor. Evelyn can shoot a mouse from a galloping horse.*

"Dad, come on, you know I don't shoot live targets," she said, desperate to stop the escalating brag session.

Billy had the kind of good looks that wouldn't stand out in a crowd but grew on you—pale hair, pale face, eyes the color of burnt caramel. Right away, her father made it clear that he liked him because he was smart and driven, and in order to survive in this new world, people had to be driven. She could tell he was the kind of guy used to getting what he wanted, and initially she didn't want to give him the satisfaction. But he was witty and could talk medicine and believed in women doctors, and despite herself, she found she was intrigued.

At the end of the blustery and frigid day, Billy had helped her light a fire and they sat and talked late into the night, long after their fathers had retired. One thing led to another and before she knew it, they were a full-fledged item. Weeks turned into months, and though Billy had to return to Annapolis, he visited when he could. Theirs was an intermittent love affair, made more passionate by the long absences between togetherness.

Billy had big plans for himself in the navy, so when it came time for him to leave for Hawaii, he didn't bat an eye. Evelyn was ready to say goodbye and continue on her own path, but he wanted to keep the relationship going. He wrote her like crazy, sending gushy letters about how much he loved her, which turned her insides to pudding. She thought he was sweet.

When things at the hospital went south, Billy jumped in to get her stationed at Pearl. He made her feel important at a time in her life when no one else did.

Now the only problem was *Lieutenant Clark Spencer.*

When Clark returned, he was carrying two drinks that looked suspiciously like Moscow mules. The orange Hawaiian-print shirt he wore brought out the bronze in his skin and she wondered if he might have a few drops of Spanish or Italian blood in him.

He handed her a copper mug and smiled. That dimple was too much. "Seems like we could both use a little pick-me-up. I'm not usually a day drinker, but figured why not," he said.

"You know this is not going to help my lessons," she said.

"Actually, you'd be surprised. Fewer inhibitions and the language flows more naturally."

She took a sip, mouth puckered. "Are you saying I'm not a natural?"

"Kimi wa nante utsukushīin daroo."

"There you go again, mumbling secrets to me. I can tell by the look in your eye it's not part of the lesson."

He looked amused, but didn't respond.

"What did you say?" she asked.

"You really want to know?"

The way he said it, like he was giving her an out, only made her want to know more.

"I do."

"I said 'You're beautiful.'"

The words nearly launched her off the chair. Clark was an impossibility. Yet here she was, thinking about him forty-two minutes of every hour. In fact, she couldn't *not* think about him. It would be easier if he would just stay in his room for the rest of the trip and she could continue on with life as planned—running away to Hawaii.

GHOST SIGNALS

Damn. He'd gone and gotten all serious on her, and then tried to lighten things up with a drink, which turned into two, and before he knew it, he was imagining taking her to that remote beach near Haleiwa and kissing her underwater. Feeling the smooth porcelain of her skin. He had to rub his eyes to wipe the image from his mind. He had spent half the previous night ruminating on whether to act on his feelings and decided there was no harm in spending a little time with her. How much could happen in a few days anyway? But Eva had a wall up of some kind, and whenever the conversation veered toward anything to do with the future, she became silent.

Clark was trying to figure out a way to dine alone with her, maybe on the upper deck of the ship under the stars, but what was the point, really? Instead, he sat with the football boys and before he could make his way over to Eva for a hello, Hank Wilson showed up in the doorway and made a beeline for him.

"Lieutenant, can I borrow you again?" was all he needed to say.

On the way out of the dining room, Clark managed to catch Eva's eye and he gave her a nod. Now she was really going to wonder, and he felt like a fool for bringing up the war with her. He had been hoping last night was just a fluke, some atmospheric anomaly that would not be repeated. But the look on Wilson's face said otherwise.

Back in the radio room, there was a yellow notepad covered in scribbles. The sound of buzzing and crackling permeated the space around them.

"We got good radio direction finder bearings, mostly from a northwesterly direction from where we are," Wilson said.

"Again?" Clark said.

He nodded. "Pretty bold if you ask me. Letter for letter the same message coming from Tokyo, which only solidifies that the signals are repeat-backs."

"How do you know?" Clark asked.

"Because I copied the original land-based signals. We don't have a recorder, but it's pretty obvious."

He wondered if the boys stuck out in the boonies at Station H were picking this up, too. In which case, the admirals would be mobilizing forces anytime now. His palms began to sweat. "What frequency did you say they're using?"

"Low frequency—375 kilocycles," Wilson said.

"Isn't that reserved for direction finding?" Clark asked.

"Yes, and it has a pretty limited range. But it's brilliant. No one's going to be monitoring for Japanese signals in this band."

Which meant it was probably lost on the boys at Station H. The immensity of what they had stumbled upon began to creep up on him. He started pacing and his armpits were now drenched, even though the room was an ice cave. "Have the signals moved since yesterday?"

"It appears they have. I'll know more if it's still going on tomorrow night," Wilson said.

"Damn, we need to get this info straight to navy HQ when we arrive."

"If it's not too late by then."

"Have you told anyone else about this today?" Clark asked.

"Nope."

"Don't. We don't want to start a panic."

"What about the captain?"

"I would say yes if our ship was in any kind of danger, but this might be a need-to-know situation."

There would be no way to get word to Honolulu without broadcasting on frequencies that anyone could listen in on. And what would he say? *Armada of Japanese ships amassing northwest of Oahu, probably getting ready for an attack.* That would not go over well. Especially if they were wrong.

"Can you be sure about all this?" he asked Wilson.

"Absolutely. I can't tell you what the Japs have up their sleeves, but you can be sure they are out there. There is no other explanation."

Unbelievable, and yet not impossible.

Clark turned on his official voice. "The report needs to be impeccable. So make sure to include every last detail that you can think of. Including your history and experience and how you arrived at all this."

"Roger that."

They continued for another hour listening to the signals, using the huff-duff direction finder, and taking down notes. If only he could decode the signals, he would be in a unique position to translate them. Whatever the Japanese army was planning, it could not be good. FDR had backed them into a corner and now they were going to make him pay. Everyone had been so sure about them sticking closer to home. Singapore, Dutch East Indies, Guam. Now it looked like *everyone* had been mistaken.

Early morning at sea was one of his favorite times. The ocean still slept, without any interruption from the wind, and

the waters were smooth as blue glass with ribbons of current.
He ran his finger along the railing and licked the salt that came
away. The swells had picked up again, big rolling mountains,
rocking the ship from side to side. No doubt people would be
sick again, but he loved the energy the sea put off. A pair of
noddy terns flitted about fifty yards out, the first he'd seen so
far. That meant land was within reach. Tomorrow.

He thought about Beth and wondered what she would think
of Eva. Though the two were from different worlds, oceans
apart, they both carried an indefinable spark. The minute
you walked into a room, you could feel their pull. At least he
could. Or maybe that was just the way of attraction. An invisible band of fire burning between two people.

A splash in the distance caught him off guard. Five seconds
later, a humpback whale shot out of the water, making a huge
whack when it landed. He looked around to see if anyone else
had seen, but the deck was empty. Either too early, or the
motion sickness had taken over. The whale breached again,
and then lay on its back and slapped a huge white flipper on
the surface, over and over again.

Beth had loved whales. One of her biggest gripes with Japan
had been their insistence on butchering whales and dolphins
in large numbers. She was outspoken about it, too, giving the
people a piece of her mind. He admired that in her, and got
the feeling that Eva was like that, too. Not afraid to speak up
for what she believed in.

Eva. The voice of reason said let her go. War was brewing
and it was looking more and more like there could be an attack
any day now. The boys in the Dungeon needed him, and he was
hell-bent on his code work. But another part of him wanted to
protect her from whatever might be coming, and to see what
unfolded. Truth be told, he was thinking about her a whole lot
more than he ought to. Those green eyes were something else,

too. Maybe he'd flip a coin. Heads—ask her to have dinner on the deck with him; tails—avoid her until Honolulu and go on his way.

He took out a quarter.

THE EXCHANGE

December 2

"What! You don't know where Carrier Division 1 and Carrier Division 2 are?" says Admiral Kimmel, after being briefed on a five-page report he'd just been handed.

"No, sir, I do not. I think they are in home waters, but I do not know where they are," says Layton.

Kimmel looks at him sternly, yet with a hint of a smile. "Do you mean to say they could be rounding Diamond Head and you wouldn't know it?"

"I hope they'd be sighted before now," says Layton.

—An exchange between Admiral Husband Kimmel and Edwin Layton, combat intelligence officer in charge of the Pacific arena, after Kimmel reads Layton's report summarizing where the Combined Japanese Fleet, aka Orange Fleet, was thought to be. Neither one of those commands had appeared in radio traffic for fully fifteen and possibly twenty-five days.

HEADS OR TAILS

Their last full day aboard the *Lurline* and not five minutes after Jo got up, she was back in bed groaning and slightly green. After bringing her a glass of water and a packet of soda crackers, Eva left to go above deck. Seasickness was terribly unpleasant to be around, and there was nothing else Eva could do to help her. Instead of seeking out Clark in their unofficial meeting place on the railing, she went straight to the opposite deck. The smooth but hilly water, the sticky air, this was the tropical feel she had imagined. The only thing was, the closer they got to Hawaii, the more she had the jitters about being found out. Here on the ship it was easy to be vague about who you were and what you did, but with the doctors and nurses at Tripler, you never knew who might have seen the headlines and paid attention, or who might have ties to Dr. Brown. The medical world had that old boy network feel. But here she was.

A strange slapping noise came from her left and she saw an enormous gray creature leaping straight into the air. She stood and stared with her mouth open.

A whale!

Forgetting her idea to avoid Clark, she sprinted down the deck, around back to the other side, ignoring the slanted angle of the ship. Her hat blew off and she had to run back and grab it. A pair of old men on deck chairs sipping coffee gave her funny looks. She thought it was probably too early for Clark to be up, but there he was.

Her breath had left her and she gasped. "Whales!"

"I guess you would have never seen them before, huh?" he said with a smile.

"You must come see!"

She was tugging at his arm.

He laughed and pointed. "They're over here, too."

A whale rose up, lifting its entire body airborne before falling flat on the water. The sound split the morning air around them.

"Why, they're so...so...massive. And majestic," Eva said.

What a spectacle! It made her want to laugh and cry at the same time. The whale was the size of a school bus.

"Pretty amazing, aren't they? They call that breaching," he said, leaning against the railing with his shirtsleeves rolled up.

Eva moved in next to him and they stood there hollering every time the whale launched out. She felt like a young girl at the circus hanging out with her best friend. The next thing she knew, her hand had latched onto his arm, squeezing. His biceps was as hard as a chunk of wood.

"This is the highlight of my whole trip," she said.

Standing there in the sun-kissed morning, watching whales breach. A day away from a tropical paradise. Two months ago, she would have never imagined herself on a ship in the middle of the Pacific. Life sure had a way of throwing in twists and turns when you least expected it. But as always, deep inside, the guilt of leaving Ruby was rooted firm.

"Mine, too," Clark said, close enough that he was almost speaking into her hair.

The hum of his voice settled below her navel, and sent a

wave of longing running down to her toes. Afraid to glance his way, Eva kept her eyes glued to the water. This was not going as planned. A few seconds later, he ran a finger along her cheek, just below the stitches.

"You're healing fast," he said.

She could scarcely breathe.

"It's the salt air. It has to be," she said.

Why was her heart skipping beats?

"You're so thin, Eva. What happened?"

If she were to open up now, it would be her undoing. *Keep him at arm's length and get to shore.* "Just Ruby. I love her so much. It's been rough, you know?"

He tilted his head to the side. "I do."

Eva still refused to make eye contact, instead focusing on the quarter in his hand. "What are you doing with that?"

He looked down, glanced back at her and held it out. "Will you flip it for me?"

"What's this about?" she wanted to know.

"Just a habit I have."

She crossed her arms. "I should know what I'm flipping for."

"How about this? Heads, you have dinner with me on the top deck under the stars. Tails, we go on business as usual and join the masses in the dining hall," he said with his eyes fixed on hers.

A bold move, to hang everything on the flip of a coin. Maybe he felt as confused as she did. Not mentioning Billy from the beginning had been a big mistake. Now it seemed impossible. The words would simply not come out. It was a rotten thing to do to someone, she knew that, which made it all the worse.

Torn between yearning for heads and requiring tails in order to keep her sanity, she tossed the quarter into the air.

Before she could blink, Clark caught it and placed it on the back of her hand.

His warm palm glued to her skin.

The wild thumping of her heart.

Tails.

After an early breakfast with Clark, in which there were long silences and periods of awkwardness, Eva moped around the room for a bit. She'd given Jo more ginger brew, leafed through an army manual and picked up a pamphlet on Hawaiian sayings, but nothing held her attention for long. *Utsukushī*…something or other…kept ringing in her ears. She had committed it to memory as best as she could, but that last word was too complicated.

Deciding it might be best to move her legs and get her blood flowing, Eva strolled through all the grand rooms of the ship again, arriving in the writing room. Ruby was deserving of a longer letter, so she grabbed several pieces of Matson linen stationery and sat down to write.

Dear Ruby,

Konnichiwa. We are almost to Hawaii, and I am doubting my decision to come, mainly because I miss you. How are you? I hope you are following orders and doing the exercises I showed you. Remember, the more you move your body the better. Get that blood flowing! Speaking of blood flowing, this ship is so huge that one walk around it and you've done enough walking for a week. That combined with the salty air is a tonic all its own. Everyone should be required to take a trip like this at least once in a lifetime, or especially when ill or depressed.

Did I mention the people? They are a whole new breed. Adventurous, worldly, fashionable. One in particular, a naval officer I've become rather fond of. He's been giving me Japanese lessons in exchange for smashing me in the face with a tennis ball. Yes, it's true, I was playing tennis! My cheek split open and required stitches. (Don't worry, I am fine.) The language is so foreign, it hurts my brain, but it's fun, too. And now I will be able to communicate with the local Japanese people in Honolulu. My only wish is that Clark and I can remain friends after the journey, as he is a fine specimen and a good man. Why is it that women and men can't seem to be friends without arousing suspicion? This is an inconvenient rule of life, and I don't like it one bit.

Anyway, we saw whales this morning. And then dolphins flying, spinning and twirling in the air. It looked like a real show for our benefit the way they rode in our massive wake. This ocean is really something you need to see for yourself. A blue you cannot even imagine, with giant sun rays shining through the depths.

I must admit, I am also looking forward to seeing this island that I've heard so much about. Is it really true that I will be walking around Waikiki barefoot and in nothing but a bathing suit, swimming in blue lagoons every day? Still, I will be counting the days until I see you again.

Take good care.

Your friend,
Eva Cassidy
PS Say hello to Evelyn for me.
PSS Konnichiwa means hello in Japanese.

She read over the letter, wondered if she should have even mentioned Clark, but then sealed it. Ruby would immediately home in on his significance, but what was she to do? She had to tell someone about him, lest she explode. Her heart was definitely jumbled, and for the first time, she dared to imagine how Billy would react if she told him she had met someone else. It would likely be inconceivable to him.

But Billy was her future. A guarantee. Clark was a big unknown. And, anyway, she loved Billy, didn't she? She had also made a promise to her father while holding his crumpled hand. Not only that, but Billy knew her secret.

Flipping tails had been for the best. So why did she feel so gut-twistingly awful?

As dinnertime neared, Eva considered staying in the room with Jo. Why go upstairs? There was no one else she was particularly eager to talk to, except maybe Dr. Wallace. The twins were fun to be around, but they would probably interrogate her about Clark and want to know how the two had ended up arriving at breakfast together.

Slipping on the green dress, the one she had saved for the final night's dinner and dance, now seemed anticlimactic. What was the point of dancing, either? Touching strangers and jumping around like a jittery bug. She wished she could snap out of her mood.

It's the last night. You have to at least show up.

Eva smoothed her hair with a rose-scented pomade and twisted it into a bun, pinning it in place with rusted bobby pins. When she leaned close to inspect her wound, which was closing up nicely, she noticed more freckles on her cheeks showing. She'd hardly been out in the sun because of her face, but the strength of it was tenfold that of Michigan's. At least it sure felt that way, scorching her shoulders through her blouse and plastering her hair onto her neck. No wonder people called it the endless summer.

Jo had decided to try sitting up, and when Eva stepped out

of the bathroom, her eyes grew wide and she whistled. "Look at you, all done up and shimmery. Meeting up with Lieutenant Spencer, are you?"

"No," Eva said a little too forcefully.

"Now, now. I was simply asking. You'd have to be a fool not to notice how he looks at you. So why aren't you?"

"Because I have other plans."

Jo sighed. "No man has *ever* looked at me like that."

Eva didn't want to talk about Clark. "Even if he did, we dock tomorrow and I'll probably never see him again. So I'm going to sit with Dr. Wallace and discuss medicine."

The dining hall was half as full as it had been the previous nights, with plenty of empty tables. Only one older couple decked out in Hawaiian-print outfits sat at her assigned table, so she scanned the room looking for Dr. Wallace.

She spotted him at a table with Bree and Sasha and the two soldiers from dinner that first night. By chance, the seat to the right of Wallace was open, so she walked over. Sasha waved madly and motioned for her to sit.

"Not bad, if I do say so myself," said Wallace when he saw her cheek.

"Your experience shows," Eva said.

"I always take more care on the face, especially with women. Most men don't give a damn about scars. They just want to be reassembled. But women, they'll take you to court if so much as a line shows," he said with a hint of a smile.

Bree butted in. "You look stunning, Eva."

"Those eyes! Why, they look positively glowing with that dress on," Sasha said.

Eva felt a blush coming on. "I figured I ought to wear it at least one night, since I'll be working straightaway once we land."

"Tripler, correct?" Wallace asked.

"Yes."

"And where did you say you worked back home?"

She hadn't said. "Here and there. A small hospital in Indiana." The lie came out stilted and heat rose on the back of her neck.

"I recently gave a series of lectures at Greenwood Hospital. Is this where you were?" Wallace said.

Her heart rate shot up. Stick with the lie or improvise? "A great place from what I hear. I was farther south, though."

Please don't ask where. Please, please, please.

He stared at her for a moment with hawk-like intensity. "You look familiar. You're not originally from Indiana, are you? You sound more north," he said.

Several photographs of Eva had been plastered across local and regional newspapers, which a visiting doctor might pay close attention to, even if he practiced in another state. Everyone loved a sensational story, as long as they weren't at the heart of it.

"Michigan."

"A wolverine, are you?" he said.

She forced a smile. "How about you, Doctor? I'd like to hear more about your lectures this weekend."

Wallace seemed happy to oblige. "I'm giving talks Thursday, Friday and Sunday. Treatments of wounds—both civilian and military—back injuries and burns. I know it sounds dismal, but war creates specific types of injuries, and the more we can be ready the better. When I went off to France I was woefully unprepared. Out in the trenches we figured out for ourselves how to dig shrapnel out of a body or not to suture wounds but to pack with gauze to stave off infection."

"Do you believe we'll go to war?" Eva asked him.

"With most of the world at each other's throats, we would

be hard-pressed not to in the coming months. Especially with Hitler in Leningrad and Kiev now."

"Would you go back to Europe?" she asked.

He took a sip of wine and swirled his glass. "No question. Those young lads on the front lines were some of the most admirable people I've seen. Taking it so that others can be free. They deserve all we can give them."

"Is the lecture for doctors only, or can nurses attend?" Eva asked.

"For doctors. It would be way over your head."

She winced. "But suppose a nurse wanted to listen in and pick up what she could? Would it hurt anything?"

"It all sounds so gruesome," Bree, who had apparently been listening in, said.

Wallace fixed his gaze on Bree. "Life and death can be gruesome… Humans can be gruesome." Then to Eva, "I imagine there should be room enough, so if you feel the need to attend, by all means come. Just don't be surprised if you get a few looks," Wallace said.

She was used to looks.

Eva picked up the menu and studied tonight's dinner options, but it was hard to focus on reading the menu, when all she could think about was Clark. She had imagined he would at least show up for dinner, but he was nowhere to be seen. While Bree and Sasha flirted with the soldiers, Eva sipped a Shirley Temple and watched the door. Guests were dressed to the nines. Suits and sequined gowns. High heels. Fancy hats. Cigar smoke.

"Waiting for someone?" Bree asked.

Was she that obvious?

"Jo said she may come up," Eva said.

"Mmm-hmm."

Beads of sweat formed along her spine. All this stuffy air

and lying were making her light-headed. "You know, I should go check on her," Eva said, pushing back her chair and rushing out of the room.

Instead of going below, she made her way up top. Salt air and one billion stars would be a cure for most any ailment. How many stars were out there? Did anyone really know?

At the railing, she looked for the North Star but felt disoriented under such a huge expanse of sky. She spun around and held up her fingers to try to count degrees. That was when she saw the lone figure sitting at a table. His was back to her. She tiptoed closer. The broad shoulders, uniform, faint smell of Old Spice. He took a drink of something, ice clinking in the glass. She had half a mind to back away and leave him in peace. Instead, she froze, memorizing the curve of his neck and the way he sat, like a football player on the bench.

"There's an extra seat here if you feel like joining me," he suddenly said, turning to look at her.

His table was just beyond a pool of light.

"How did you know it was me?" she asked.

"Your rose lotion gave you away. If you want to sneak up on someone, never wear perfume or lotion. That's your tip for the night," he said.

"Hang on, I wasn't trying to sneak up on you. I just noticed your silhouette there and was trying to get close enough to see who it was," she protested.

A smile crossed his face. "I was hoping you'd come," he said with a tenderness that softened the backs of her knees and swelled her chest.

Staying would only invite trouble, but Clark didn't wait for a response. Instead, he stood and pulled out the chair for her. "Sit. I could use the company."

She obeyed. What else could she do? Such a perfect setting could not have been manufactured. The air temperature was that of early summer in Michigan—halfway between warm and cool—not another soul in sight, and the buzz of steel guitars wafting up from below. Here she was, plopped in the middle of the Pacific Ocean counting stars as though she had not a care in the world.

It felt like someone else's life.

"Did you notice the phosphorescence?" he asked.

"Where?"

He pointed. "In our wake."

A luminous ribbon of glowing blue water trailed out a mile behind the ship, like a pathway to Neverland. "I was too busy looking at the stars, I can't believe I missed it."

"It's like the ocean's version of starlight," he said.

"What causes it?"

"They're tiny plankton that send off light when disturbed. The glow happens in ship wakes, or when waves break against cliffs, stuff like that."

"But we didn't have a trail like this on the past nights. Why now?"

He shrugged. "Probably to do with the tides and water temperature."

"Well, if there are any Japanese submarines out there, they sure won't have any trouble spotting us now. It's like a big neon sign that says 'Here we are!'"

There she went, worrying about submarines again. But being on a ship in the ocean, even though it was a grand ship, made her feel like a giant target. No solid ground, no place to hide. Only miles and miles of water and sky.

"We aren't at war with Japan…yet," he said, swigging the last of whatever was in the glass and staring off into the night.

They sat quiet for a time.

"You know something, don't you?" she said, finally breaking the silence.

Just then, the music grew louder. Jimmy Dorsey was cooing "Green Eyes," one of her favorite songs. Without a word, Clark took her hand and pulled her up. He moved her like she weighed nothing. One hand went to her low back, wrapped partway around her hip; the other, warm and calloused, gripped her hand. An electric current skimmed along her limbs.

"I couldn't leave without a dance," he said softly into her hair.

She leaned against his collarbone and could hear the thump of his heart. This was not meant to be happening. But the sweetness of the moment was too lovely to stop. As much as Clark was impossible, he was also inevitable.

He was a good dancer, too, leading confidently and right on time with the music. It seemed as if good old Jimmy was singing the song just for the two of them. Everywhere Clark touched her, her skin burned.

When he pulled away and looked down at her, a sheer smile brushed his lips. Their eyes fixed on each other and a shiver of longing ran to the base of her spine. He smoothed back a wisp of hair on the side of her cheek. *Go ahead, kiss me*, her body screamed. At that moment, she would have given up everything to feel his mouth on hers. It had already happened in her mind so many times. His salty lips, warm hands. But Clark seemed to be unsure. The song ended and a lively jitterbug started up, immediately breaking the spell and causing a moment of extreme awkwardness.

He led her over to the railing, where a cool and salty breeze rose up from the water. "This music isn't my thing," he said.

Having hardly had time for dancing in recent years, Eva had to agree. "I would just embarrass everyone around if I tried those moves."

"Why are you always so hard on yourself?" he said.

"I'm not—"

"You are. I get the sense that you blame yourself for your sister, and there's something else you're not telling me."

Her throat caught. "It's just been hard back at home, losing my father last year and feeling responsible for my sister. My family is everything to me, and now Ruby, the only one I have left, is sick. It terrifies me."

"You were close to your father?"

She nodded. "My father was tough but he was my biggest fan. When he died, a huge light went out in my life. He instilled in me a reverence for medicine and healing and making a difference in the world."

"Your father was a lucky man," Clark said.

"I know we don't get to choose our parents, but if we could, I would have chosen him over every other man on earth," she said.

"I hope my children say that about me one day," Clark said.

"You still want children?"

"More than anything."

"I give you credit, Clark. For not letting yourself be shut down by your loss. I've seen it happen so many times. But you, you are still a part of the world, still smiling at life."

He blew like a horse. "I'm working on it. It hasn't been easy. I lost thirty pounds, didn't sleep for six months and was like a ghost in the world. I didn't want to be here."

"What changed?" Eva asked.

"One day I saw a young father playing in the ocean with his daughter. The absolute love between them was so clear. I thought to myself, I don't want to leave without knowing that."

Eva was on the verge of tears, so she wasn't conscious of his bending down until his lips met hers. Softly at first, like butterfly wings but more insistent, until his whole body was pressed against every nook and cranny of hers. She liked how he tasted, his warmth and his hardness, and how his hands firmly held her waist. All that wanting built up inside over the past few days welled up and she felt her body give way. No one had kissed her like this before.

Ever.

She leaned back into the darkness, waves lapping below, and let him tangle his hands in her hair. His stubble scraped against her chin, but she barely noticed. A soft moan escaped. Her whole body was trembling with need. He clutched her even tighter, and yet still he wasn't close enough.

The way his tongue teased the inside of her mouth, slow and soft and hopeful—as if they would be here all night— was causing a strange humming on her insides. She wrapped one leg around his, as high as she could, and pulled him in tighter, if that were possible. Her back arched against the cold, hard railing.

Stop, a small voice inside whispered. Eva ignored it and kept on kissing.

She was conscious of him hoisting her up and swinging her around, placing her on a nearby bar stool with one leg on either side of him. He had to hunch down a little to see eye to eye. Maybe it was starlight or maybe she had grown accustomed to the darkness, but she could see every contour of his angular face, every fleck of light in his eye.

"You taste like the ocean," he said, his voice hoarse.

"I hope that's a good thing."

One side of his mouth curled up. "Very good."

Leaning in again, his lips hovered an inch away from hers. Steamy breath. Eva felt herself on the edge of not being able to stop where this was headed. His palms moved up along the outside of her thighs. She closed her eyes, summoned bravery.

It had to be now.

Eva put her hand on his chest and pushed him back. She took a deep breath and smoothed her skirt down over her knees. "Look, Clark, I know we've spent a lot of time together on board—" Each syllable was a hunk of meat lodged in her throat. "And I have grown very fond of you, as I'm sure you can tell, but there's something I haven't mentioned, which I certainly should have right from the very start." A sore pause.

He waited in silence for her to continue, a strained look on his face. She wanted to pull him back close, to kiss instead of talk. But there was no chance of that now.

The rest came out jumbled. "There is a man—I mean I have a man, a boy…friend, in Honolulu waiting for me."

Saying the words aloud was a shock to her system. She felt like keeling over then and there, or retreating into a shell if only she had one. It would have been better if Clark said something, but he made no move to answer. He just slowly turned and looked out at the ocean. She wished she could have rewound the clock to that first night at the captain's dinner table. She would have casually told the table that Billy was expecting her in Honolulu.

Still, Clark stood in the worst kind of silence.

Her heart was pounding. "Say something?" she said.

"What's there to say? The trip is over and we'll each go our own way," he said, in a flat tone as though he was entirely disinterested.

"Can we be friends still?" she pleaded.

"My work keeps me busy, Eva."

Here she'd gone and made him loathe her, detestable human that she was. She deserved it. Even worse was the searing thought of not seeing him again. Her confession had ruined all chances of that. She looked down at her trembling hands. Fought back a sob.

"Well, then."

He stepped aside. "Well, then, I have some business to attend to, if you'll excuse me."

Her lip quivered as he walked away. Tears slid down her face. When she turned to see the phosphorescence once more, it was gone, as though someone had switched off all the lights in the ocean.

THE WOODS WING

September 21, 1941

The Woods Wing was part of Hollowcreek General, but a wall had been built to separate the two and keep the dreaded germs contained. Now you had to walk outside the building to enter. For some nurses and even a few of the doctors, an assignment in the Woods Wing was a game of Russian roulette. It was easy for adults to catch the polio virus and then pass it on to their own children. Hence, no one but hospital staff was allowed in. But Evelyn never minded. She had no kids.

"What are you doing here?" Milly Upton asked when Evelyn walked in the door.

"Dr. Brown sent me," she said.

"Again?"

"I must have that effect on him."

Last time he had sent her to Woods Wing, it was after she had politely suggested to ease off on the ether based on the patient's pupils. He hadn't liked that one bit. But what was the point of having a trained anesthetist if you refused to listen to her? She wished she could be more forceful with him, but he was such a bully.

Milly handed Evelyn a folder. "I could use another hand here. We have two new cases, brothers aged four and seven.

One completely paralyzed, the other has a hunched and slug-gish gait, but he's still able to move around."

After scanning over the chart, Evelyn went straight into the room. The older brother, Jimmy Dalloway, lay in his bed with a frightened look on his face, while the younger one snored like a goose. Her heart ached for the two boys. Greasy orange hair and freckles, and slightly malnourished.

She sat next to him and picked up his clammy hand. "What's your favorite animal, Jimmy?"

"I dunno," he said.

He looked like he would burst into tears at any moment.

"Do you like dogs?"

"I think so."

She laughed. "You think so, huh? Well, then, you're in luck. We have a doctor here named Dr. Jones, who happens to bring his dog, Scout, to work with him every other day."

His eyes widened. "Into the hospital?" Jimmy asked.

She nodded. "Yep, and she's the sweetest thing this side of cherry soda. The only thing you have to worry about is get-ting licked to death."

In four short months, since Jones began bringing Scout around, she had seen kids go overnight from hollow-eyed and hopeless to smiling and asking when Scout was coming back. Administration had balked in the beginning—*dogs carry disease*—and a few parents complained, but when they saw the results, people quit fussing. Jones, Dr. Brown's peer, was one of two doctors who could get away with such a thing. Where Brown ruled the surgical ward, Jones ruled the Woods Wing.

"When is she coming?" he asked.

"Tomorrow morning, and I'll make sure you're the first person she visits, okay?"

His lower lip stuck out and a small bob of the head was all he gave.

"You're going to be fine, Jimmy, stay brave for your brother. Can you do that for me?" Another nod.

She brushed aside his damp and matted hair. "Good."

"Nurse?" he said in a very small voice.

"What is it?"

"What does Scout look like?"

"She is sleek and gray like mercury, with yellow eyes and big floppy ears. And all she wants is to please you and make you laugh. If you don't fall in love instantly, I'll give you a quarter. Deal?"

A thin smile appeared on his face. "Deal."

Ten seconds later, the hospital alarms went off. A feeling of dread whooshed through her limbs. Instincts told her to run straight back to the operating room, but she was terrified of what she would find. Nor would Dr. Brown want her, of all people, showing up to help. Maybe it was something else. Please, let it be something else!

She knew it wasn't something else.

THE ONE-TWO PUNCH

December 2

Never show weakness. The rule applied not just to combat, but to women. Even though Clark felt like his insides had been detonated, he had somehow managed to maintain coolness. How could he not have seen this coming? Even when they were dancing and he was holding her close, taking in the smell of roses, he sensed a hesitance. Something was holding her back.

Damn.

The walk to the radio room was a death march. With each step, leaving behind the only thing in recent memory that had stirred some feeling in him. He had finally thrown away his reservation, worked up the nerve to kiss her and then this. Hell, the drive to Waimea Bay with her was all planned out in his mind. In a week from now, her cheek would be healed enough to swim, and he couldn't wait to see the expression on her face when he pulled up to the overlook. In that way her eyebrows arched up just before she smiled. Eva would be tough to forget, but he was good at turning off pain. He'd had lots of experience.

Wilson was waiting for him. "I'm glad you're here."

"So am I," Clark said. The radio room situation would be the best kind of distraction.

"I can say with certainty that the signals are coming from moving objects. They are moving away from Japan, closer to Honolulu," Wilson said. "Signals are being sent on the same frequency as the last two nights."

"And you trust your direction finder?"

"Absolutely."

"Let me have a listen," Clark said.

He put on the headphones and turned the knobs. His mind spun along with them. A fleet of Japanese ships approaching Oahu could only mean one thing. He thought back to his last meeting with Ford and Admiral Kimmel down in the Dungeon, before he had flown to San Diego the previous week. They had been debating the location of the Japanese subs and carriers. One thing both Station HYPO and CAST agreed on, was that the Japanese Navy was up to something in the South China Sea. A strong offensive movement was likely there. Less clear was what was happening closer to Hawaii. Station CAST maintained that there were no forces in the Marshall Islands, but Ford and Clark's team at HYPO had been tracking submarines there. At least fifteen or twenty. As far as aircraft carriers, indications were one, possibly two. All of this was purely based on radio intelligence. They informed Kimmel and Washington of this, but the Marshall Islands were 2,500 miles away. Hawaii was not a target. If anything, Japan was bolstering its defenses for when it attacked Singapore or the Dutch East Indies.

After listening for a time, and registering coded signals, he put the headphones down and turned to Wilson. "Something doesn't add up here," Clark said.

Wilson looked grim. "It seems pretty clear to me, sir."

"How has no one else picked up on this?"

"No one else is looking on those low frequencies."

"When do you head back to California?" Clark said.

"On the fifth."

"The sooner the better, with what's out there."

The implication hung in the air between them.

Wilson frowned. "In all my years, I've never come across anything so puzzling. No one seems to think the Japs are coming for Hawaii, but here they are."

Thirty years at sea could take a toll on a man, and Wilson had the creased and leathery skin to prove it. But Clark could tell he was as sharp as the day he started, with triple the experience of anyone else aboard.

"Keep this between us, okay? The guys in Honolulu will know what to do," Clark said.

"I hope so," Wilson said.

A feeling of dread swept over him. He and the boys at HYPO had missed something. Station CAST in the Philippines had missed something. Washington had missed something. Something big. "I'll stop by in the morning to pick up your report. Make sure to include anything and everything, so no one can dispute it."

"Does this mean what I think it means?" Wilson asked.

"I'm afraid it does, sir," Clark said.

Sleep was elusive, but in the end, he managed a few hours. He woke early, packed his bag and shaved. One look in the mirror and he felt like he'd aged ten years overnight. The evening had started off so well, only to turn into a one-two punch to the gut. First Eva, then Wilson. He'd spent the first few hours tossing and turning and getting tangled in his blankets, picturing her face and the smooth curve of her neck. The next few hours were spent trying to figure out what the Japanese Navy had up its sleeve. Hawaii was not prepared in any way for an attack. Carriers were at sea, planes were in the

Philippines and people were still going on as if they lived in a tropical paradise immune to any invasion.

The thing that bothered him the most was whether or not he should warn Eva. This wasn't the kind of information you shared with civilians, or even low-clearance military. Telling her would be breaking the law. But how would he live with himself if anything happened to her and he could have prevented it? He shook his head, told himself to stop ruminating. Eva wasn't his concern. At this very moment, she was probably giddy about seeing her man and getting gussied up for Boat Day. No, he would go eat breakfast and steer clear, then find Wilson.

Focus on the situation northwest of Oahu.

On the walk up, his mind began to wander. In China, he'd heard about the green recruits of Japan's Kwantung Army and how they were required to blindfold prisoners and tie them to poles and then bayonet them to death. Straw dwellings of peasants were set on fire. Hundreds of thousands of innocents were killed in the bombing of Shanghai. Women raped. Human beings turned into fighting machines and drained of all decency. It happened in war, he knew that. A strange fluke in our design.

Would there be anywhere safe to hide on Oahu if it were invaded? His neck began to sweat. By the time he reached the dining room, he was so worked up, he turned around and headed straight back down.

Screw it.

NO TURNING BACK

December 3

Circular twenty four forty four from Tokyo one December
ordered London, Hong Kong, Singapore and Manila to
destroy Purple machine. Batavia machine already sent to
Tokyo. December 2 Washington also directed to destroy
Purple, all but one copy of other systems, and all secret
documents. British Admiralty London today reports
embassy London has complied.

—*A message sent from OP-20-G, Captain Laurance Safford
to Admiral Kimmel at Pearl Harbor and the Fourteenth and
Sixteenth Naval Districts.*

UP IN FLAMES

The consul general is burning his papers.

—*An intercept from the FBI telephone tap in Honolulu, listening in on a conversation with the Japanese consulate's chef and someone else in Hawaii.*

BOAT DAY

Boat Day had finally come and Eva was miserable. She felt like a rotten, selfish person. Leading Clark on like that. What had she been thinking? The truth was, she hadn't been thinking. Clark had been a burst of color in her black-and-white life. The missing Ruby, the guilt over leaving, and the lying, all of that erased in his presence. He had made her forget, if only temporarily.

A soft knock on the door.

Jo glanced at her. "Are you expecting anyone?"

"Nope, it must be the bellman."

Eva opened the door and found herself face to chest with Clark. Bleary-eyed, he looked around her toward Jo. "Look, I'm sorry to barge in like this, but can we talk in private for just a moment?"

Eva's hair was pinned up to set the curls and she was in a bathrobe provided by Matson. "If you wouldn't mind, I can get changed and meet you in the lounge in fifteen minutes?"

Jo cleared her throat. "I was just leaving. Come in, Lieutenant, by all means."

"Don't leave on my account," he said, but Jo was already out the door.

The poor woman was probably weak with hunger by now. The seas had calmed a little, and Eva swore she could hear Jo's stomach growling before she climbed out of bed. But now she would be alone with Clark. A warning bell went off in her head. He stepped in and shut the door behind him.

"About last night—" she started to say.

"Look, I'm not here because of that," he said, making no move to sit, cornering her between him and the bed. His face was all buttoned-up and stern.

"What is it?" she asked.

"I need you to swear to secrecy," he said.

She swallowed hard. "All right."

Ruby always swore her to secrecy, but it usually involved a boy she had a crush on or something Mrs. Green, the town gossip, had told her. This had a whole different feel.

"Tell no one. Friends, coworkers." He paused. "Boyfriend."

"I swear."

"When Wilson came and got me the other night, he was picking up Japanese radio signals somewhere northwest of Honolulu. Over the past few nights, we determined without a doubt that a fleet of ships is approaching Oahu from the northwest," he said.

"What kind of ships?" she asked.

"Imperial Japanese Navy ships. Warships."

He was close enough that she could smell the Ivory soap on his skin. The fleck in his eye seemed darker this morning. Here Clark was, telling her something dangerous and life altering, and all she wanted was for him to take her in his arms and kiss her. Boy, did she have her priorities wrong.

"Did you hear me?" he said.

Her heart felt like it had dropped into her abdomen. "What does this mean? Everyone says the Japanese would never attack us," she said.

"I'm turning in our report straightaway, and I'm sure by now our stations on Oahu are onto them. But I wanted to warn you. In the off chance of an invasion, there's a place on the North Shore I want you to know how to get to."

"You're scaring me," she said.

"This is worst-case scenario. But you should be prepared."

"Is that where you'll be?"

He shook his head. "It doesn't matter where I'll be. Once you get to the bay I told you about, with the big surf, find a place to park your car out of sight. You'll see two gun turrets on each side of the beach, but you want to go back into the valley, not stay near the beach. Follow the stream back about a mile and you'll come to a concrete bunker built into the hillside. Two miles back is another one."

For some reason, her fear was peppered with anger. "So I should just waltz in there and tell them you sent me?"

"Eva, this is serious. There are actually pillboxes all over the island, but this is somewhere you could hide out for a long time if necessary. The military isn't using them. There are banana trees, guava trees and even big fat prawns in the stream. And, of course, water."

"How far from Pearl Harbor is it?" she asked.

"About an hour, maybe less."

She pictured Japanese soldiers coming ashore, shooting and burning and taking prisoners at every turn. Clark's vision sounded like a better option. If she could make it there without being caught. The roads out there couldn't be very good and she had never been good at fishing. "Maybe I should do a practice run." Her voice sounded panicky even to her own ears.

"It wouldn't hurt," he said, shifting around on his feet.

He seemed like he was gearing up to kiss her goodbye, then thought better of it. Eva couldn't help it, she jumped forward and wrapped her arms around him as a child would. He was like a big, warm rock. At first his arms just hung there, but a few seconds later he pulled her tight enough to squeeze the air from her lungs. Tears streamed down her cheeks. When he kissed the top of her head, a sob escaped from deep in her chest that sounded more animal than human.

"It just wasn't our time," he said in a soft voice.

A moment later he was gone.

Eva ignored the breakfast bell and spent the next hour on the opposite side of the deck from where she usually found Clark. Staring out into the ocean was supposed to be a balm for tattered nerves and yet all she wanted to do was cry. Such a lovely sight with high cotton clouds and yet it did nothing for her. People showed up in shockingly bright fabrics and the kind of getups you would only see on a tropical island— strapless with flowery prints and exceedingly bright colors.

"Look, there it is!" someone nearby shouted.

Sure enough, a faint green outline loomed on the horizon. She remembered clearly, while reading the Matson brochure, how it had seemed so alluring and so distant, "...the first view of the jagged cliffs of Oahu brings a wave of excitement, an ineffable feeling of romance and mystery." Here they finally were, and there was none of that. Nowhere in the brochure had it mentioned a fleet of Japanese troops lurking off Oahu. Or the possibility of war breaking out at any moment.

As they neared enough to see the coastline, two young girls ran past her, screaming, "Diamond Head, Diamond Head!" Smaller boats streamed alongside them now, with sepia-skinned people hanging halfway overboard and waving. The rolling seas that they'd encountered yesterday had lain down and the water was now a brilliant turquoise. Pretty soon, welcoming crews climbed aboard, bringing garlands of flowers that they called lei, and draped them around every-

one's necks. Eva had never seen such an extravagant greeting. A tugboat called the *Mikioi* guided them into the harbor,
where Hawaiian boys were leaping into the water to retrieve
quarters. They had been warned the boys would only go for
quarters, not nickels or dimes, and especially not pennies. It
was all so festive.

If only.

Amid the hundreds of faces, blurred by serpentine stream-
ers, Eva searched for Billy's. A troupe of women in long leaf
skirts danced the hula, while a band of men in white uniforms
played Hawaiian tunes. Once off the ship, she struggled to push
through the masses, looking and looking. In his last letter, he
had said he would do his best to meet her at the pier, and on
the odd chance he couldn't make it, he would send someone.

The heat was for the record books, or maybe this was normal for Honolulu. Either way, her shoes were going to melt
into the pavement at any moment. Half-clad women held up
cardboard signs. *Holzman. Rigg. Abernathy. Spencer.* Eva spun
around. Would Clark be leaving with one of these beauties?
With women like this around, who needed a wife?

What also struck her was how colorful the people were. Not
their clothes, their skin. She tried not to stare, but they were
honey, ochre, copper, chestnut and everything in between.
Some were voluptuous with thick manes of hair, others were
rail thin and had jet-black hair glistening in the sun like strands
of glass. All of them were smiling. *Aloha! Youkoso!* Just then,
someone grabbed at her arm from behind.

"Excuse me, are you Evelyn Olson?" a man in uniform said.

Her body went rigid. "Who wants to know?"

The shock of hearing the name *Olson* was like someone
pressing a hot iron onto her neck. Her paperwork into the
Army Corps said she had attended University of Lewistown
nursing program in northern Indiana, with experience at

Greenwood Hospital, where her close friend Eve Cassidy had studied and subsequently worked. In a desperate state, Eva had borrowed Eve's transcripts and changed the *e* to an *a*, hoping no one would notice. Eve had agreed, with the stipulation that she would forever claim ignorance if anyone found out. The army had been so pressed for nurses to send overseas, they hardly checked. Thank goodness for friends who believed in you. And in one day, Evelyn Olson had become Eva Cassidy.

"Billy sent me, ma'am, my name is Dan Underwood." Dan looked at the slice on her cheek but was polite enough not to ask.

She let out a big sigh. "Please, call me Eva. Where is Billy?"

"Something came up at work, he said to tell you he will pick you up for dinner this evening in Waikiki."

Half disappointed, half relieved, she welcomed a little more time to pull herself together. Clark's Ivory soap smell was still stuck in her nose. The kiss imprinted on her heart. Here she had been aching to see Billy for the past seven months and now everything had been turned upside down.

She spun around, trying to catch sight of Clark as Dan led her off. All she saw was a tangle of people covered in flower lei and shirtless lads mingling through the crowd.

"So how was the trip?" he asked.

"Just lovely," Eva said.

"Imagine you're happy to be on solid ground again."

She smiled. "I fared quite well actually."

Eva wanted nothing more than to turn and run back to the ship. Just a few more days on the *Lurline* was all she needed.

It seemed like the whole island had taken off of work to witness the ship's arrival. Either that, or no one worked on a Wednesday afternoon. They passed an open market with hanging roosters and pigs, then drove toward a tower with an enormous pineapple atop of it.

"What on earth is that?" she asked.

"A water tower for Dole cannery. Sharp, isn't it?"

Under such glaring blue skies, with flowers spilling off every bush, she wondered how anyone ever got anything done here. It would be like living in a perpetual postcard.

The nurses' quarters were several blocks away from Tripler General. The buildings here all had more windows than a Southern plantation house. Tripler was no different. It looked like a place you would sit on the big veranda and sip tea while watching a game of croquet. Palm trees lined the street.

The house matron, a silver-haired woman named Myrtle Milton, showed her to her room. "You're going to love it here," she said as she huffed and puffed up the dusty stairs. "The quarters are nothing fancy, but you won't be indoors much. Either you'll be working or out exploring the island."

"Do you know who I'll be rooming with?" Eva asked.

"This is Grace's room."

"Grace?"

"Grace Lane. She's a doll."

A voice behind them said, "Are you my new roommate?"

Eva turned to see a nurse dressed in a crisp white uniform walking down the hallway toward them, cute as a pixie with short blond hair and a wide smile.

"I'm Evelyn—call me Eva."

There she went again, forgetting her own name.

"Welcome, Eva. And look at your cheek! What happened to you?"

Eva steadied herself against the wall. "Say, I'm feeling a little peaked from the heat, would you mind grabbing me a glass of water?" she said to Myrtle.

The events of the past months and the buildup of coming to Hawaii and meeting Clark and falling for him and now, finally being here, it was all too much.

"Come inside and sit," Grace ordered.

Myrtle returned and handed her a glass of water, then left the two to get acquainted.

The room was barely twelve paces across, but it smelled like sun and tangy vanilla blossoms, if there were such a thing. A screen door opened to a tiny porch with an overhanging tree and twittering birds.

Grace pointed to one of the twin beds. "This is yours. Have a rest."

Eva all but fell onto the mattress.

"A rough crossing?" Grace asked.

"For some. I managed to dodge the seasickness only to barely survive a deadly match of tennis."

The sweetest smile crossed Grace's face. "I am hopeless at tennis, too. I think you and I are going to get along just fine. Where have you traveled from?"

"A small town in Michigan. No place anyone has ever heard of."

Grace sat down on her own bed. "I'm from Seattle, and I can hardly tell you where Michigan even is," Grace said, cheerfully. "Say, are you married?"

"I thought we couldn't be married," Eva said.

"Oh, we can't be, but I know a few gals who secretly are. Not me, though. I'm single and looking."

Eva laughed. "I'm sure there is no shortage of men here."

"Yes and no. Most of them visit the brothels in their time off. I want quality."

"Quality is good. Hold out for that."

"How about you? Do you have someone special?"

"I do have someone. He's actually stationed here and I haven't seen him in half a year."

Grace looked confused. "Well, why isn't he here right now?"

"I guess he had to work."

"You'd have thought he could get out of it on a day like today."

One would have hoped.

After unpacking and getting acquainted—they were both bookworms, both at the top of their classes and both small enough that they could share clothes—Grace led Eva to the hospital. "You'll be starting tomorrow, but may as well see the place so you know where to go in the morning. I will say this, you really lucked out in getting sent here. We do work, honestly we do, but it's also a bit like being on vacation. Even the doctors. They spend more time playing golf than they do seeing patients."

That could change sooner than you think, Eva wanted to say. Going on as though everything was normal was going to prove challenging. Hopefully Clark would get the information into the correct hands and measures would be taken. But so far, no one around here seemed the least bit concerned.

"Anyone I need to watch out for?" Eva asked.

"Everyone is pretty easygoing. But you may want to steer clear of Dr. Newcastle."

"Why is that?"

Grace reached up and picked a pink flower from a tree and handed it to Eva. "He thinks he owns the place."

Eva sighed. "There's always one."

THE DUNGEON

Clark and Wilson went directly to Naval Intelligence. They arrived in the administration building above the Dungeon with their shirts plastered to their backs despite the breeze. They had cabbed it with a speeding Chinese man who, instead of braking, screamed for people to get out of his way. Lieutenant Commander Lawson was out, but his second in command, a man by the name of Lieutenant Irving, invited them into his office. Clark had never met Irving, but he'd seen him around.

"Sir, we have urgent information to get to Lieutenant Commander Lawson," Clark said.

"He's off at He'eia. I can probably help you," Irving said.

Clark knew that his boss, Ford, regularly met with Lawson, but Ford had never mentioned Irving being included.

"It's sensitive."

Irving folded his arms and leaned back in his chair. "Lawson won't be back until tomorrow. Can it wait that long?"

"No."

"I have top clearance. Fire away."

Clark slid the report in front of him. "We just came in on the *Lurline*. Hank Wilson here is the radio officer aboard. A few nights ago, he picked up Japanese coded signals, and those signals continued for the past two nights. They were repeat-backs to ships."

Irving hadn't made the connection. "And?"

"And the ships are northwest of Hawaii, moving east," Clark said.

Just speaking the words out loud made his skin crawl.

Irving frowned. "You're mistaken." It wasn't a question.

"Sir, at first we thought the same thing. I couldn't tell you what the Japs were saying, but I do know they're out there. Our DF is top-notch," Wilson added.

"Hank has been doing this for thirty years, sir. And I know my way around a ship's radio room," Clark said.

He sized up Irving, who was about the same age as him, a little shorter and half as thick. It was hard to pinpoint, but there was something about the guy he didn't like. Maybe it was his smug expression, or his air of superiority. Weren't they all on the same team?

"So, you think there's a Japanese fleet sailing our way and we wouldn't know about it by now?" Irving said, lighting up a cigarette and looking at them as though they were incompetent.

Clark began to wish he'd waited for Lawson. "Read the report."

After a few minutes of reading, Irving shut the folder. "This is a bold claim, for which I'm sure there is a reasonable explanation—probably fishing vessels—but you can be sure Lieutenant Commander Lawson will see this as soon as he returns. In the meantime, not a word of this to anyone. This is how dangerous rumors get started."

Ford would want to know.

"Not even Ford," Irving said coolly, as if reading his mind.

Clark acknowledged with a tip of his head.

"I mean it. National security."

★ ★ ★

Down in the Dungeon, when he walked into the wall of smoke, Clark felt like he'd returned home. He was the only one of the twenty-eight who didn't smoke, but felt like the blend of cigarettes, pipe smoke and Cuban cigars added credence to the mystique of the place. No one aboveground knew what they did, though speculation ran rampant.

Ford wasn't at his desk, but Huckleberry, aka Lieutenant Tom Finn, looked up from his makeshift plot table and gave him a nod.

"Look who the cat dragged in," he said.

"Hello to you, too," Clark said.

Tex, Ford's right-hand man, was on the phone, gesticulating with his massive hands, and Hal Dunn stared intently at a sheet of paper spit out by the IBM, probably looking for patterns that no one else could see. Nothing had changed—except for Dunn's beard. He now looked like a bona fide lumberjack. The guys in Washington would not be pleased. Which was exactly why he did it. A sign on his desk said YOU DON'T HAVE TO BE CRAZY TO WORK HERE, BUT IT HELPS!

Clark walked to the north wall, where Captain Alvin Lassen was seated, reading a string of Japanese lines. Lassen used green eyeshades to block out the fluorescent lights, and if he noticed Clark, it didn't show.

Clark cleared his throat. "Hey, Captain, would you mind getting me up to speed?"

Lassen looked up as if just noticing Clark. "Welcome back, Spencer. You really want to know?"

He doubted much could be worse than what he and Wilson had discovered on the *Lurline*, though nothing in the newspaper he had read on the way over signified anything big. "Absolutely."

Clark had been briefed on the latest before leaving San Diego. But a lot could happen in five days.

"First off, on December 1, the Japs changed their call signs," Lassen said.

"Again? But they just changed them."

Lassen nodded. "Every damn one of them. Which you know means they're up to no good."

Too true. Wilson's report would be shared soon enough, but Clark was itching to say something. "How about diplomatic talks?"

"Done, over, up in smoke. Admiral Stark went so far as sending out a war warning memo, and just this morning Ford was told by Lawson that Tokyo has instructed all of its consulates to burn the codes."

"Jesus."

"Thing are heating up."

Wait until he heard about the report. "Where is Ford?" Clark asked, still undecided if he would tell his boss anything yet.

"Checking on the guys at He'eia. They've been around the clock listening for the Winds message, but so far nothing."

"The Winds message?"

Lassen took off the shades. "You really are out of it. The Brits intercepted a message that in case of an emergency, a warning will be added in the middle of some Japanese news broadcast saying 'east wind, rain.' That means war with us. 'North wind, cloudy' would mean war with Russia and 'west wind, clear,' Britain."

"Have any of the stations picked it up yet?" Clark asked.

"No, but based on everything else, I think we're looking at days, not weeks before they attack someplace. Probably the Philippines, but Tex and Mike are convinced those missing carriers are headed our way. In fact, Kimmel was flipping out in his meeting with Lawson that we can't be sure of where they are."

"Any more on their movements? Have the guys at He'eia heard anything else unusual?" Clark asked.

"There's been a complete absence of calls, from the three carriers back in Japan home waters, which is unusual. Radio traffic is at a real low ebb."

Clark had heard enough. Here he was, with the knowledge neatly packed away in his brain, but he had to keep his lips sealed. Maybe he should talk to Irving again and find out who had clearance on this.

He uncrossed his legs and stood up, thinking about Eva and where she might be right now. Probably reunited with her guy and strolling down Waikiki Beach, arm in arm. He tried to convince himself he was better off without her, but his heart refused to listen. Maybe he should track her down and try to talk some sense into her. What happened between the two of them had not been meant to happen, but he knew it hadn't been one-sided. The way she had closed her eyes and fallen into the kiss. And how she'd clung to him for dear life this morning. She was in as deep as he was.

"I'll be at my desk catching up," he said to the boys.

Being back at work with an important mission would do him good.

NIGHT AT THE PINK PALACE

Eva walked back and forth on the grass in front of her barracks. She was a bundle of nerves. What if being with Clark had erased all her feelings for Billy? The truth of the matter was a big portion of her love affair with Billy had been through letters, and a week here and a week there. She had fallen for him even harder once he had up and left. Living for his letters and colorful descriptions of life in the islands and where he would take her once she arrived. An easy dream to conjure. Now it was time to see how real it all was.

Grace had pinned a yellow plumeria in Eva's hair and now she felt hot with self-consciousness. Who was she trying to fool? She was—and would always be—a fair-skinned girl from the Midwest. On the verge of hyperventilating, she took a deep breath and ordered herself to relax.

A few minutes later, a shiny gray Plymouth rumbled up to the curb and slammed to a halt. She could feel her heartbeat in her ears. Billy hopped out and ran around to her side. He was not as tall as she remembered.

"My sweet Evelyn, welcome to Honolulu!" he said with an ear-to-ear smile as he carefully placed a white flower lei over her neck and hugged her close.

"Eva," she said softly in his ear.

It would have to be second nature, so the sooner the better.

"Eva," he said, drawing out the *e*.

He felt less substantial than Clark. More bones and less muscle. Did she smell cigarettes on his skin? And yet there was a soothing familiarity in his presence. This was Billy. *Her* Billy. The Billy who knew her life, her father, Ruby. Her secrets, too.

"Did you get into a brawl on the ship?" he said with a grin when he pulled back.

Her hand went to her cheekbone. "A minor accident. A stray tennis ball."

"I hope the guilty party was made to pay," he said.

She forced a smile. "He did."

Clark was the last thing she wanted to talk about now. But had she honestly thought he would fade away?

"Seriously, though, you look rail thin. This has all been hard on you, hasn't it?"

Achingly, agonizingly hard. She nodded.

"We'll fatten you up in no time, I promise. I'm glad you're here, Eva."

"Me, too," she said.

Billy deserved a chance, she would give him that. Plus, it wasn't as though she could go crawling back to Clark after what she had done. She turned away and concentrated on what was outside the window. They drove past Chinatown's neon lights and a heavy stone building, which he informed her was Iolani Palace, then along the coastline toward Diamond Head. The sun was about to set and rosy clouds dotted the sky. They held hands the whole way, and his palm was damp with perspiration. She kept catching him staring her way.

"What?" she finally asked.

He winked. "You're even prettier than I remember."

She touched the flower to make sure it was still there. "Oh, come on."

In Eva's household, looks had never mattered. It was your brain and your heart that made you who you were. And, anyway, Ruby was the real looker in the family. Taller, more curvy and a smile full of straight, white teeth.

As they passed through Waikiki, sailors in their liberty whites spilled out of storefronts and saloons. Eva was too busy taking it all in to say much, plus the engine was almost too loud to speak over, which was really a blessing. How could there be so much to talk about and yet she couldn't think of one thing to say?

"There are so, so many of them," she mustered.

"Close to twenty thousand on the island. Ready to defend." She sure hoped so.

Billy parked outside of a grand pink building six stories tall. The Royal Hawaiian Hotel in real life! It sat right along the beach, skirted by grassy lawns and coconut trees. An American flag waved lazily on its top dome.

"Here we are. The Pink Palace. They always have a nice party on Boat Day," he said.

She froze. If they ran into Clark, she would climb under a table and hide. "Does everyone from the *Lurline* come?"

"Half the island comes," he said, leading her down a sandy path toward the shoreline.

She had no choice but to follow along, slipping off her sandals. The sand between her toes was warm and grainy and her feet sank with every step. But it was the ocean she couldn't take her eyes off. One hundred shades of blue. White foamy rollers.

"Look, they're surf riding!" she said, temporarily forgetting her worries. Men on long wooden planks rode the breakers like they were flying. "Do women do it, too?"

"They usually go tandem with a beach boy."

"I want to try it," she said.

Billy looked nervous. "First things first, honey. There's a hospital waiting for you."

The smell of torch fuel and seaweed drifted in the air around them. Light from the first stars began to pop. It was about the most romantic setting you could imagine, and yet she felt a bottleneck forming in her throat. Unable to bear it, she pulled up her dress and plopped on a patch of thick green grass.

She looked up at him. "Sit with me?"

"Are you okay?" he said.

"I think the heat is getting to me. And maybe I'm just a little overwhelmed by all the newness."

Dusk and ninety degrees. Something she would need to get used to.

"You're a long way from home, darling. I was going to wait until we were at the table to give this to you, but maybe this'll help." He drew an envelope from his pocket.

"To Eva" read the words on it.

"Ruby!" Eva cried.

"She said she didn't know when you'd be settled in so she mailed it to me, and asked me to give it to you."

She tore open the letter with trembling hands.

Dear Eva,

I am dying to hear about your trip to Hawaii. Was it everything they say and more? I bet it was! And Billy, did he officially propose yet? I still plan on coming, you know. Nurse Sylvia is like a drill sergeant about those exercises, but we have to do them in secret because Dr. Badger starts yelling at me to rest if he catches me so much as lifting my hairbrush. He does let me get wheeled around twice a day, though, and it is the highlight of my day going to the picture window and watching the squirrels. That and seeing Scout

I love that dog. If only I could go outside myself. This stale air is getting to me. I'm feeling well, other than the fact that my legs are still uncooperative. I've been having lots of conversations with God about this, and He has assured me that, in time, I will walk. Do you want the good news now? I wiggled my big toe yesterday! At first I thought it was a fluke, but no sirree, that toe was moving on its own. I'm going to look into traveling out there next month, by rowboat if I have to. That may sound soon to you, but I have faith. Send news as soon as you can.

Love,
Ruby

Eva held the letter to her chest and closed her eyes. She tried to catch any familiar scent of Ruby and her favorite lemon-scented balm, but the paper smelled like gasoline. Above all, she had been hoping to hear that Ruby's legs were better. But she knew that nerves took their sweet time in healing and they could be fickle as the devil. No change for weeks and then a sudden, small improvement. Then the same thing a month later. She remembered one young man in particular who had fallen while hunting and pinched his spinal cord. He spent hours staring at his legs, then pleading with them and finally screaming at them, *Move, you hear me? Move!*

Billy asked, "How is she?"

"The same ridiculously optimistic Ruby. At least she's in good spirits, but her legs still don't work and she has the notion she's coming out here next month."

He gulped. "Next month? You better talk some sense into her."

"I'll ring the hospital tomorrow if I have time," she said.

The unfortunate problem was that Ruby was a patient at Hollowcreek General.

"You don't want people snooping around Pearl Harbor, asking about you. Be careful what you tell Ruby," he said.

"I have it worked out, thank you," she said a little sharply.

Billy leaned in and put his arm around her. "I know it's been rough on you. What do you say we go find a cocktail and forget the outside world for a bit, eh?"

It sounded like a splendid idea.

While Billy ordered drinks at the outdoor bar, Eva watched the guests standing around in small clusters, many she recognized from the *Lurline*. It looked like a band was setting up under a cloth tent and dancing would be in the grass under the stars. Here they were in December wearing nothing but summer dresses and sandals. Some people were even swimming. It was certainly a life one could get used to.

Billy handed her a pineapple-shaped mug. "World-famous Royal Hawaiian pineapple cocktail."

"You must come here a lot, you seem to know your way around."

He shrugged. "I appreciate the finest, and this place is it."

The drink was tart with a fruity twist. She felt herself lightening up after a few sips, thank goodness. Was it even legal to be unhappy in Waikiki?

"Yum!" she exclaimed.

"The boys and I come here now and then, and this here is my favorite." He moved closer, eyeing her lips and then meeting her gaze with longing. Instinctively, she stepped back.

"Are you not happy to see me?" he said.

The kiss with Clark loomed. She *was* happy, but she was having a hard time erasing that memory and the feelings of guilt that came along with it. She took a huge sip and gave him her best smile. "Of course I am. It's just—"

"Eva!" said a familiar twangy voice.

"Fancy meeting you here, love."

She spun around to see Bree and Sasha hurrying toward them across the lawn. She should have known they would be here. Nothing but the finest for those two, either. Seeing them here made the world feel small and friendly, and she was happy for it.

"So, this is the lucky bloke," Bree said.

"Sasha and Bree are friends from the *Lurline*," Eva said to Billy, introducing them all.

"A pleasure to meet you, ladies. Double trouble," Billy said with a nod and a hint of a smile.

Was he flirting? All this time away from him, and she'd never given much thought to what he did in his time off, other than golfing and going to the beach. Maybe living in such a small town had made her naive, but the lovesick letters had given her confidence and caused an unflinching trust.

"Poor Eva, you should have seen the ball she took to the face," Sasha said to Billy.

"She took it like a champ, though. And Lieutenant Spencer is no weak fish, I'll tell you that," Bree added.

Billy perked up. "Clark Spencer?"

"You know him?" Eva asked, doing her best to keep her voice casual.

"I know *of* him. Big guy."

For a split second, Eva was against his chest again, listening to his heartbeat.

"Very," Sasha said.

"He was your tennis partner?" Billy asked.

"He was Bree's." She nodded toward Bree.

"Lucky for me," Bree said with a grin.

"How long you ladies here in the islands?" Billy asked.

"Not long enough," Sasha said.

"Three weeks in Waikiki and then we hop back on a ship."

Eva realized she wanted to see more of them before they left. "Maybe we can meet up on my day off."

"What fun that would be! We're staying here at the Royal. Just drop on in."

The twins floated away as quickly as they'd come, two bright spots of color in the night. They would want to make the rounds and chitchat with everyone from the hula dancers to the waiters to the guests.

Soon, Billy led her onto the dance floor. At first he felt like a statue, awkward and stiff and stepping on her toes. But the moment she relaxed into him, he softened. The lazy pulse of steel guitars wafted through the night around them. Despite his lack of dancing skills, he held her with care. They danced and sipped on pineapple drinks in between. He brushed his lips against her cheek, stirring up a familiar fondness that she had begun to doubt was still there.

"Evelyn," he whispered in her ear. "I want to marry you. Please, say you will?"

The blood rushed from her head. He pulled away and looked at her, his fingers gripping her arms a little too firmly. A proposal had been the furthest thing from her mind. Eva was conscious of his breathing and hardly noticed that hers had stopped until she broke into a coughing fit. This was too much, too soon. Another helping of confusion piled onto an already towering mound. But she had gone and gotten herself into this mess. Now how was she going to get out of it?

A MASSIVE CIRCLE

December 5

With such finicky weather, they have to alter their formation often. Today, four destroyers lead, followed by heavy cruisers *Tone* and *Chikuma*. After them come the six carriers—*Sōryū*, *Hiryū* and *Zuikaku* in one line and *Akagi*, *Kaga* and *Shōkaku* in another. Three submarines cruise along underneath. Behind them are the oil tankers and more destroyers, and then battleships *Hiei* and *Kirishima* taking up the rear. They move at sixteen knots, as fast as their slowest vessel. Expanding out from here, in a massive circle around Hawaii, the First, Second and Third Submarine Fleets, along with a Special Attack Unit, are all in place.

Up until now, by some strange miracle, the fleet has remained invisible. Passing no other ships. And then a strange thing happens. A trawler appears, close enough to read the name. *Uritzky.* Soviet.

Both keep on sailing by without any acknowledgment.

BLACKFISH

Five miles outside of Pearl Harbor, US destroyer *Ralph Talbot* makes underwater contact with an unidentified vessel. They believe it is a submarine and ask permission from the squadron leader on *Selfridge* to drop depth charges. The squadron leader denies, telling them it's an orca.

"If this is a blackfish, it has a motorboat up its stern," is the reply from *Talbot*.

SISTERS

December 4 & 5

The next two days were a blur of activity for Eva. Meeting the Tripler General staff, being assigned to Maternity—not what she expected—and learning the ropes. Meanwhile, going through all of this with one phrase playing over and over in her head and causing a strange throbbing in her temples.

I want to marry you.

Couldn't he have waited until she had her bearings? To spring it on her while her legs were still wobbly from the crossing seemed unfair. She hadn't said yes, but she hadn't said no.

The atmosphere in Tripler Hospital was unhurried and carefree, to say the least. The rooms were painted a light sunshiny yellow, with white window trim on oversize windows. The effect was bright and cheery and a lovely welcome to the world. Two young army wives were close to giving birth, and the doctor had ordered them on bed rest. Another two had new little pink bundles with them and would likely be discharged in a day or two. The other two nurses on duty, Sally Watts and Judy Walton, wanted to fill her in on all the hot spots around town.

"The football games are always a hoot. There's a big one tomorrow, if you'd like to join us," Sally said.

"I'd like that. The boys from Oregon were on the ship with us," Eva said.

Clark would probably be there, too, of course, unless he had work to do. On both Thursday and Friday, Eva had grabbed a newspaper first thing to check for updates about the approaching Japanese ships. But there was nothing. Still, she was on edge and the knowledge scratched away at her insides.

Eva felt like a novelty item, the way Judy and Sally were peppering her with questions. *What happened to your face? Was there anyone famous on the* Lurline *with you? Do you like dancing? Have you ever been to a luau? Do you have a man back home?* Sally had one in Ohio, and Judy was engaged to Sid, a pilot she'd met on Waikiki Beach. Sid was teaching her how to surf, and she invited Eva and Billy to join them the following weekend.

"Have you heard any scuttlebutt about the Japanese attacking?" Eva asked.

"Attacking where?" Sally said.

"Attacking here."

Both women laughed. "Oh no, that won't ever happen. Sid says the Japs are smart enough to know they can't defeat us," Judy said.

Sally lowered her voice for the moms-to-be. "It does sound like there's going to be conflict over in Asia soon, and we may get transports of wounded from there. So our easy days may be numbered."

How could absolutely no one be aware of the danger lurking just offshore? It seemed impossible.

"May as well enjoy it while we can," Judy said.

With three nurses on duty and only two mothers and babies, there was plenty of time to stand out in the hallway and talk in between wiping bottoms and taking temperatures. Midway through the morning, Judy stepped outside for a fifteen-minute break and came back with an armful of long red torch-like

flowers and an assortment of ferns and vines and began pluck-
ing them apart and arranging them. The vines were covered
in tiny green blossoms that perfumed the whole building.
Sweeter than honeysuckle and far more potent.

"I never want to leave this place. Year-round flowers and
moonlight swims. You'll be hooked in no time," Judy said.

Eva believed her. "Will you be getting married here?" she
asked.

"As soon as my year is up. Right on Waikiki Beach, where
we met. I'm learning the hula," she said, waving her arms
around and swiveling her hips.

"I can teach you, too, if you'd like."

Here they were, living every person's dream, and yet Eva
sensed a change about to come. She'd heard too much on the
way over to rest easy. In the other room, one of the babies
started a wailing fit, and Sally and Eva hurried in to help the
poor mother, who looked desperate for help.

When they came back out, Judy hung a lei over Eva's neck.
"You deserve a proper welcome. We consider ourselves sisters out here, being so far away from family and all. So now
you're one of us."

At the word *sister*, Eva choked up.

"Lord knows us nurses have to band together," Sally said.

Wasn't that the truth.

In the middle of her shift on Friday afternoon, Willa Smart,
head nurse on duty, came in. "We need to borrow one of you
for surgery. Gladys went home with a fever."

"Who's on?" Sally said.

"Dr. Newcastle."

Sally and Judy exchanged glances and said in unison, "Eva
will go."

Despite Grace's warning, Eva was happy to have something

to do that involved tending to patients. Anyway, Dr. Newcastle couldn't be worse than Dr. Brown.

When she walked into the operating room, Dr. Newcastle was all scrubbed up. He was younger than she had expected, with a shiny bald head, and was barely taller than Eva.

No greeting, no smile. Just a quick once-over with steel eyes. "I've never seen this woman before, Willa. Can you get me someone who knows what they're doing?"

"I'm sorry, Doctor, everyone else is gone or busy. Give her a chance," Willa said before she turned and walked out the door.

Eva stood quietly, giving a small smile. Her heart was pounding more than it should be. Right away, she could smell his dismissal. The hair on the back of her neck went up.

Newcastle handed Eva a chart. "Appendicitis. What's your experience?" he said.

It was hard not to give him her full qualifications, but that was part of the deal. "Three years of surgical experience in Indiana, all kinds."

"Where was your training?"

"Greenwood Hospital."

"Never heard of it."

Good. Eva didn't give him any more.

"I don't know about the doctors in Indiana—I'm from New York—but I expect you to follow my orders and I don't like to be questioned. You got that?"

She nodded. "Yes, sir."

"What happened to your face?"

"Tennis accident."

"Nice work."

"Dr. Wallace stitched me up. Aboard the *Lurline*."

He looked impressed, leaning in and inspecting the work. Rancid breath in her face. She'd remember to bring some chewing gum next time. "Dr. Wallace is a legend," he said as if she didn't already know.

"Will you be attending his lectures?" she said, hoping they might have some common ground.

He pulled his spectacles down to make his point. "Does it look like I am?"

"Well, no, it doesn't. But Sunday I'm—"

"I don't have time. Now, get cleaned up."

Private Allen Dean had been having stabbing pain in his lower right abdomen for several days now, with bloating and constipation. A simple procedure, Dr. Newcastle assured her.

"Are there signs of rupture?" she asked.

Newcastle rolled his eyes. "You worry about his blood pressure and pupils."

Eva had to clench her jaw to keep herself from saying more. Surely, Newcastle knew what he was doing, but she had so many questions. When he pulled out the drop ether, she was relieved. Private Dean seemed as though he was on the edge, with a weak pulse, clammy face and skyrocketing fever. The last thing she wanted was to have to make any suggestions.

"Nurse, am I going to be okay?" Private Dean said.

She smoothed back his hair. "You're in good hands. We'll have it out before you know it."

Newcastle eyed her. Was she not allowed to talk to patients? Touch them?

The minute they sliced him open, the putrid smell of pus almost knocked Eva back. "Rupture," Newcastle said through his surgical mask.

She nodded, feeling smug about her diagnosis. As Newcastle went to work removing the diseased organ, she had to admit he was good. His small hands and delicate fingers maneuvered around the abdomen easily, and he snipped and scraped with great precision. As much as possible, Eva stayed out of his way. And when it was all over, despite the rupture, she got the feeling that Private Dean would survive.

Outside, Newcastle pulled off his mask. "Well done, Nurse, but leave the talking to me."

She was taken aback. "Why, I was only trying to comfort him."

"I've had nurses say the damnedest things to patients, so do me a favor and keep your thoughts to yourself, okay?"

"Yes, Doctor."

They had two more surgeries that afternoon—a badly fractured leg and a tonsillectomy—and Eva was walking on eggshells the whole time. *Hand me the scissors. Cut me some gauze. No, not like that! How are his pupils?* With the leg fracture, Eva wanted desperately to suggest a different length pin, but held her tongue. Blending into the background was her only shot at keeping her new job, which she was lucky to have in the first place.

THE VISIT

December 4

Clark was poring over a stack of decrypted messages when Ford came over and sat on his desk. Pipe smoke poured from his nostrils. Ford was in his usual orange robe, a strange habit he'd taken up mainly because the room was so dang cold.

"I just got off the phone with Special Captain Jensen. He said he'd just been informed by the FBI that Consul General Kita was ordered to burn his codes. All telegraph codes and codebooks, all secret records, and not to arouse outside suspicion," Ford said.

"Jesus."

"He was supposed to wire the word *haruna* when he finished. What does it mean?"

"Literally—'spring,' or 'clear weather.'"

"The buggers are elegant, you have to give them that," Ford said.

Clark's mind was spinning. Should he tell Ford now? Ford was cleared for Ultra, so why had Lieutenant Irving ordered him not to tell? "Did he wire it?"

"Last night. You ask me, Admiral Hart is going to have his hands full in the Philippines any day now. I sure hope he's ready." Ford took another puff from his pipe. "I'm going to take this over to Kimmel. In the meantime, can you go see how the guys at Station H are doing? This 'east wind, rain' message is sure elusive. They've been there around the clock for the past week with nothing to show, and I want them back."

Either Ford knew, and he thought the info was above Clark's clearance, or he was still in the dark. Everyone knew Ford kept an iron grip on their raw intelligence, but Clark liked to think that Ford trusted him. Looking at his face now, in the dim light and through the smoke, it was hard to get a read.

Just then, Tex came over. "Boss, Lawson's on the line."

"I need to take this, we'll talk more tomorrow."

The thirty-mile drive to Station H, over the Pali, was not for pussy-foots. It took every bit of focus to navigate the rugged and narrow road carved into the side of the Ko'olau mountains. One wrong turn and you were airborne, plunging a thousand feet down a vertical cliff. As Clark bounced down the mountain, he stole glances at the calm waters from Kaneohe clear up the coast. Small islands popped up here and there, making it look very South Pacific.

Eva would love this. He wished he could have watched her expression change from fright to awe as they came down the Pali. She would have likely been clutching his arm. Or maybe sitting in his lap if he was lucky. *Stop wasting your time with dumb thoughts. She belongs to someone else.*

Once he got to the bottom of the cliff, Clark hung a left and followed a muddy and little-used road. It was tricky— slow down and get swarmed by mosquitos, or speed up and knock yourself out on the roof. The road was in danger of being swallowed by banyan trees and a thicket the Hawaiians called *hao.*

Being out in the jungle, Station H had a phone, but it was a party line. Of all the dumb things. Ford was infuriated by the useless setup, but his pleas for a fix had gone on deaf ears. Someone had to drive out there or back to Pearl Harbor daily in order to communicate securely, so information was always days late.

The boys at He'eia were happy to see him. Sitting around in the ramshackle stone building must have grown old pretty darn quick.

"Count yourself lucky, Spencer. While you were wining and dining on the *Lurline*, we've been holed away here, listening for a pin drop on the other side of the ocean," Brody said.

He couldn't argue there. "Ford wanted me to see what you've got and to tell you that the Japanese consulate has been ordered to burn everything."

Brody lit up a cigarette. "No shit."

"And yesterday, the same in Washington," Clark said.

"Which means we already know what we need to know. Once they burn the codes, it's only a matter of days, right?"

Cronin, a gangly redneck, chimed in. "I say we head for the hills."

"Don't be stupid, it's the Philippines they're gonna hit," Brody said.

"I don't trust Washington. I bet they know something they aren't telling us," Cronin said.

"Why do you say that?"

"Because did any of us know what a Purple machine was until yesterday? They only tell us what they think we need to know."

It was true. None of them had ever heard of Purple, which Ford found out yesterday was what the boys at OP-20-G called a cipher machine that Japan used to swap messages between Tokyo and their foreign diplomats. Here they were working on the Japanese Flag Officers Code, and not even close to solving it, while Station CAST was tasked with decrypting

JN-25 Naval codes and Washington had their own project, Magic. It seemed like a bad case of the right arm not knowing what the left was doing.

"Have you guys picked up anything else of interest? Any odd transmissions on unusual frequencies?" Clark threw out.

"Nothing that shows they're heading our way. Why?" Brody said.

"Just curious."

Cronin scratched a festering red bite on his neck. "Something's fishy. All that lack of traffic can't be good."

Had he and Wilson been wrong about what they had heard? Was there another explanation?

Out at sea, a mountain of dark clouds boiled up. Rain blew in quickly here, and Clark gathered the latest recordings and aimed to cross the Pali before the road turned into a waterfall. Ten minutes into the drive he spotted a car in the road up ahead, hood up. It looked civilian.

When he got closer he leaned out and called, "Everything okay?"

Two men were leaning on the fender, standing in a cloud of smoke and mosquitos. "Mind giving us a hand? We're stuck."

The shiny black Ford seemed out of place, as did the men in their button-up shirts and fedoras. His gut told him something was off, but he couldn't just drive on by without helping.

He pulled to the side of the road and got out. "Where are you fellas headed?"

One of the men looked vaguely familiar. He was thick enough to be a linebacker, but too short. The other was Hawaiian with a shiny and pocked face.

"Lieutenant Clark Spencer."

It wasn't a question. His skin tingled. He glanced around for a way to hightail it out of there if need be, but the forest was dense and the trees woven together with a web of ropy vines.

"What do you want?" he said.

Linebacker said, "A bird told us you turned in a report yesterday from the *Lurline*."

"What if I did?"

"Who else knows about this besides you and Wilson?"

He stepped back. "I don't even know who you are, and you want me to answer sensitive questions?"

"All you need to know is that we work for someone above you. Way above you. We know about the report and we know that you were friendly with an Eva Cassidy on the boat coming over. Did you tell her anything?"

A fierce protectiveness filled him. "Hell no. Leave her out of this."

"We don't take orders from lieutenants in the navy, but, anyway, you sure you didn't tell anyone else? Ford? Brody? Any of your Dungeon buddies?"

"I gave the report to Irving and that's it."

Maybe he should have told Ford, or somebody.

"Is it true that you lived in Japan for several years?" Linebacker asked.

"Yes."

"And you are fluent?"

He didn't like where this was headed. "I was sent by the navy to learn the language."

"But you made a lot of friends."

"What are you implying?"

Linebacker pulled his jacket aside, revealing a gun. Clark had a sudden thought that these two guys could easily stuff him in the back of the truck and dump him in the ocean with a brick tied to his leg, and no one would be the wiser. He might be able to take on one, but not both.

"We have a message for you. Keep the information to yourself or evidence may arise linking you to the Japanese. The United States doesn't tolerate spies."

"Are you threatening me?" he tried to say coolly, all the while panting like a tired dog.

How did they know about Eva?

"I am. Either that or you and Miss Cassidy might end up as sugarcane fertilizer."

"This is outrageous."

"Would you rather we just take you out now?"

Beads of sweat collected on his neck. A fly circled his face. Who *were* these thugs? "I don't understand. The information in the report is critical. And classified."

"All you need to understand is that you don't breathe a word of this," Pock Face growled.

Clark tried to make sense of it all. He and Wilson must have been correct in their assessment. But who wanted it kept hidden? And had anyone else seen the report besides Irving?

He was backing toward his jeep. "So you want us to get caught with our pants down? Is that it?"

Linebacker followed his move and came six inches away, blowing tobacco smoke and spit in his face. "Here's what's going to happen. You're going to get back in your car, forget about the report, forget about this meeting and go on translating the Jap talk. Your country needs you."

He almost laughed. "What my country needs is to know about that fleet."

"The problem with guys like you is you're small-minded. You can't see the big picture."

"Oh, I can see it damn clear, and it's not pretty," Clark said, picturing the island in flames.

The man put his hand on the gun. "Get out of here, Spencer, before you make me shoot you."

SUNKEN WORDS

December 6

Pardon your neglectful son for the lack of letters
these long months. Now that fall has turned to winter,
I imagine you are setting aside your nets to mend
and readying for the snowfall. I only wish I could
be there to help, but we are departing soon for an
unknown destination. If I fail to write, do not fear,
for it means I am performing my duties sensibly. Should
anything happen to me, and I do not return, rest in
the knowledge that your son died serving Japan in the
most honorable way. Goodbye.

 —*Letters like this were sent home from Japanese submarine
  pilots to their parents before they climbed into their subs with
  a bottle of sake and boxed lunch, locking the hatches and
  sailing off into Hawaiian waters.*

FINAL SONGS

Battle of the Bands is held at the shiny new Bloch Rec Center at Pearl Harbor. The crowd dances to ballad, swing, jitterbug and all the latest tunes, showing off their new moves. Favorites like "The Jumpin' Jive" and "I Don't Want to Set the World on Fire" have the joint hopping. Tonight is an elimination round, and troupes from battleships *Tennessee* and *Pennsylvania*, and transport *Argonne* compete, each trying to outdo the next. Meanwhile, the audience loves every minute of it, cooling off in the pool hall with 3.2 percent beer. When *Pennsylvania* is finally declared the winner, the whole place breaks into Kate Smith's version of "God Bless America."

The band from *Pennsylvania* wins the honor of going up against the other finalist, *Arizona*, on December 20.

THE RUN-IN

Billy picked Eva up bright and early Saturday and drove her toward the east end of the island. He pointed out sights—Mount Tantalus, Koko Head, and then a ten-mile stretch of coast with nothing but coconut trees and tidal pools that he said were used as fishponds by the Hawaiians. They stopped and got out along the way, collecting shells called cowries and spotted cones.

As of yet, there was no discussion of his proposal. He had taken the hint well, and she was grateful. Billy had what her father called "people smarts." He was good at reading those around him and always knew the right thing to do or say. When she had first told him about Ruby, he had told her that if and when the time came, he would come get her himself and bring her to Hawaii. For Eva, that had meant everything.

Once they rounded the eastern portion of Oahu, the scenery changed dramatically. Tall cliffs and rough seas. No beaches there, only rugged windswept rocks. Beyond the corner, a verdant wall of mountain rose straight up, at least several thousand feet, disappearing into the clouds.

Eva craned her neck. "It reminds me of King Kong."

"Only, there are no gorillas here. Or any kind of wildlife

for that matter. No bears or cougars or crocs or wolves. The only creatures you need to worry about are sharks." He paused for a moment. "Or the two-legged kind. A lot of those on the loose here."

He was wearing a mischievous grin, though Eva detected an undertone of seriousness.

"Good thing I have you to look after me, then," she said.

He reached over and grabbed her hand as they bounced down a rutted, sandy road toward the shore. Eva closed her eyes and willed herself to feel something, anything. He squeezed, and she squeezed back. But she might as well have been holding Grace's hand, for all the electricity she felt.

Give it time.

They pulled up at a white sand beach that went on for miles, and Billy produced a picnic basket from the backseat. He kicked off his shoes and she did the same. They were the only two in sight. Eva could not believe that a place this post-card perfect existed. The sand was sugary white and hot to the touch, the water a turquoise blue that looked almost drink-able, and the air felt just right on the skin of her bare arms.

Eva forgot about everything for a moment and ran toward the water. Once she hit the wet sand she slowed and turned to see Billy running after her. She wanted to plunge in head-first, but he stopped her, pointing at blue bubbles with thready tentacles littering the sand.

"Portuguese man-o-war. They have a nasty sting. We can dip in Waikiki on the way home if you want."

It was her first proper day at the beach. "Can't I just dunk?"

"Not unless you want to end up with burning welts wrapped around your whole body. Trust me," he said.

That was the end of that. They sat on a beach sheet and munched on sardines and Saloon Pilot crackers and something called poi: a gray paste made from the taro root. Billy said he'd brought it just because she ought to have a taste. The Hawaiians loved poi with everything they ate. After the first mouthful, she wasn't sure she could tolerate another bite. Sour, mushy and thick tasting, like a cross between porridge and clay.

"It's a nice sentiment, but save it for those who can appreciate it," she said, handing the spoon back with half a bite still on it.

He laughed. "Don't worry, it's an acquired taste."

"Do you like it?"

"I do. Say, remember that time that Ruby was so proud of her first mincemeat pie, but she'd forgotten the sugar?" Billy said.

Being with someone who knew Ruby made her feel right at home. "She was beside herself, and when she saw my father's face..."

"He tried to keep it straight, but God, that pie was bad."

They laughed. As smart and talented as Ruby was, her big failing was in the kitchen. Her mind was usually thinking about ten things at once, and ingredients often got left out. Eva hated to imagine what Ruby's future husband would have to endure, but she made up for it in a hundred other ways.

They sat and listened to the shore break. Sun melted onto her shoulders. Within ten minutes, a fine layer of sand coated every surface of her body, including her scalp, though she wasn't complaining. Being with Billy was like being with an old friend, and for the moment, it was enough.

In his letters, he'd rarely talked about work. She knew he was in Intelligence, but not much else. There was only so much he could say. Today, she pressed him.

"We make sense of information gathered through clandestine sources, I'll leave it at that," he said, as tight-lipped as ever.

Surprising he didn't know Clark. And if this was his area of expertise, maybe she should ask him about the Japanese ship signals. The information was gnawing away at her.

She summoned courage and spoke. "What if I told you I overheard something on the *Lurline* while coming over?"

"I'd say 'What did you hear?'"

"Two men were talking about a fleet of Japanese ships approaching Honolulu. They seemed to think these were warships and were planning an attack any day now."

A look of surprise flashed over his face before he chuckled. "Good one. The guys were probably just speculating like everyone does. You'll notice the rumor mill is highly active here, since people have a lot of spare time on their hands."

She stood her ground. "These guys weren't speculating. They talked about Japanese radio signals and discussed technical details and both seemed certain."

"Where exactly did you hear this?" he asked.

"Two men were out on the back deck late on the last night. They didn't realize I was there since it was dark. Nor did I get a good look at them, but I was interested, so I didn't walk away."

"They may have sounded certain, but I'm sure they were wrong. In the meantime, this is the kind of thing you keep to yourself, Eva. Okay? Promise me? You don't want to draw attention to yourself." He had a point. And maybe he was right about the signals, too. Who knew how experienced this radio operator was.

She picked up a stick and began breaking off pieces and tossing them toward the water. "Fine. I just don't want anyone to get hurt. If it's true, I mean, and they attack us and we aren't prepared. Can you at least ask around? Have a plane sent out or *something*?"

He sighed. "Oh, Eva, you're so beautiful when you're upset, you know that?"

"I'm not upset," she said, crossing her arms.

He put his hand on her shoulder. "Just focus on yourself and your job, and everything will work out."

"Easier said than done. We could be invaded at any moment."

"If the Japanese are so bold, they'll find themselves up shit creek. And they'll have brought us into the war, which may not be a bad thing."

She couldn't believe what she was hearing. "War with Japan may not be a bad thing?"

"The Allied forces need us. Trust me, if Germany takes over Europe, and Japan the Pacific, life will change as we know it. You want to live under Hitler? With your dark hair, you'd run the risk of being exterminated."

"Of course not. I can see sending help over to Europe, but being attacked by the Japanese would mean fighting a war on two sides of the world, and here on American soil. It scares me, that's all," she said.

"It scares everyone."

Of course she had heard about the Nazi camps like Mauthausen and Auschwitz, where people went in and didn't come out. Jews, Roma or anyone who the Germans deemed as dangerous or inferior. Recently, horror stories had been leaked in the news about new methods of killing involving gas vans, where the Nazis would fill the vans with people, seal it off and connect the exhaust. Things in Europe did seem to be spiraling out of control. But why not go straight for the Germans?

Suddenly, raindrops the size of tadpoles started to dump down on them. They dashed to the car. Eva's mind was churning with questions. What if he knew something? Or even worse, what if he was right?

That afternoon, she, Grace, Sally and Judy drove to the university stadium for the football game. The road in front of them steamed from another bout of rain on the scorching black pavement. Weather here was highly temperamental with sun one minute and a downpour the next. Happily, snow was out of the question.

Eva felt like she was back in college with all the chitter chatter and howling laughter. It was hard to feel like she fit in, with her tarnished life, but she found when she put on a good front, her mood seemed to improve. While Judy, with her blond ringlets and shiny red lips could have been a movie star, Sally was pretty in an understated and wholesome way. The two of them wanted to discuss every last happening at the hospital.

"Millie Andrews told me that Dr. Newcastle made a pass at her yesterday," Sally said.

"No!" Grace said, covering her mouth.

"Cross my heart. He told her she was filling her uniform out nicely, and gave her a little pat on the rear as she left."

Eva couldn't picture it. "Is he married?"

The girls all laughed. "He's married to the hospital, and bags an unsuspecting nurse now and then. But I think he secretly dislikes women," Sally said.

"He's a good surgeon," Eva said, unsure why she was defending the man.

"Just be careful. He's unpredictable."

Wonderful.

Sally kept on going. "Mary said that three more soldiers came in with sore throats today that turned out to be the clap. All of them failed to mention pus coming out of their short arms. I swear to you, these boys cannot keep it in their pants."

Eva had never heard the term *short arm* before. All this military slang was entertaining if not baffling. Earlier in the day, Billy had offered to spray her with bug juice. One look at her face and he'd rolled over laughing. *Insect repellent, my dear.*

"Be thankful you're not on pecker-checker detail, Eva. It's the worst. They put me in there when I first came and I had a crash course in male anatomy," Judy said.

Grace laughed. "That and how to keep a poker face."

"Where are they contracting it?"

All three said in unison, "Chinatown."

Sally stuck her hand out the window, diverting the hot wind into the car. "Hotel Street is crawling with pickup girls."

"Is it legal here?" Eva asked.

Judy rolled her pretty blue eyes. "The cops ignore it. With the amount of soldiers roving the streets like wild animals, it would be impossible to stop it. The military brass can only do damage control by passing out condoms and Pro-kits to all GIs."

In her almost nonexistent training, Eva had been shown a Pro-kit—sulfa ointment, directions and a soaped-up cloth—and told to hand them out to every soldier who left the hospital. A Good Soldier Will Not Get Venereal Disease was stamped across the front.

"The problem is, there are a hundred men for every woman on this island. No wonder they're desperate. Those call girls are exotic, too. Chinese, Japanese, Hawaiian, Filipino or all of the above," Sally said.

Eva thought about Billy. And Clark. Did they visit these kinds of places? Feeling lonely and full of need. Needing a woman's touch. For some reason, the image of Billy hitting up Hotel Street was more believable than Clark. Now, why would she think that? Maybe it was how he went on and on about how much he craved her touch. Before it had felt romantic. Now it seemed almost desperate.

"Men will be men," Grace said.

"Speaking of men, how's it going with your sweetheart?" Judy asked.

"Fine." Eva wasn't in the mood to discuss her jumbled emotions. Grace was the only one she'd told about the proposal and she wanted to keep it that way. In her experience, the more you talked about something, the muddier it became. Usually, her first instinct was trustworthy. Except in this case. One minute she was positive Billy was the one, the next she was convinced she couldn't live without seeing Clark again.

"The offer still stands to go surf riding with Sid. You're going to love him. He's the finest man around, not to mention the most skilled and the dreamiest," Judy said with a sigh.

"Skilled at kissing," Sally said.

If he was half as good-looking as Judy, he was probably a dish. Those poor soldiers with the clap must have about died when she sauntered into the room. Fortunately, Judy didn't seem to notice—or care—what effect she had on people. Eva liked her.

At the stadium, the women found seats near the fifty-yard line. Grace and Sally went to find a restroom, while Eva and Judy guarded their seats from the hordes of people. The smell of popcorn and rain and sweaty people surrounded them. The bleachers kept on filling up until there was standing room only. And all for a college football game. As soon as the game began, Eva could see that the Oregon boys were in trouble. Not eating for five days would have that effect. The rumor was more than a few had hardly left their rooms during the crossing.

At halftime, under a misty drizzle, Eva and Judy left to purchase hot dogs and Coca-Colas. Eva was fascinated by the mixture of races all blending together and she tried not to stare. A young Japanese woman with a mouth like a button. The shocking blue eyes of a Hawaiian boy. She was so distracted, she almost walked right into a man's chest.

"Excuse me," she said, before realizing she was speaking to Clark.

"Eva."

The deep vibration of his voice. His face in the rain. She could see the tiny water droplets on his lashes. The dimple. Her mouth went dry.

"What are you doing here?" She hadn't meant it to sound like an accusation, but the words tumbled out anyway.

"I'm here to cheer on the Bearcats. How about you?" he said.

Judy stepped in and locked arms with Eva. "We're on the Hawaii side."

"I have a thing for underdogs," he said, not even glancing at Judy.

Eva wanted to throw her arms around him and say, *Pick me up in the morning and show me your secret beach! Please?* If only she could have one more day with him, maybe she would know. "Clark—"

Another man appeared and handed him a beer. "Here you go, buddy."

"Thanks," he said, still not taking his eyes away from Eva.

The friend did a triple take when he saw Judy. "Who are your friends?" he asked Clark.

"This is Eva Cassidy, and..."

Eva chimed in. "Judy Walton. We work together at Tripler."

"How's the assignment going?" Clark said.

"So far so good."

Eva could have stood there for a year—was it legal for a man to be so handsome?—but the band stopped playing and loud cheering cracked through the sun-slanted afternoon. Behind them, stomping feet shook the bleachers.

"I thought about—" Clark said.

A burst of static. "Ladies and gentlemen, the second half is underway. Hawaii up by ten and we'll see if the Bearcats have anything left in them to turn this game around," boomed from a loudspeaker three feet away.

"Fellas, it was a pleasure, but our food is getting cold and our friends are waiting," Judy yelled above the noise.

"You'd better get back, then," Clark said, and Eva realized he probably thought they were with their boyfriends.

"Wait," she said.

Say something, silly. Anything.

He looked at her expectantly, but this was not the time nor the place. Any blind idiot could see that. "It was nice to see you, Lieutenant."

His jaw tightened. "Stay safe, Eva."

And then he turned away.

"Who *was* that?" Judy asked once they were in the clear.

"He was on the *Lurline*."

"Not to be nosy, but did you two have a thing?"

A question Eva wasn't quite sure how to answer. "We spent time together. I met him the first night at dinner because we were some of the only people not green in our rooms. But I had Billy waiting for me here and whatever *might have been* ended when we docked."

Judy looked her in the eye. "Not from the looks of it."

The Oregon boys lost the game. They simply ran out of steam. Eva felt badly for them, traveling all this way, but they'd have another chance in a week, and by then they should have their strength back.

She was exhausted, too, and ready to curl up in her twin bed. As they approached Pearl Harbor, she admired what appeared to be the whole of the Pacific Fleet.

"All those ships sure make an intimidating sight," Eva commented.

"Isn't that the truth. If someone were going to attack, now would be a good time. They could take out all our defenses in one swoop," Sally said.

The words caught Eva off guard, but Sally was right. Battleship Row shone in the fuzzy yellow of streetlamps. Hulking masses of steel and gun power. Floating fortresses. Surely, no one would dare. The moment gave Eva pause. She suddenly felt proud to be a nurse and proud to be an American. Even if she'd had to lie to get here, she would do her part. *Whatever that meant.*

HELL DIVERS

December 7
0300

The pilots of Operation Z write goodbye letters to their families back home. They are ready to die. In the envelopes, they include strands of hair and nail clippings so their families will have a part of them to cremate. Some slip pictures into their pockets, all say silent prayers. Many wear thousand-stitch belts made by mothers or wives or sisters who asked passersby to add a stitch for good luck and victory. For the mission, the galley has prepared each man a bento box. Rice ball, pickled plums, a biscuit, chocolate, amphetamines. If they run out of fuel or are in danger of being captured, they are told to find a target and crash into it. Everyone nods in agreement. There is no fear, only honor. They are *hell divers*, after all.

The seas are so rough that thunderous waves slam into the carriers and spill across their decks. The ships pitch and roll, tilting the flight decks to more than ten degrees. The morning is black but for blinker lights atop of each ship. Wind screeches through the planes in an eerie wail. It is decided—the mission will continue as planned. Before the pilots climb into their cockpits, they tie *hachimakis* around their heads. *Hisshou.* Certain Victory.

Spirits are high as the flight deck comes to life. Plane engines hum, lamps wave in circles. The first takeoff is postponed for fifteen minutes due to the wild seas. It must be timed perfectly. *Go!* The Zero fighter begins its run, increasing speed. Everyone holds their breath. Liftoff happens just as the deck pitches back down. Cheers erupt and are instantly swept away in the dark wind.

THE BIG MISS

Privates Skip Lewis and Danny McVay have been on duty since 0400. It is a dreary Sunday morning with no action. Skip fusses with the radarscope, which has a history of acting erratically. A short two-week history. All of this is new to them, as it is General Short, who has been recently given the radar equipment by the War Department. Neither man is particularly happy about being here and they are still in training, but they take their job seriously. The third guy on their team decided on sleeping in this morning, and Skip and Danny assured him they could handle the Sunday workload. Nothing much happens on a Sunday anyway.

The phone rings. Skip answers.

"Lewis? You guys are relieved of duty. You can shut the scope down and head back."

He hangs up. "That was HQ. They said we can call it a day."

"May as well wait until the truck actually comes," Danny says.

The truck is often late.

"Sounds good."

The two men continue to work the radarscope, and at 0654 a small flicker appears on the screen, 130 miles to the northeast.

"Here's something," says Skip, letting Danny take over the dials. "You wanna practice?"

"Sure."

At 0702, a big blip appears.

"Hell! What is that?" Danny says.

"Damn thing must be busted again, I've never seen anything like *that*. Here, let me have a go."

They switch places, but it soon becomes clear that the radar is working just fine. What they are looking at is a shitload of aircraft coming their way.

Danny goes to plot the position—137 miles north, 3 degrees east. When he goes to radio Fort Shafter, no one picks up. "They must be eating," he mumbles.

"Use the phone," Skip says.

He reaches a switchboard operator named Private Todd Allenton and fills him in. "I'll pass on the message, but I'm the only one here."

A few minutes later, Allenton calls back. "Look, fellas, I consulted with Lieutenant Stone here and—"

Skip takes the phone. He doesn't like what he sees. "You don't understand, these blips have gotten bigger and are moving fast. Put Stone on."

He hears shuffling and mumbled voices, and then, "This is Lieutenant Stone. Look, what you're seeing are a group of B-17s coming in from the mainland. Nothing to worry about."

After they hang up, Skip and Danny look at each other and shrug. At least they know the radar is working.

THE REAL McCOY

0755

Hawaii laughed in the face of wintertime. Trees burst with leaves, vines meandered across walls and flowers colored up the landscape. Eva sat on a bench outside Queen's Hospital, enjoying the warmth and solitude. A cluster of sparrows picked at worms in the grass and when the clouds parted, a rainbow shone through.

She had persuaded Grace to drop her at the medical conference on her way to an early church service with Judy and a few gals from Tripler. None of the other nurses had wanted to come to see Dr. Wallace. *We're not invited*, they'd all said. Church, followed by a beach picnic sounded like a better option to them. But Eva wouldn't miss this lecture for anything in the world.

The bronze plaque on the wall read Mabel Smyth Memorial Building and she wondered who Mabel Smyth was. It was unusual to have a hospital building named for a woman. The auditorium and the hospital grounds were impressive for such a remote island and she was finding Honolulu to be full of pleasant surprises. For all its remote island feel, the city was also a bustling port with one foot in the future.

No one else had arrived yet and she appreciated the time

alone. No roommate, no man, no bedpans to change. She looked at her watch. There was still over an hour before the presentation started. Enough time to take a walk and get back in time to catch Dr. Wallace before his talk. She wanted to thank him again for patching up her cheek so nicely.

When she reached the corner of the building to cross the street, the drone of an airplane engine grew louder and louder. The sky hummed around her. *Strange that they fly so low over the city.* A moment later a plane whizzed over her and skimmed the roof of the hospital, filling the air with the taste of fuel. The navy must be doing drills. Nevertheless, it ramped up her pulse. She kept walking under a dense tree canopy, down the block in the direction of the palace, but two more planes zoomed past heading toward Diamond Head. A minute later an explosion sent shock waves blasting through the morning. In the distance, a pillar of red smoke erupted into the sky. Some training they were doing!

Then, through the branches, she thought she glimpsed red balls on the underbellies of the planes. It resembled the Japanese meatball insignia. She'd seen it in the papers.

No!

Time shifted, folded in on itself. Like the exact moment when she had realized Tommy Lemon was gone. How you knew when you knew. Something was terribly wrong. Eva broke into a run back toward the hospital. So early on a Sunday and there were no other people out on the streets. A loud *bang* rocked the atmosphere.

It was happening.

All the blood in her head turned to sludge.

A metallic taste in her mouth.

Lord help us all!

Eva poked her head into the auditorium. A couple of men stood around chatting, seemingly unconcerned by the planes.

This put her at ease and she talked herself into calming down. *Deep breaths, Eva, deep breaths.* Maybe it was just a drill, after all. A very realistic one. The taller of the two glanced her way, but made no acknowledgment. Soon a couple more men trickled in, and then Dr. Wallace showed up, looking flushed and off-kilter. Still an intimidating figure in his white coat and spectacles. All part of the physician mystique, of course, but her father had been the opposite. A people's doctor all the way in rumpled clothes and never afraid to rub elbows with the poorest of poor. He made it clear that he was no different than the average person. *We are all sewn together with skin, Evelyn. We have hearts and lungs and livers, and we all need food, water and love to survive. Remember that.*

"Dr. Wallace, it's lovely to see you again," Eva said, seizing the moment to talk to him before he was swarmed by others.

Wallace looked up and recognition dawned. "Well, if it isn't the little tennis star. You made it. I was beginning to wonder if I had scared you away."

"They put me to work straightaway so I missed your last two lectures, but here I am, ready to learn more on burns," she said like an eager pupil. "Say, is this kind of drill normal for a Sunday?"

Wallace seemed to be breathing more heavily than normal. "My word, you haven't heard, then?"

"Heard?"

His face drooped. "Pearl Harbor is under attack. The Japanese are bombing the island."

A violent flash of panic ran through her. "But why are we still here?"

"We may as well make ourselves useful. If you will excuse me, I need to get started on the talk."

Wallace pushed away and went toward the podium. Eva was left standing there in shock. Her mind immediately went to Clark. Where would he be? Her breaths were now coming in shallow bursts. Billy was playing golf on the other side of the island, thank goodness, and Grace and the girls were nearby on Queen Emma Street.

In the distance, another huge explosion split the air. Windows rattled. Uneasy looks on faces. The auditorium had not filled up as expected. Only forty or fifty men where there should have been hundreds. The buzz of excited voices filled the room, yet no one seemed to know what exactly was happening. *You hear all kinds of stories, don't believe it. The Japs are coming ashore in Waikiki. The Navy is stepping up their drills.* Eva felt like a trapped rat. It suddenly seemed imperative that she return to Pearl Harbor.

The microphone crackled on and Wallace cleared his throat. "This reminds me a bit of France in 1918," he said with an uncomfortable laugh.

It all seemed so *wrong.*

He continued, "'You also must be ready, for the Son of Man is coming at an hour you do not expect.' A fitting message from Luke for this Sunday, don't you think?"

One thing kept running through her mind: *How did this happen? We knew they were there, didn't we?* Had Clark not delivered the report?

Somewhere nearby, a concussive blast, and then another. Eva smelled smoke, heard more planes. War had arrived from the sky, not the sea as she had imagined it might. All along, she had assumed the navy would neatly handle the Japanese ships, yet here she was in the midst of an air raid. Another blast rang through her teeth. She tried to rein in her dizzying fear.

A few seconds later the doors burst open and a man slid in and shouted, "This is not a drill! Surgeons are needed at Tripler on the double! They say the wounded are coming in by the truckloads."

Wallace turned to the man, then looked out at the audience and very calmly said, "I guess we should wrap it up here. Let's go save some lives."

If we aren't blown to smithereens first.

Murmurs erupted and the room cleared faster than if someone had let loose a bagful of snakes. Eva ran down the aisle and hurried after Dr. Wallace, who was being ushered out by another man carrying a worn black medical bag. Her legs felt as wobbly as they had when she'd first stepped off of the ship.

"Doctor, might I catch a ride?" Eva called.

The other man turned. "Where we're headed is the last place you want to go."

"I'm a nurse, sir. I'm stationed at Tripler."

Here she went again, running toward trouble. It seemed to be a habit. But why fight it?

Wallace motioned for her to follow. "She's with me."

She felt like kissing him at that moment, and swept out after them and into a jeep. Outside, in the direction of Pearl Harbor, the sky was smeared black with billowing shafts of smoke. A new line of planes zoomed past, strafing the steeple of an old stone church.

"Step on it, Joe," Wallace said, leaning his head out the window and looking skyward. "Jesus, it looks like Armageddon out there."

Bombs were coming down, bombs were going up, or maybe that was antiaircraft fire. The whistle of bullets. The *rat, tat, tat* of machine guns. And above all, the swarming hum of airplane engines.

Joe turned on the radio, but it was all static. "Find us a station," he yelled to Wallace.

All of the sudden, Webley Edwards's voice came on. Wallace turned it up so they could hear above the noise. In the backseat, Eva sat in disbelief at the nightmare unfolding around them. There was a strange feeling of numb detachment, that this could not be real.

"All right now, listen carefully. The island of Oahu is being attacked by enemy planes. The center of this attack is Pearl Harbor, but the planes are attacking airfields, as well. We are under attack. There seems to be no doubt about it. Do not go out on the streets. Keep under cover and keep calm. Some of you may think that this is just another military maneuver. This is not a maneuver. This is the real McCoy! I repeat, we have been attacked by enemy planes. The mark of the rising sun has been seen on the wings of these planes and they are attacking Pearl Harbor at this moment. Now keep your radio on and tell your neighbor to do the same. Keep off the streets and highways unless you have a duty to perform. Please don't use your telephone unless you absolutely have to do so. All of these phone facilities are needed for emergency calls. Now standby all military personnel and all police—police regulars and reserves. Report for duty at once. I repeat, we are under attack by enemy planes. The mark of the rising sun has been seen on these planes. Many of you have been asking if this is a maneuver. This is not a maneuver. This is the real McCoy!"

EGG LAYING

0730

Clark ran as much for his mind as he did for his body. Nothing could beat the peace and quiet of an hour of running. His body craved the movement and his mind required the trance-like state he fell into step after step after step. Running had been his salvation after Beth died, when the agony of living had been almost too much to bear. Today, it had taken him longer than usual to settle in. Too much on the mind. Eva, and that damn Flag Officers Code that was stubborn as a blind mule with three legs.

Under patchy clouds and a light drizzle, he had taken the road toward Ford Island and headed south along a rocky path, through kiawe trees with one-inch thorns and down to a marshland where long-legged birds hunted for fish.

As always, he admired the might of Battleship Row. *Arizona*, *Maryland*, *Nevada*, *Oklahoma*, *Tennessee*, *California* and *West Virginia* all lined up along the southeast side of Ford Island. Of the bunch, the *Nevada* and the *Oklahoma* were the navy's first super-dreadnoughts, and Clark, like any good soldier, got a lump in his chest just looking at them. Triple gun turrets, a radical new armor scheme, geared steam turbines, and they burned oil instead of coal for fuel. There was no doubt in his mind that here were the greatest battleships afloat.

At Hickam Field, he circled the long runway, waving at a couple of airmen getting ready for the B-17 Flying Fortresses that were scheduled to come in. Hickam housed the bombers—B-17s, A-20s and B-18s—whose pilots loved to razz their sailor neighbors with screaming flybys. But when the carriers came in, the navy hotshots gave them a run for their money. Clark got a kick watching their antics. No carriers today, though.

Being Sunday, Ford was off and had a family picnic planned, but Clark had decided it was time to bring up the matter of the radio signals. He had waited three days, and in those three days not one person had mentioned anything about ships being detected northwest of Oahu. Even the boys at He'eia. They were focused on radio activity in the South China Sea and the Dutch West Indies. *There is no activity of importance observed in the Sub Force*, they'd told him. Clark was more confused than ever. He would swing by Ford's this afternoon.

His T-shirt stuck to his back as he hit the grass for a round of push-ups. Once a football player, always a football player. Show him a green grassy field, and he would show you fifty push-ups. Sometimes, he felt like a show-off because he could outwork most of the younger guys, but he believed in keeping himself finely tuned and ready for action.

He heard the planes before he saw them, thinking it would be a treat to watch those babies come in. *Forty-six, forty-seven.* Beads of sweat dripped down his nose. He jumped up, dusted the grass from his palms and looked north, facing the middle of the island. A formation of bombers in a perfect V flew toward them.

"Here they come!" someone shouted.

Damn, what a sight.

"We're going to have an air show," another guy called.

The bombers began to peel away and swoop down, coming straight at Hickam faster than they ought to. Something seemed off. Clark moved closer to the men.

"Hey, those look more like navy fighters," a stocky mechanic next to him said.

Everyone was squinting to get a better look.

"What the—"

Several of the planes swerved around and dived straight at the harbor. On the underside of their wings were big red circles. Everyone stood for a fraction of a second, mouths hanging open. Half the formation was still making a beeline for them.

"Holy shit. It's the Japs!"

The crew scattered like schoolchildren after the bell, some heading for the barracks, others for a line of trees. Clark was in the bunch scrambling for the barracks. The dive-bomber was a mere two dozen feet over their heads. Close enough that Clark swore he saw the screws in the underbelly of the plane. The pilot smiled before opening fire, strafing the grass where only a minute ago, he'd been exercising. Clark wondered what was going through his mind. The guy's lips had been moving, and what Clark would have given to know what he said. War suddenly seemed different when it was down to the lowest denominator. Man on man.

The next thing he knew, a detonation flattened everyone to the ground. He had a second to think, as the ground came up at him, *So this is how it ends.*

One of the nearby soldiers screamed, "I'm hit, I'm hit. Oh God, I'm hit."

That was how Clark knew he was still alive. He could still hear. Men screaming, the thrum of engines, bombs cracking the sky. Hangar Seven went up in flames. The taste of dirt and blood filled his mouth, but otherwise he seemed in one piece. When he jumped up, two guys were pulling the wounded man toward the building, leaving behind a dark red streak in the grass.

How could this be happening?

Another dive-bomber swooped down on them. There was nothing to do but run. A moving target ready to be peppered with bullets. Miraculously, he made it to a truck and slid underneath just as the front door of the barracks burst open and soldiers spilled out—some still in their pajamas, others in their skivvies—carrying guns. Colt .45 semiautomatics and several old Springfield rifles.

What the fuck? Clark thought. *As if we stand a chance with those.*

Two guys on the parade ground had managed to get a Thomson submachine gun, and he watched in horror as the Zero shot through them as easily as if they'd been pieces of paper. Strangely, he felt nothing. Between the passes of the fighters and dive-bombers, he ran out and checked to see if either man had survived, even though he knew they hadn't. Both were full of holes. Gagging, he grabbed the gun and sprinted back to the truck, where he leaned against it, ready for the next round. He'd be damned if he didn't shoot down one of these devils.

Fires were popping up everywhere. The planes on the tarmacs made easy targets, exploding and spilling their gas into burning streams that lit up anything they touched.

A man came out of the building yelling like crazy. "Help, help, Lieutenant Braden is hit!" Of all things, a small dog on a rope cowered behind him.

Clark followed him into the mess hall, where a hole had been ripped through the roof.

Bodies lay on the floor with limbs at unnatural angles, or missing altogether. The metallic smell of blood hit him hard but he kept on going. One man had opened a five-gallon pail of pickles and was handing them out.

"In case we have to hide out in the hills. Here, take one," he said to Clark, completely shell-shocked. Clark took the pickle and stuck it in his pocket.

He was determined to help the panicky kid. The weird thing was, everywhere the kid went, the dog was right at his heels, panting.

"Where'd the mutt come from?"

"She's a stray, sir. Me and a couple of the guys started feeding her and I think I've become her favorite." The kid knelt next to a man on the floor. "Here he is."

Blood oozed out of Braden's chest and he was moaning and wheezing. They lifted him onto the counter. Someone was calling an ambulance. As if an ambulance would be able to make it through. Clark was ready to move on to others who seemed more likely to survive, but the kid begged him to stay. He found a rag and pressed it firmly to the man's wound.

"Hang in there, buddy, your men need you," Clark said.

Oddly enough, five minutes later, an ambulance came screeching to a halt in front of the blown-up building. Clark and the kid carried Braden out and laid him in the back of the vehicle. The dog followed with its rope dragging behind.

The ambulance driver helped them, then took one look at Clark and said, "Come on, I'll get you to Tripler."

"I'm fine. I wasn't the one hit."

"Sure, sure," the driver said, grabbing his arm and trying to pull him into the ambulance, too.

The guy was so persistent, Clark got in, crawled over the passenger seat and left through the back door. Walking away, he looked down and saw that his entire shirt was soaked in blood. His hands had turned red and he hardly recognized them.

A new roaring overhead as another round of planes approached. These looked like bombers. "Get outta there! You'll all get killed," someone screamed to a bunch of men on the field.

What were they *doing* out there?

Clark and the kid and the dog ran to the side of the building, looking for a way underneath it. The kid was shaking, and Clark couldn't tell if he was injured, too, or just covered in Braden's blood. "You okay?" he asked.

The kid ignored his question. "Are we going to have to move into the mountains? I heard they skewer their prisoners and eat dogs."

"Let's worry about getting out of here alive first."

He felt as though he were watching a war movie, his eyes unable to believe what he saw. He kept thinking about that first Zero and how close it had been. The bastard had actually waved. That face, he would never forget. He rubbed his eyes, trying to make sense of it all.

"For Chrissake, someone save that plane!" a man barked. Most of the planes on the airstrip had been strafed to hell, but one appeared to be untouched.

Clark watched another guy, dressed in shorts with no shirt, leap into the plane. The engine roared to life.

The kid next to him yelled, "Damn, I sure hope he knows how to fly that thing."

Another round of Japanese fighters bunched up over the harbor. "Shit," Clark mumbled, running out for the submachine gun, which he'd left under the truck.

When the fighters flew over, whoever was in the American plane didn't try to take off, but zigzagged her across the runway. By some miracle, he managed to avoid strafing from the Zeros. Clark blasted away at the low-flying planes, feeling pathetically undergunned. A second later, one blew up just beyond the barracks and rained down fiery metal and glass. Everyone in the vicinity cheered.

"Was that me?" Clark said to the kid.

"Beats me. Either you or the antiaircraft guns."

The tiny moment of victory was short-lived as a new formation of bombers arrived. Blinding explosions rocked the ground. Right in front of their eyes, the jeep he'd been hiding behind evaporated. A P-36 exploded in a fiery ball. Chunks of shrapnel sprayed out and lodged in anything within a fifty-foot radius. Clark was torn between hiding out in the building or staying outside. Either way, it was luck of the draw. Over the bushes, he could see a soldier without legs bleeding out into the grass. He wanted to help, but knew there was no point. The break in fire wouldn't last long. The kid bent over and started vomiting on his shoes.

"Make it stop. Can you make it stop?" the kid said.

"What's your name?" Clark asked.

"Jack. Private Jack Singer," he said to the ground.

"Jack, it looks like they're coming back, so you need to hold yourself together. We'll get through this," Clark ordered. "This dog needs you, too," he said as an afterthought.

Jack reached down and stroked the dog tenderly. Her tail was tucked so far under her legs you couldn't even see it. Still, she looked up at him with adoring brown eyes. "Brandy, you're my girl, aren't you?" he said.

Clark patted Brandy on the head. "Stay with us and you'll be fine."

If only.

This time, there were dive-bombers and fighters lined up, coming at them from two directions. He watched the bombs fall, first on Hangar One, which lifted entirely off the ground, and then into some kind of fuel storage building that sent a shock wave through the whole block. Next, they must have hit an ammunition depot, because the aircraft machine guns popped like firecrackers before the whole place detonated. Without any foxholes or trenches, they were shit out of luck.

Now, the way the barracks and hangars were being targeted with such precision, he thought it better to remain outside and ask God for an extra string of prayers. A bushy hedge with delicate white flowers was all that stood between them and half the Imperial Japanese Navy.

Whoever let this happen was done for, Clark would see to that—if he made it out alive.

"Sir, we are at war," Jack said, as if it needed to be announced.

Despite himself, Clark was damn impressed with the Japanese pilots. Perfect formation, perfect timing. People liked to talk about how the Japanese were an inferior breed, but he knew differently. Here was the proof.

Never underestimate your enemy.

The lead bomber now tucked into a steep dive and headed straight for them. "Cover your face," Clark cried, rolling over facedown into the sandy dirt. Jack was next to him with his body over Brandy.

He thought of Beth, and then Eva and how he'd let her slip away so easily. *Idiot.* Why hadn't he fought harder for her? *Tat, tat, tat, tat. Boom.* Twenty feet away, half the building wall ripped off. A scream next to him. A yelp. Shards of wood and metal and stone whizzed past. He found it hard to suck in any air. Something heavy on his leg. Had he swallowed sand? And then a warm tongue licked his face, nipping and barking. For a while, he tried to stay with it, but the darkness tugged at him.

And the smell of roses.

PURPLE HEARTS

A pale-faced sentry stood in front of the gate at the entrance to Pearl Harbor. He held both hands up as though he would stop the car with his own body if they tried to plow through. "Military only, we have a war going on here. You'll have to turn around, and I'd advise you to get the hell away—fast," he yelled.

Time had seemingly changed directions, with the yellow morning light turning back into twilight. A smoky darkness had settled around them. Eva wondered if she'd made the right call by coming here to ground zero. Who knew if the hospital was even still standing.

Wallace reached into his pocket and waved a badge around. "I'm a colonel in the United States Army. Let us through, boy," he roared.

The sentry squinted, trying to inspect the badge, but Wallace pulled it away and tossed it onto the backseat. Eva picked it up. New York Transportation System, it said.

"Sir—"

"Do you still want a job when this thing is over?" Wallace said.

Joe revved the engine, forcing the sentry to jump aside and

let them through. Eva wouldn't have wanted that job any more than she wanted hers at the moment.

"God bless you," Wallace said as they sped past into the fury.

When they screeched to a halt in front of Tripler, it looked like a battleground. Ambulances and American Sanitary Laundry trucks were lined up in front, unloading wounded. One truck had a bedsheet with a red cross painted on it, and even that was strafed. One hundred years of house calls and nursing school could not have prepared her for this. Men on makeshift stretchers—or no stretchers at all—were laid out in the grass out front. The line of cars hardly moved. All the while, Japanese planes were still busy crack shooting Battleship Row and Ford Island.

Thank God Ruby hadn't come.

"We should have pulled over back there, at this rate we'll never get to the front. Come on," Wallace said to Eva, opening his door. "We'll see you in there, Joe."

Neither of them were in uniform, but that hardly mattered. She followed closely at Wallace's heels as he barged through the front door. Nurses scurried everywhere, setting up cots in the hallway and ushering newcomers into closets. There was a sickening smell of blood and burnt skin and fear.

"Who's in charge here?" Wallace asked the first nurse whose attention he could get.

She shrugged. "I have no idea," she said, turning back to the tattered soldier leaning against the wall.

"I know where the operating room is. Follow me," Eva said.

A feeling of calm determination overcame Eva. Whatever it took, she would not let these boys down. She would stay here until the building blew up—a real possibility—if she had to. Moving through the hospital, Eva felt as though she were in some unearthly place. One man they passed lay moaning on a cot and hugging his severed leg like a teddy bear. There was an *M* and a *T* marked in ink on his forehead. Another appeared dead except for the gurgling coming from his chest. Eva wanted to bend down and help these men, to hold their hands and assure them everything would be fine, but there were too many just like them packing the hospital. More than she could count.

No one wants to die alone. In the end, you just sit with them and hold their hand. Nothing is more important. Her father's voice. *And don't be afraid to look 'em in the eye.*

Wallace announced himself at the nurses' station outside the OR. "Dr. John Wallace, head trauma surgeon at your service. Show me where to go and I'm all yours." He motioned to Eva. "This gal needs to be put to work, too."

"In there," the nurse said to Wallace, and he was off.

Eva explained who she was. "I've been assigned Maternity. But I have plenty of experience in surgery."

"You could be a first-year student and we'd use you. Anyway, the women and babies have all been transferred to an underground bunker."

"I'm not in uniform," Eva pointed out.

The nurse snorted. "The closet to your left. Grab one and make yourself useful."

"Where should I start?"

"Anywhere."

The closet door was already open and on the floor lay a wide-eyed soldier with blood-soaked bandages wrapped thickly around both his arms. He looked all of seventeen. "Nurse, I think I lost my hands," he said.

Eva couldn't imagine him being conscious and talking if he'd lost both his hands. "It may feel like that now, but we'll take care of you. You just rest, you hear me?"

"But my hands," he said, this time more softly.

His eyes closed. Eva quickly slipped off her dress and stepped into the crisp white uniform she pulled from the shelf. Whose dumb idea had it been for nurses to wear white? The dress was for someone twice her size, but it was the only one left. She took the belt from her own dress and cinched it around, feeling half-ridiculous but ready to get to work.

This time, back at the nurses' station, a woman directed her to the front lawn. "We need help with the new arrivals. We can't keep up." She handed Eva a tray with syringes. "Give them a shot of morphine, and if they aren't critical, or if they're beyond saving, keep them outside. And don't forget to put an *M* on their foreheads."

Eva wanted to do more. She knew she could. "But I have experience in anesthesia."

The nurse eyed her. "Maybe later. We need you outside now."

The wounded kept pouring in. Civilian automobiles, grocery trucks, you name it. Eva went about greeting them and directing them where to go. Most of the time, she managed to keep her expression even. *Never show them how bad it is*, her father used to say, *even when you want to turn around and make a break for it, or throw up your breakfast*. But every so often, one was so awful, tears began to leak out of her eyes. She said an extra prayer for those.

A few raindrops began to fall and she cursed. Not now, for heaven's sake, not now. The cloud soon passed. With every arrival, she was almost afraid to look for fear of seeing Clark's face among the dead. In most cases, she could tell right away just from their size. A strange mixture of relief it wasn't him, and sorrow for the injured man. Some were so far gone, she directed them to be carried to the far side of the field, where the dead were being laid out and covered in blankets or any available material. They were probably the lucky ones, who never knew what hit them.

Sometime in the next half hour or so, Grace ran up to her. "Eva, you're alive! We could see the fires from church and it looked like Queen's Hospital had been hit."

They hugged briefly, but tightly. Grace still smelled of lavender and soap. Eva thought how easy it would be to collapse into a sobbing mess. She ordered herself to hold it together.

"I could use a hand. Go grab me some more morphine syringes and blankets and anything else you can find that would be useful out here," she said.

Grace darted off.

"Miss, can you help me?" said a man on a litter. His whole left side was crinkled like pink parchment paper and he was stark naked but for a towel draped over his groin.

No, I probably can't.

"What do you need?" she asked.

"My buddy Ralph. Is he here?"

"What does he look like?" she said, taking hold of his good hand.

"Like a bulldog. Black hair, freckles."

Ralph could have been one of hundreds. "Tell you what, I'll see if I can find out. In the meantime, you just keep on being a hero, okay?"

"I'm no hero, miss. Ralph is the one who pushed me into the boat. He gave me his spot," the man said.

Suddenly, the whine of an engine grew louder and louder. She turned to see a plane trailing thick black smoke beelining toward them. The red circles under the wings were like big fat targets. Everyone just stood and stared, frozen in place.

Eva was caught between wanting to run and wanting to scream, and doing neither in the meantime.

Where were all the antiaircraft guns? Or American fighters?

"He's gonna crash!" someone yelled.

The plane came so low—just skimming the kiawe trees—

that Eva saw the pilot's face crack into a smile. One gold tooth. Burning fuel stank up the air. At the last minute, the pilot waved and pulled the nose up so it squeaked past the roof of the hospital by a hair.

"Someone kill that motherfucker!" the man she had been helping screamed.

If only Eva had a gun now, she would put her shooting skills to good use.

A few minutes later, Grace came back with a white face and a tray of syringes. "I don't know if I can do this," she announced.

"You don't have a choice."

Grace's voice cracked. "Eva, there are arms and legs in the hallway and the blood is two inches thick on the floor in there."

"How do you think the men feel? Hold yourself together for them. They need you at one hundred and twenty percent," Eva said softly.

Grace's lip quivered and her pale blue eyes scanned the mess around them. Broken men, burned men, dead men. Eva silently prayed. *Please, God, stand by us here, we need all the miracles You've got.*

"We better get to work," Grace finally said, standing up straighter and pulling out a tube of lipstick.

Eva gave her a puzzled look.

"They're out of markers," Grace said.

They took turns injecting morphine and tetanus vaccines and marking foreheads with lipstick. An *M* and a *T*. Wounds were cleaned and debrided and sprayed with sulfa. Clouds came and went and the skies were quiet once again. It seemed like the Japanese planes had flown back out to sea. For the moment. The boys were saying it was only a matter of time before the ships came to shore and then the real trouble would begin.

Soon, more burn victims started coming in, in droves, and Eva and Grace returned to the hospital. Men had been dipped in fuel head to toe. You could smell them coming a mile away. Grace disappeared and came back with a bucketful of tannic acid. They ended up dipping the gauze into the acid and draping it over the burned body parts. In some cases that meant the whole body.

"We need plasma to treat these burns," Eva said.

"Good luck. We'll never have enough."

At some point, Grace, who wasn't even in uniform, took a good look at Eva. "Why is your dress so big?"

"It was all they had."

A flicker of a smile. "You look like you're playing dress up."

"Don't I wish that was the case. And that this whole thing was make-believe. I keep expecting to wake up at any moment."

"I feel like I should be doing more," Grace said as they moved down the hallway to the next room. There were more soldiers than beds. Several of the men had blackened skin and they went to them first.

"There's only one of you and hundreds of them," Eva pointed out. "But I know what you mean, especially because I have experience with anesthesia."

Grace looked surprised. "You do? Why didn't you mention it?"

"Long story."

One of the men passed out the minute Eva shot him up with morphine, which was probably a good thing, since his legs looked like used campfire wood. Grace followed up with the soaked gauze.

"You should be helping with the surgeries."

"I know. But they sent me here."

"Go back and tell them for heaven's sake."

"I can't tell them," Eva said.

"Why not?"

Eva sighed. "Because I had to lie to get here. I promise I will tell you everything later, and trust me, it's not what you think."

Grace didn't press it. "It's bound to be chaos. They're probably desperate for your help. Just act like you're meant to be there and no one will know the difference."

"You think?"

"I do."

Eva left Grace to sort through the injured. Half past ten and every room and every bed in the hospital was now full. It was the first time she had looked at her watch since the first plane flew over her at five past eight. In a little over two hours the world had gone from a lazy Sunday morning to a desperate fight for survival. Nothing would *ever* be the same.

She looked through the rooms for Dr. Wallace, but couldn't locate him. Upstairs, two doctors and Judy Walton came out of the operating theater with down-turned faces. Judy gave her a worn-out look. One doctor was saying, "Any abdominal or thoracic wound needs to be brought in right away."

The nurse nodded toward the line. "Every one of these is an abdominal or thoracic wound."

"God help us," the one with his back to her muttered.

Whether or not people figured out she hadn't been totally honest was irrelevant at this point. She straightened her hat. "Excuse me, but I'm here to help in surgery. Willa sent me."

No one argued.

"Help me get this man in here, then, and check his vitals," he said, turning to face her. "I'm Dr. Izumi."

Eva felt her cheeks flush. Once the initial shock wore off, she realized he might be Japanese, but he was also on their side. Up until this morning, he was simply a man being a doctor on a Pacific island.

Throughout the first surgery—removing shrapnel from Bobby Angelo's arms and chest—Dr. Izumi maintained a steady hand and calm demeanor. They worked in near silence, oblivious to the other surgeries going on just feet away. He used just the right dose of ether and gave Eva a certain amount of autonomy. It wasn't until the third patient that things went south.

"Get him away from me!" the wounded soldier on the table screamed. "No Jap is gonna touch me. He's a spy!"

Eva and Dr. Izumi locked eyes. Luckily, most of the patients in the room were in some form of unconsciousness, otherwise the whole place was liable to chime in.

"Dr. Izumi is not a spy and if you let him, he'll save your life," she said coolly.

The man tried to sit up, but fell back down, clutching his stomach and wailing, "Murderer! I don't want to die…" His voice faded away.

They quickly got to work, pulling a piece of metal the size of a small saucer from his side. By some miracle, his spleen was still intact and he hadn't bled out. Eva was loading him with gauze when she noticed rivulets of sweat pouring down Dr. Izumi's forehead. The words surely had struck a chord, and she felt for him.

At the end, he said to her, "I shouldn't be here."

"How many lives have you already saved?" she asked.

"I've lost count."

"There's your answer," she said, surprised that he was talking to her, of all people, about this. "That soldier was talking from fear. I don't know if you've been outside, but those pilots have been flying so low you can see the whites of their eyes."

A nurse wheeled over another patient, and they immediately stopped talking. "He's bad, Doc, severed left leg and a crushed pelvis. Jack Singer is his name," she said.

The man—a kid, really—was whiter than the sheet, and Eva could barely find a pulse. Something about him reminded her of Tommy Lemon, and her heart picked up speed. She could tell he wanted to open his eyes by the way they kept fluttering, but couldn't muster the strength. Finally, he succeeded.

"Brandy," Jack moaned.

Eva touched his shoulder and leaned close. "We have something even better, it's called morphine."

"Where's Brandy?" he said even louder.

Eva felt something rub against her leg. "What the—" A second later, a small sooty dog stuck its nose out from under the table and began a barely audible whine.

Jack's hand dropped down and the dog licked it lovingly. "Can you make sure my Brandy is okay?" he said, staring as deep into Eva as he possibly could, diving past her defenses. A pleading *I know I'm not going to live* kind of look. She'd seen it one too many times today.

"Don't you worry, Jack, you'll be able to take care of her yourself," she assured him.

Lacking any strength, he reached out and squeezed her hand. "Promise me."

"I promise."

What was she doing? Making promises she couldn't keep to a dying kid. Over the years, this same kind of weakness in her father had turned their home into a sanctuary for orphaned animals.

Across the table, Dr. Izumi had attached a plasma bag and was readying the anesthesia. When he turned and saw Brandy, he froze. "How did that dog get in here?"

"I have no idea, but she's with him," Eva said.

"No dogs allowed. Dr. Newcastle would have a fit."

Even though he was under two blankets, Jack's teeth started chattering. "Us guys at Hickam are all she has."

Under normal circumstances, a dog would have been thrown out without another word, but Dr. Izumi just shrugged and said, "Keep it under the table, then."

Brandy seemed to understand what was happening and curled up below Jack's one remaining foot. Fortunately, someone had used a belt as a tourniquet to keep him alive. But the shock was what worried her.

"Let's run another bag of plasma," she suggested.

Dr. Izumi looked at her questioningly. "Why do you say that?"

"Because he's in shock. Look at him."

She thought he was going to override her, but he agreed. "Go get another bag."

By the grace of God, the hospital still had plasma, but how long it would last was anyone's guess. While Eva ran the other line, Dr. Izumi drank down a glass of water that someone handed him. Suddenly, Dr. Newcastle appeared next to him. She moved to block the dog from his line of sight.

"Do you need a break? I can take over on this one," Dr. Newcastle said.

Eva stiffened.

"There's a whole line of boys all the way out to the front lawn, so I won't be resting anytime soon," Izumi said.

She almost cheered. Nor was the irony lost on her. Two surgeons. Both competent. One white. One Japanese. She would have chosen Izumi over Newcastle any day. Even today.

Dr. Newcastle slapped him on the back with his hand and spoke in a hushed tone. "I like your attitude but we've been getting a lot of flak for having you here. We know you're one of us, but all they see are those damn Nip pilots."

Eva couldn't help herself. "But, Doctor, he's already saved a half-dozen lives or more."

Dr. Newcastle ignored her. "They could use you in the morgue."

"No disrespect, Frank, but you need every surgeon on deck and then some. You need me," Dr. Izumi said.

The injustice of it burned at her. Helplessness was not her strong suit, and all Eva wanted to do was grab Dr. Newcastle by his bloody scrubs and shake him.

"Not if it causes distress," he said.

Dr. Izumi pulled off his surgical mask and tossed it on the ground. "I'm not going to stand around here and argue. Have at it."

She opened her mouth to speak, but Dr. Newcastle shut her up fast. "Not a word from you."

Still reeling, Eva went about her business of readying young Jack—scraping out rocks and glass from his wounds and checking his blood pressure and pupils. He seemed to be responding well to the extra plasma, but his skin still looked dusty white. Maybe if she worked hard enough, she could reverse it.

Dr. Newcastle put Jack under and got to work. Every time he moved to the foot of the table, Eva was sure he was going to kick Brandy. But somehow, the dog eluded him.

Halfway through the operation, she caught sight of a man who looked like Clark being wheeled past. Same size, same chocolate hair, only it was soaked in oil and the skin on his face was charred beyond recognition. She closed her eyes, refusing to believe it was him. *He would not have been out on the water. No. No. No.*

She heard the doctor say, "Why are you bringing this man here? He's dead."

A stone in her throat.

Dizziness.

A small tattoo on his forearm.

Not him.

"Nurse?" Dr. Newcastle was waving his hand in front of her face.

A shudder ran through her. "Sorry, I thought I saw someone I knew."

"Don't check out on me again like that, or I'm sending you to the morgue, too," he said.

"I swear I won't."

By now, she had been able to piece together what had transpired. Two waves of attack. A complete surprise. For many of the men aboard the battleships, the choice had been to go down with the burning ship or leap into the flaming water. Battleship Row and Hickam Field seemed to have been the hardest hit. *Half my friends are stuck in the belly of the* Oklahoma *as we speak. They blew us up while we were sleeping. Suddenly I was looking at sky where the roof was supposed to be. I watched Andy Bustard get cut in half.* Just looking out the window, down onto the mayhem of Pearl Harbor, full of rescue boats and fire engines and plumes of black smoke, was enough to cause a breakdown. She felt her armor cracking, but summoned strength by looking at all the brave souls around her.

Jack survived the surgery, hanging on by a thumbnail, and was moved to a room across the hall. The minute Dr. Newcastle left to wash up, Eva scooped up Brandy in a towel, ran her over and set her under his new cot. It was hard to tell how much of the black on her coat was real and how much was soot. Eva filled a stainless container with water. Brandy sniffed her hand and looked up at her with cautious eyes. Her tail was tucked all the way under her little body and she was shivering. Eva scanned for any signs of injury, but the dog seemed outwardly fine.

"You take care of him now," Eva said, rubbing behind the

dog's ears. Her hand came away black. She wished she could stay longer to comfort the poor thing but she had men to tend to. She slipped out of the room with no one the wiser. Everyone else was too busy to notice.

They worked and they worked and they worked. Grace came back inside and Eva was glad to have her nearby. At some point, a small cocoa-skinned woman came by with a tray full of fried chicken and cups of a bright red drink.

"What is it?" Eva asked, hardly able to understand the woman's accent.

"Proot punch."

"She's saying fruit punch," Grace said, taking one and handing it to Eva. "Thank you, Mrs. Mac, you're a lifesaver."

"Whose bright idea was it to serve red liquid today?" Eva wanted to know.

Grace shook her head. "Lemonade would have been a better choice."

"Or Tennessee whiskey. But I'll take what I can get."

At least as far as drinks went. Food was another story. She didn't think she could stomach a bite of anything right now. Especially fried chicken.

At some point head nurse Willa came in and rounded up anyone in sight. "There's talk that the Japanese have eighty transports off of Diamond Head and they're landing parachute troops in the cane fields. We need to patch our soldiers up, so they can get back out there and keep fighting."

The nurses all stared at each other. The mood went from dark to black. At least half of these boys would not be leaving the hospital anytime soon. In fact, they would be lucky if they ever left. As for the others, many needed to be strapped down in order to keep them in place. One soldier with a jagged head wound and sixteen broken teeth told Eva, *I gotta get back to the* Utah *to find Johnny. He went down the bilge manhole.*

He's going to be trapped. She knew that the *Utah* was now resting on the bottom of the harbor.

After Willa left, Grace looked Eva square in the face. "This must be what hell is like."

BLIND ASSUMPTIONS

September 21, 1941

Evelyn had spent the rest of the morning fixated on her conversation with Dr. Brown before he kicked her out of the operating room. It should not have happened, plain and simple. Top of her class in nursing school, highest accolades in nurse anesthetist training, residency at the Mayo Clinic, and yet still she was not immune. What nagged at her the most was that she had accepted her fate and walked out instead of putting up a fight. Leaving the operating room had seemed like the only option, but had it been?

Don't ever suggest that you know better than me. You can be excused, Nurse.

The scene was etched on the backs of her eyelids and she replayed it every few seconds. What if she had stood up to him? Refused to budge. Or gone and found another doctor to complain to and reported him for being unfit to operate. Would anyone have listened?

It was hard to concentrate on anything other than the blue face of Tommy Lemon on that table. In this field, deaths were commonplace. But in all her years in the field, none had died as the result of pigheadedness. Maybe this one time, Brown had finally done himself in. *Seen himself to the door,* as her father would have said.

Evelyn was taking Jimmy Dalloway's temperature when Milly walked in with a pale face.

"What is it?" Evelyn asked.

"I had lunch with Madge, and she said that Jed Lemon was standing in the hallway screaming obscenities at Dr. Brown."

No one screamed at Dr. Brown. *Ever.* "He could lose his job over this," Evelyn said, imagining how pleasant things would be around the hospital without him. But it should have never come to this. No one should have to die to get the man ousted.

Milly suddenly became interested on a crack on the wall. "That's the thing."

"What do you mean?" Evelyn said.

A long pause.

"There seems to be uncertainty over what the cause was."

"His heart stopped beating due to the fact that he was already in shock when given sodium thiopental, that's what happened," Evelyn said.

"Dr. Brown will never admit to any fault."

A rush of horror sucker punched Evelyn in the gut. She felt panicky and guilty and began explaining herself to Milly over and over again, as if Milly was the one who needed to know. "I suggested to use ether instead and he refused to even consider it. You know how he is. Tommy Lemon would have had a chance if he had listened to me. I can't say with one hundred percent certainty that he would have lived. But I have a hunch he would have, he was young and strong and full of life."

Milly gave her a sorry look. "Oh, Evelyn, I know you did your best. We all do. Accidents like this are the downside of the business. They happen to the best of us."

Evelyn threw her hands up and began pacing. "This was not an accident. I'm going to go talk to him."

Milly grabbed her arm. "Wait. Madge said he's hysterical. If you show up, things could get ugly."

"But I need to explain what happened. Don't I?" Evelyn said.

Milly sighed. She had been around long enough to know how things went. "Give it a little time, let things settle, and, anyway, what are you going to say? *Dr. Brown killed your son because he was negligent?*" she said.

Evelyn fought the urge to crumple to the floor in resignation. "What if I talk to Mrs. Lemon? She's a kind and reasonable woman from what I've seen of her."

Milly shrugged. "Anything is possible, I suppose."

That was about as unlikely as Dr. Brown coming out and admitting his mistake.

"I need to try," Evelyn said. She ran out of the Woods Wing and into a blast of cold air.

Later on, she wondered if things might have turned out differently if she had listened to Milly's advice, but the need to tell her story burned so brightly she could not ignore it.

THE LITTLE FELLA

December 7

At two o'clock, the prostitutes showed up. Eva was in the supply closet looking for more tannic acid when she heard unfamiliar female voices. Peering out, she saw three women standing around the nurses' station talking animatedly to Willa. Two white women and a copper-skinned beauty, all dressed like they were going to church. The way Willa was shaking her head, Eva could tell she was upset. She walked over to see what the fuss was. One with balloons in her blouse—or so it looked—said, "We've already donated blood and we can help in any way you see fit."

"This is a hospital, not a brothel," Willa said.

No wonder the room suddenly smelled like a perfume factory. First a dog, and now a group of call girls. Yet Eva supposed there was no rule book on how to react when ambushed by the Imperial Japanese Navy. All normalcy had gone out the window at about 7:55 this morning.

One of them put a hand on Willa's arm. "Nurse, we want to be of service. Even if it's just to sit with them and pray. Please."

Willa noticed Eva standing there. "Why don't you give these gals something to do?" she said.

Eva turned around, hoping to God there was someone behind her.

"Me?"

"Yes, you. Take them to Burns. They can spray and pray."

One of the ingenious nurses had found a shelf full of flit guns for insect repellent and decided it would make a handy spray device for the tannic acid. Eva had been impressed. Not only about that, but how the whole world had come together to help these poor boys. Laundry trucks as ambulances, regular people off the streets dragging the injured in and now the prostitutes. What was next?

"Do any of you have any kind of first aid training?" she asked, unsure what to expect, having never been in the company of a call girl before.

"I do," the Hawaiian one said. "I've, uh, serviced one of the heads of the Red Cross here. He told me they're all stocked up since they knew this was coming. I bet they'll be sending out some Gray Ladies soon."

The words stopped Eva cold. "Who knew this was coming?" she asked.

"The folks in Washington."

"And your friend knows this for certain?"

"Apparently. All the money and supplies got switched to wartime levels. He told me it was imminent, but not to breathe a word. I guess the secret is out now."

"Well, I'll be damned," Eva said.

Donna, Mary Ann and Lehua were their names and they were genuine in their desire to help. Just the fact that they'd come to the hospital spoke volumes. She led them down the hallway, stepping over patients and ignoring the catcalls. Wounded men were still men.

"The burns are the worst," she warned them. "It's like someone dipped them in a chicken fryer and left for the afternoon.

They lose a lot of fluid and then are in danger of going into shock. So keep an eye on the IV bags and let us know if you see one empty."

In the burn ward, the smell about knocked you over. Mary Ann held a handkerchief to her face. Donna turned gray and braced herself on the wall. Across the way, Judy was rubbing ointment on a skinless man. Eva went to her and attempted to hand off the women.

"I'll take 'em. At least we know they have experience in comfort," Judy said.

Lehua wasted no time in sitting on the edge of a bed. "What's your name?" she asked softly.

Eva left them. What a strange twist of fate that she had been sitting in the auditorium this very morning waiting for a lecture on burns. Traumatic surgery, back injuries and burns of all things. As with the timing of the Red Cross supplies, it seemed oddly coincidental. Was it possible Dr. Wallace had been brought here based on foreknowledge of the attack?

Inconceivable. And yet…

Back in the operating room, Dr. Newcastle singled her out again, calling out as she tried to sneak on by behind him.

"Nurse! I want you to help me on this one. He's critical," he said, and Eva didn't know whether to be flattered or frightened.

Cyanosis is something you can't imagine until you actually see it. People can be lots of colors, but blue should not be one of them. In all her years, she had never seen a person be this purple and still have a pulse. Not only that, he was swollen from head to toe, as though someone had put a straw in his mouth and blown him up like a balloon. He was thrashing around. Shrapnel had torn apart his chest, leaving the air to bleed out into his tissues.

The man was gasping for air. They had to do something on the double. "Just cut him there. I'll aspirate," she said, pointing to a spot just above his sternum.

He surprised her by taking his scalpel and slicing right where she had indicated. No anesthesia. A few moments later, the patient's breathing eased, and a minute after that, a hint of color returned to his skin.

They worked in silence, she drawing fluid from the patient's trachea and Dr. Newcastle controlling the blood. By the time they finished, her hands were trembling and her legs wobbly. She needed fresh air and sunshine. She needed a hug. Where was Grace?

Dr. Newcastle walked away without a word.

Over in Jack's room, Eva found Grace tending to a soldier with a bandage around his whole head. "She sure was pretty. Bird boned, shiny black hair. We were going to go roller-skating this morning," he was saying.

Grace held his hand. "You just worry about getting better so you can skate again."

"No one will talk to me if I associate with a Japanese girl."

"Seeing that more than half the island is Japanese, I think they may forgive you, Don," she said.

Eva wasn't so sure. Anything Japanese would always remind these boys of today, December 7, for the rest of their lives. Be it short or long. She bent forward to make sure Jack was breathing. He was, with Brandy still tucked under his bed.

Eva knelt down. "Hi, sweetie." The desire for ear scratches won out over fear, and the dog soon rolled onto her back and offered her spotted pink belly up for petting. The doctors were all out of the room, so Eva invited the dog over to see Jack.

Brandy stood on her hind legs and sniffed the whole of his body. Not a big dog, she was about knee-high and narrow like a whippet. Her eyes were dark and inquisitive and rimmed in coal. When she got down, she moved on to the next bed, and the next. Don was the only one alert enough to notice her.

He whistled her over. "Brandy? Come here, girl."

At the sound of her name, Brandy ran over and leaped onto the side of his bed, careful to avoid landing on him. The maneuver was pure love. A spot of sunshine on a thunderous day.

Grace watched in utter surprise. "Horsefeathers, there's a dog in here!"

"She came in with Jack."

Don's face had gone from pained to smiling in one second flat as Brandy lay by his side and thumped the bed with her tail. "This here is our mascot at Hickam, Brandy. Smartest dog this side of the Pacific."

"They let you have dogs in the barracks?" Grace said, doubtful.

"Not at first, but she kept coming back. I think it was because Jack and Henry gave her sardines, and she was hooked. I was damn sure the bombs had got her. Thank You, Jesus, for keeping her safe."

He touched his forehead and chest.

"I'm happy she's alive, but she has to go. We can't have dogs," Grace said.

Eva disagreed. "We had a dog at the hospital back home and everyone loved her. I say we keep her until someone tells us not to."

"Dogs carry germs."

"We can wash her. She'll be a big boost to morale in here, you'll see."

Don looked concerned. "Our barracks were hit pretty bad. Where else will she go?"

Grace sighed. "Do what you want. I have to go get some more supplies. But don't say I didn't warn you."

Once Grace left, Eva searched around for a place to keep Brandy hidden from the doctors. In truth, it was only a matter of time. But you did what you could. The best solution ended up being to hang an extra sheet off the side of Jack's bed. Washing the dog would have to wait, but she wetted down a towel with warm water and wiped all the dirt and blood and ash from her fur. Most of the black came away, leaving only one big spot remaining on Brandy's side. Brandy made no fuss, even letting Eva get between her toes. She could see why the boys at Hickam had kept her.

Once she was cleaned off, they visited the other men in the warm and stuffy room. Eva was impressed at how Brandy approached each man differently. For one in traction, she stayed off the bed, for another with both legs bandaged, she stood near his upper body. And with another, who was sitting cross-legged and seemed fine, she jumped right into his lap.

"I think the little fella likes me," he said, beaming.

Not everyone knew her, but every single one of them wanted to pet her and rub her. Brandy couldn't have been happier. After the rounds, she sat by Jack's side, staring up at him as though she could will him better with enough love.

If only they could have one *little fella* for each man in here.

In the midafternoon, Eva finally took a break. Her movements had begun to feel leaden. She needed fresh air. No one objected; everyone was too busy tending the injured. Cars and ambulances were still pulling in, and she circled behind the hospital to seek space and a place to just *be* for a minute. She sat beneath a sprawling tree and watched a trail of ants move a leaf, oblivious to the madness around them.

That's just the way of the world. It keeps on spinning, her father would have said.

For the first time that day, she had time to think about

her own troubles. There had been no word from Billy and no sign of Clark. Word had been coming in that the bases on the north and east ends of the island had been hit, which was where Billy had been going to play golf, and while she had concern for him, Clark was the one she ached to hear from. There was also the matter of Ruby. Surely news of the attack would have made it to the mainland by now, and her sister would be worrying herself half to death. Eva would send word as soon as she could, but for now, these men took priority.

A loud banging noise erupted from the front of the hospital and she headed back to see what it was. Inside the main entry, two men in uniform were nailing a piece of wood over the picture window and another hung heavy army blankets on the smaller ones. Blackouts had been ordered and no one was taking any chances. The night would be a long one.

On the way upstairs, Eva bumped into Judy, whose eyes were rimmed in red. Her expression was stone.

"Are you all right?" Eva asked.

Judy fell into her arms and buried her face in Eva's neck. "They got Sid. He's gone, Eva."

"Oh, honey, no!"

"My beautiful Sid, strafed in his plane before he even got off the ground."

Judy let out a moan that was so raw, so gut splitting, that Eva felt it reverberate through her bones. All she could do was hold Judy tight. There were no words. By the time they separated, the left upper half of her dress was soaking wet with Judy's tears and snot.

"You know, we were supposed to get married on Christmas. We were going to elope. Just he and I on Waikiki Beach. Now I can never, ever go back there," Judy sobbed.

What could Eva say to that? If he had known the Japanese were coming, maybe he would have been flying already and on the offensive. Eva felt a sudden, overwhelming surge of guilt. She should have marched into Admiral Kimmel's office and told them about the ships. Demanded that something be done. Billy had dismissed her, and she had let it go too easily. Why hadn't she pushed? Billy was turning out to be different than she remembered.

"You're in shock, sweetie. Do you want to go lie down?" Eva said.

"No! I'm not a deserter."

"No one in their right mind would call you a deserter."

"They need me here."

"You sure?"

Judy's lip quivered, but she nodded bravely. "And, anyway, most of them have a woman out there somewhere. Nobody should have to go through this, and if I can keep just one man alive, well, then, I've done my part. I need to keep working to keep me preoccupied."

"If you need anything, come find me," Eva said, squeezing her hands.

"By the way, they brought a man in a little while ago who looked like your friend at the ball game last night," Judy said.

The stairway spun around her.

THE PATIENT

Eva started off in the burn ward, going from bed to bed looking for Clark's familiar face. Each man waged his own battle for survival and Eva choked back the tears. Scorched skin began where the clothing had ended. Since the attack had come early on a Sunday, a white T-shirt and shorts were standard attire, leaving arms and legs to be seared.

War's brutal message had stamped itself across the island in big red letters. And the smell of tannic acid and burnt skin was something she would never forget.

"I use a perfumed hankie. It's the only way," one of the nurses told her, seeing Eva's hands clamped over her face.

When Eva had finished looking there, she moved on to Orthopedics. But Clark was not there, either. Dr. Wallace was, though, checking on patients. He looked as though he'd aged thirty years since morning.

"Have you seen Lieutenant Spencer come through?" she asked.

"As a casualty?"

"Yes."

"Not to my knowledge, but someone could easily get lost in here. How are you holding up?"

It was the first time anyone had asked her that. "Well, I

haven't had time to consider it, really. I'm still standing, so that's a good sign."

He wiped his forehead with the back of a gloved hand, clearly not acclimated to the tropical heat yet. "You nurses are doing a fine job, everyone stepping up to the plate and then some. Making me proud."

Why couldn't all doctors be like this? "Thank you."

Once she had covered the whole second floor, she went back downstairs and made the rounds there, too. Along the way, she held some hands and said a few prayers. Clark was nowhere to be found. The last place to search was the morgue. She stood in front of the steel door trying to summon the strength. *Do you really want to know?* In the end, she couldn't bring herself to go in. Her job was with the living.

While downstairs, Eva made herself useful and grabbed several pails of water. Instructions had been given to fill all containers to capacity because the local Japanese sympathizers were poisoning the water sources. Who knew if it was true or not, but she didn't want to find out the hard way.

A few more cots had been crammed into the ward, and Grace and Judy were monitoring the new patients. One of them was begging for a cigarette, another wanted to hear the twenty-third psalm over and over. When Eva neared Jack's bed, she heard a tail thump.

"There you are. Willa said someone was asking after you on the operating table," Grace said.

Eva's knees almost buckled. She had just finished convincing herself that Judy had been mistaken, and Clark was working cracking codes in his secret office. She squeaked out, "Where?"

"She didn't say."

Eva flew out of the room and down the hallway, barging

in on more than one surprised doctor. "Sorry, wrong room," she said.

In the third room on the right, Dr. Newcastle was hunched over a large man. She didn't know the nurse assisting. If he noticed Eva, he didn't show it.

"Nurse, can you shine the light this way? I can't see what I'm doing," he said.

From this angle, Eva couldn't see the face, and the only exposed body part was a hairy leg. Nevertheless, she *knew*. She tried to swallow but couldn't. It was one thing to treat strangers, another to treat loved ones. This had become glaringly apparent when Ruby had fallen ill. Brave nurse Evelyn reduced to a panicky mess.

"What's wrong with him?" she heard herself asking.

The nurse looked up. "He was shot and filled with shrapnel."

Dr. Newcastle glanced up. "What are you doing in here?"

"He's a friend."

Moving closer, she tried to assess what was going on, catching sight of his square jaw and the shadow of stubble against chalk-white skin. If there had been any doubt, it drained out of her then. *Clark.* To her horror, his breaths were shallow and he was hooked up to an IV, which meant they were using sodium thiopental on him. Her heart free-fell.

"He looks too pale," she commented, knowing full well that she might end up fired or found out. Or both.

No response.

She kept going. "Look how his chest is barely moving up and down. He's going to go into arrest if you aren't careful."

Once you had seen the signs, they were hard to miss.

"Miss Cassidy. Out, now!" Dr. Newcastle bellowed and she was surprised he knew her name.

The reliving of a nightmare. That was how it felt. But

where she'd walked away the first time, she couldn't bring herself to now.

"Doctor, I've seen this before. I have experience in anesthesia. Bring him out now, or you're going to lose him. It's the sodium thiopental."

He stared at her. "Excuse me?"

She stared back, ready to stick to her guns. "I said, if you keep using the sodium thiopental, he's going to die."

Whatever training Dr. Newcastle had had as a surgeon, he was bound to know about the dangers, but possibly not firsthand as she did. In such a setting, and with so many men in shock, the choice to operate was a fine line.

He gave her a look that would have brought down a Japanese plane. "Out."

The other nurse spoke up. "Doctor, his heart rate *is* dangerously high."

Without another word, Newcastle turned his attention to Clark. He listened with the stethoscope and took his pulse. He must not have liked what he heard, because he quickly adjusted the IV. "This chest wound is going to have to wait. Whoever he is, you may want to notify his next of kin," he said to Eva.

Eva remembered his last words to her. *It just wasn't our time.* Her head resting on that same chest and the solid thud of his heart as they danced in the starlight. How he had held her with such tenderness. And the kiss that still simmered on her lips. What kind of fool had she been to let him slip away?

Words poured from her mouth. "Now is not your time to die, Clark. You hear me?"

Whatever happened to *never let them see your fear*? Or the bedside manner that had been drilled into her head. *Always meet the patient in a cheerful and sensible manner, endeavoring to inspire confidence.*

"For the last time, get out," Dr. Newcastle said.

She turned and pushed through the doors, gulping down air, trying not to trip on her own feet. At least they were bringing him off the anesthesia. That meant he had a chance. But how would she be able to impress upon these doctors the need to use drop ether? Surgeons did not take orders from nurses, plain and simple.

Back in the recovery room, Grace was sitting on one side of Jack, Brandy on the other. His eyes were open and he looked dazed but alive. Eva leaned against the wall next to them and buried her face in her hands. She slid to the floor.

"What is it?" Grace asked.

"It's Clark."

"Your friend from the ship?"

She had told Grace about Clark, but kept it light. Just a handsome companion to flirt with on the trip over. Nothing more.

She nodded. "He was about to go into cardiac arrest on the table."

"Lieutenant Clark Spencer?" Jack said.

"Yes. You know him?" Eva asked.

Grace butted in, eyes wide. "Wait, you went in there?"

"I know, I'm probably out of a job. But I couldn't help it," Eva said.

"He helped a bunch of us out there. Saved my ass. Is he your sweetheart?" he said.

Did wanting him to be count? "We spent time together on the *Lurline*, as friends."

Jack tried to sit up to get a better view of her, then winced. "Damn it to hell, that hurts. Anyway, I see it written all over your face."

Grace laughed nervously. "That's a pretty bold statement coming from someone as young as yourself."

"I *am* fond of him," Eva said.

He shrugged. "You ain't foolin' me none."

Was she that obvious? Her hands were shaking. "The point is, he's in bad shape. Were you there when he got hit? What happened?" she asked.

Hold it together, Eva.

"We were hiding under a hedge. With the Japs blowing up buildings and shooting up the airstrip, it was anyone's guess where to be safe. One of them dive-bombed us and that's all I remember."

She flashed back to the gold-toothed pilot out front. The terror of it.

"Clark is in good hands. Dr. Newcastle might be a crank at times, but he's top-notch," Grace said, taking Eva's hand in hers and pulling her in for a hug. Eva rested her head on Grace's shoulder and inhaled the faint scent of her shampoo. Falling apart now was not allowed. Brandy watched them, then jumped off the bed and approached.

"Come here, you. Why so timid?" Eva said, pulling away and holding her hand out.

"She was beat before we found her. I don't know by who, but if I found out, I'd be more than happy to return the favor," Jack said.

Two seconds later he was snoring.

Jack was probably Ruby's age. Not even a proper adult, and yet here he was, full of holes and more concerned about his dog than himself. She said a silent prayer, *Please, let this one live.* Eva patted her leg and Brandy jumped right up. Something about the curve of fur and the warm contact soothed her immediately.

"We have to figure out what to do with the dog. She won't last long in here," Grace said.

Whenever Eva stopped petting, Brandy nudged her hand.

"No one will see her under the bed. We have to keep her while Jack is here."

Grace kept her voice low. "Storming into the OR and keeping a dog in the recovery room are good ways to get yourself shipped right back out of here. And if you're already here on shaky grounds, best to follow the rules. Can you tell me now?"

No one was paying them any mind, and it would be nice to have an ally, someone who knew and she could talk to. Eva told Grace an abbreviated version of what had happened at Hollowcreek.

Grace kept shaking her head. "Someone needs to do something about this. It's not fair."

"Tell that to Jed Lemon."

"This is your life we're talking about."

"I told Dr. Newcastle."

"Told him what?" Grace asked.

"That I have anesthesia training. I wasn't specific, but I had to. Clark was going to die. Let's hope in all the madness he forgets," Eva said.

Grace groaned. "Dr. Newcastle doesn't forget."

It was too much to think about. "Then I'll be fired."

All the while, Ruby's hospital bills were mounting and Eva hadn't even received her first paycheck. Some sister she was.

"We'll figure something out," Grace said.

Eva felt like she'd just earned a new sister.

After pulling herself together, Eva decided it was time to make herself useful in the operating room again, only this time she would seek out someone other than Dr. Newcastle. On her way out the door, she ran smack into Billy. He looked crumpled and frantic and gathered her into his arms like a pillow.

"Dang, I've been wanting to get here all day, but I was stuck out at Bellows until an hour ago. All our planes were sitting ducks—it's a mess out there. Are you okay?" he said, holding her out and doing a once-over.

"On the outside," she said, meeting his concerned eyes and feeling nothing.

His clothes carried the stench of burning fuel. "We really are at war," he said, as though she might not have noticed. He cleared his throat. "Listen, can I talk to you in private for a minute?"

"There is no private in here. We have patients in the hallways and storage closets, practically on top of each other."

Eva tried to push past him. She had no time for this. Not now. Not with Clark possibly dead on the other side of the wall.

"What are you doing?" he asked.

"I need to check on a patient."

Billy wouldn't let go. "I want to tell you a few things. About staying safe." He pulled her in again, this time slipping a heavy, metal object into her pocket. She knew exactly what it was.

"What in the dickens—"

She stepped away.

"Shh," he said, frowning.

At that very same moment, two nurses wheeled in a new patient fresh from the operating room. The unmistakable smell of sulfa powder wafted off him. Eva glanced down and saw the faint rise of his chest.

Clark, alive.

"Dear Lord, thank you," she said to no one in particular.

Billy looked down. Something like recognition crossed his face. "Is that a friend?"

"Someone I helped operate on. We thought he wasn't going to make it."

A moment of awkward silence.

"Isn't that Clark Spencer? The guy who smashed your face?" he said at last.

His words stung.

"It was an accident. And yes, that's him," Eva said.

One of the nurses pushing Clark scanned the room and said, "Looks like no place for him in here."

For Eva, it was imperative Clark remained in this room with Jack and Brandy. "Wait! I'll go scrounge up a cot, leave him next to Jack for the moment," she said. Then to Billy, "I'm so relieved you're alive and unhurt, really I am. I want to talk to you more, but these boys need tending."

She saw a hardening around his eyes. "Right, of course. I'll check in with you later."

He gave her a peck on the cheek and was out the door.

Deaths accumulated in threes, heartache in pairs. Eva fought to see any good in what was going on around them, but it was something her father had taught her. *In everything, there's a silver lining.* All of Honolulu had banded together to help. That was a real thing. The Japanese had not returned yet—as far as she knew. Clark and Billy and her friends were alive. *She was alive.*

Clark took his sweet time in waking up. His eyelids fluttered a few times, but then he fell off again. As much as she'd wanted to go help with surgery, Eva couldn't pry herself away. Instead, she sent Grace. She busied herself by hooking Clark up to more plasma, which was far better than whole blood for shock. By some miracle they still had plasma, but Grace had informed her that Honolulu had its own plasma bank. At first Eva hadn't believed her, but then she'd heard the appeals on the radio for anyone and everyone to donate.

Ten minutes later, Dr. Newcastle came in to check on his patients. She felt her blood pressure skyrocket. While everyone else in the hospital looked haggard and spent, Dr. Newcastle had somehow managed to appear as though it was just another day at the office.

"How is the kid?" he asked.

"Jack seems stable. Respiration is a bit fast, but other than that, he's hanging in there."

"And the big guy. Is he awake yet?" he said.

"Not yet."

He walked around, carefully examining each man in the room. The fact that he wasn't reprimanding her made her cautious. In all the bustle, had he decided to let it go?

When Dr. Newcastle neared Jack's bed, she moved to the opposite side and quietly snapped her fingers under the table for Brandy.

Whatever you do, don't thump your tail. Hot breath warmed the back of her hand. She lightly held the top of Brandy's head. Heaven forbid she lick Dr. Newcastle.

"The danger with these shrapnel wounds is infection," he said.

Of course she knew that. "Oh?"

"Make sure to keep an eye on their wound sites."

"Yes, Doctor."

As soon as he turned to leave, she sucked in a deep breath.

He stopped in the doorway, turned and said, "You and I will be having a talk when this is over."

Just after sunset, Eva was holding the hand of a young man named Samuel Matthews, who had woken up convinced he was still in Mississippi on a bird-hunting trip.

"You bumped your head pretty bad when your truck was blown up. We're in Hawaii. Pearl Harbor's been attacked by the Japanese," she repeated.

He looked annoyed. "But I've never been to Hawaii."

After a while, she gave up trying to persuade him. She glanced at Clark. His eyes were open, staring straight at her.

"Have I died?" he asked in a gravelly voice.

Eva rushed to his side. "Dying is forbidden in this room."

The very edge of his mouth curved up, almost imperceptibly. "It sure feels like I have, and what about the kid I was with?"

She nodded toward Jack. "He's right there."

"Can you come closer so I can see your face?" he asked.

Unaware of anything else in the room, Eva knelt next to his cot. His eyes were glassy and rimmed with dirt, and his face as pale as a hospital sheet, but he was breathing, thank heavens. The way her heart raced along at two hundred beats per minute, you'd have thought she just ran a hundred-yard dash.

"How did I end up with the prettiest nurse in the whole Pacific?" he said.

"Shh. Save your breath, sailor," she said, smoothing down his hair.

He closed his eyes. "It hurts."

"What hurts?"

"Everything."

At the sound of Clark's voice, a soft *thwack thwack* started up under Jack's bed. Eva checked the hallway for doctors and then invited Brandy over to Clark's cot. If someone walked in and found her, Eva would go to bat for the little dog with everything she had. The only smiles she'd seen all day had been brought about by Brandy. It seemed fitting she was white, as if she was born a nurse.

"Someone wants to know you're all right," she said.

It was easier for Brandy to get close on the lower cot. She stood on her hind legs, with her ears down in the dog version of a smile.

Eva saw their eyes lock and his face brighten at the sight. "You made it, girl," he said.

He looked like he was concentrating on lifting an arm to pet her, but couldn't muster it up.

"You can pet her later."

Brandy hopped down and once again, several of the wounded called her over. She went to Samuel Matthews first and nuzzled into his side.

"Good job today, Bubba, we're gonna be eating duck for weeks," he said.

Clark gave Eva a confused look, and she knocked on her head and mouthed, *Head injury.*

"That Brandy…" he said, and the words faded out.

If it had been at all possible, Eva would have crawled onto the cot with Clark and curled up as he slept, just like Brandy had been doing with all the men. She would have rewound the clock to December third. To that moment in her cabin, when she'd been wrapped in his arms. Or standing at the rail watching the whole ocean light up blue. The smell of Old Spice. She noticed herself shivering, not from cold but from nerves and outrage and blind fear. Men had done this to each other.

Why had it been allowed to happen this way?

INFAMY

No one in this room was in the clear yet, not even close. In fact, no one in the hospital was in the clear yet. Or the island, for that matter. As night began to fall, lights were turned off and flashlights covered with blue cellophane were handed out. Some help that was.

Eva was standing at the nurses' station when she heard familiar voices coming down the hallway. She spun to see Bree and Sasha dressed in white tennis outfits, bright points of light amid the gray ash of a day. Impossible but true.

Sasha rushed forward and threw her arms around Eva. "Eva! Some man in scrubs sent us upstairs and said to get busy. We were hoping we'd see you and that you were okay, and look at you, all in one piece and beautiful."

"Are you sure you want to be here?" Eva asked.

"We were meant to be here, love, otherwise we'd have gone straight on to Oz," Bree said.

"Put us where we're most needed. But before we start, any word on Lieutenant Spencer?" Sasha said.

Eva didn't want to jinx his survival. "He's alive."

"He's hurt?" the twins both said in unison.

Holding herself together was proving difficult, but Eva was

determined. "He took some shrapnel, but he's out of surgery and stable."

"That tennis match seems like another lifetime ago now, doesn't it?" Bree said.

Eva couldn't think about it. "Come on, let me get you two set up. You can help make the rounds in our room and the others on this floor. But I have to warn you, you're going to need to summon every bit of strength you ever had and more."

"We're in."

Eva led them around and watched them fight to maintain composure. She was impressed at how they managed to keep their faces in order. No tears fell, at least not in front of the men. Not only that, but the wounded sailors and airmen perked up in their presence.

"Sit with me a little longer, will you?" one man asked.

"As long as it takes," Bree said.

It didn't take long and he was gone.

At about eleven o'clock, Eva rounded up the twins and Grace and Judy and sneaked outside for a break. She was bone tired and hungry and weak, and she wondered how much longer she could keep it up. They found a curb across the street to sit on. Grace had managed to find a package of Saloon Pilot crackers and three Coca-Colas, and handed them out.

Sasha waved it away. "You need these more than we do."

Grace pointed toward the harbor, where the bottoms of the clouds glowed orange from fires scattered across the waters and airfields. "Would you look at that. They blacked out our windows, and yet any Japanese plane for miles will know exactly where to come. We're sitting ducks."

"It's hard to hide a burning island," Bree said.

Eva felt the weight of the day pressing down on her. "This is going to make *some* story for those of us who survive."

"We'll survive," Sasha said.

Eva shivered. "Look at all our ships, most of them are on the bottom of the ocean."

"But our planes are out there," Grace said.

Judy said in a very flat voice, "Don't count on it. The Japs shot up all the airfields before they even arrived at Pearl Harbor."

She might have been right, seeing in what shape the boys from Hickam had arrived at Tripler.

Around them, the street was eerily deserted. Everyone had been ordered inside after dark and a strict curfew was going to be enforced. Eva was thinking about the Japanese transports mentioned earlier, dropping parachute troops, and she kept her voice low when she spoke. "How are you holding up, Judy?"

Judy let out a heavy sigh. "I died this morning and now I can't feel anything. There's simply none of me left."

"You're a brave girl," Grace said.

She and Eva were on both sides of Judy, and they each held an arm around her. "That's normal. But when the feelings do start to come, and they will, you come and find one of us. No matter what we're doing, okay?" Eva said.

Judy stared straight ahead. Even if Judy couldn't feel her pain, Eva could. So real and alive, it might as well have been sitting between them on the sidewalk.

Grace added, "You are not alone in this, nor will you ever be."

Judy said, "I'm here just for the boys."

Eva felt hard inside. Furious and mad with pain. She was no stranger to death. "His light will always be in you. Remember that. I know it seems black now, but Sid's spark is there."

Eva felt guilty that the grief belonged to someone else this time and not her. They sat there arm in arm, leaning on each other and listening to the far away sounds of motorboats and sirens, while the clouds glowed above them. Bree and Sasha remained quiet, too.

"Have you thought about being captured and what you would do?" Grace finally asked.

The only time Eva had given it any real consideration had been that last morning on the *Lurline* when Clark had warned her. In truth, her thoughts had been more on Clark and Billy and her new job than the Japanese.

"Hardly, what about you?" Eva said.

Grace held a plumeria flower up to her nose. "I never want to be captured by those bastards. I'll walk into the ocean and swim out to sea if it comes to that. Drowning is supposed to be a peaceful way to go."

"But if you're dead, you can't be rescued. Our guys could come in the next day and get you. Have you thought about that?" Eva argued.

"You've heard the stories, haven't you? About what they did to the Chinese," Grace said.

Of course she had. Looting, raping, killing at whim. She hated to imagine herself at the hands of such captors. But she was an American surrounded by American soldiers. Wouldn't that make her immune?

"That would never happen here," Eva protested.

Judy jumped in, her voice dead serious. "Sid gave me a gun, and I plan on using it if I have to. Shoot as many of them as I can…and then shoot myself."

Eva felt Billy's gun in her dress pocket, pressing against her thigh. "Clark told me about a place on the other side of the island where I could hide. It's up a stream and in the jungle. I suppose we could try to get there if we had to."

"But what about all of our patients here?" Judy said. "You two can go where you want, but I'm not leaving them behind."

"They won't be the ones getting raped," Grace said.

A small explosion ripped through the night. They all jumped. Talk about frayed nerves. Every person on the island was going to be shell-shocked for the foreseeable future.

Eva tried to imagine running off alone into an unknown forest. "Whatever happens, I hope you will at least think about coming with me."

"How will you get there?" Grace asked. "And what about food?"

"We can take your car. And Clark said the place is full of fruit trees and there are prawns in the stream."

"Count us in," Bree said, and Sasha nodded.

"You'll need weapons," Judy said.

"I have a gun," Eva said.

Grace looked surprised. "How did you get a gun?"

"Billy thought I might need it."

"I mean machine guns, that kind of thing. If I end up with you out in the boonies, I'm going down fighting. Those men will not take me alive."

At least Judy was considering it.

"An impossible choice, really," Grace said.

"I guess we won't know until it happens, but it's good to have an idea."

No matter which bottle you drank from, the outcome did not look good.

They worked all night, surviving on adrenaline and catnaps. Willa had dragged a few sheetless mattresses onto the hallway floor. Eva blocked out thoughts of their earlier conversation and focused on keeping the men alive. Between the dense heat and overflow of patients, she felt like she was working in a field hospital in the jungles of Asia.

That the doctors were still operating was heroic in and of itself, and Eva attached herself to Dr. Hall, a young surgeon with one quarter the attitude of Dr. Newcastle, but also half the skill. Her suggestions didn't seem to bother him, as he appeared to be awake solely due to caffeine. She kept drilling into his head, "Drop ether is the only way to go with these shock patients." Whether or not he was safe to be wielding a scalpel was another story, but you took what you could get.

Every chance she had, she checked on Clark, who went from dazed and awake, to restless dreaming. His forehead was hot and she didn't like his weak pulse, but Dr. Newcastle had informed Willa, who told Grace, who told Eva, that Clark needed to regain some strength before they operated again. A piece of shrapnel was lodged close to his heart.

Clark's presence in that room was never far from her mind and it reminded her of the last days with her mother. The feeling of wanting to hold on so badly that you could hardly breathe. A lot of bargains had been made with God. *If You let us keep her, I promise to never ever complain about another thing in my whole life.* Eva would sit by her bed and imagine her mother's lungs clearing and returning to normal. The finality of her death loomed big and inevitable, and yet Eva fought it every step of the way. Even when her mother had given up, Eva refused to.

Later, her father said to her, *Evelyn, dear, life and death are part of the same cycle. There is such thing as divine timing and once you accept that, you've won half the battle. It was simply your mother's time.*

That was a lot easier said than done, she realized. But the notion of divine timing had stuck with her. Meeting Clark had felt like the opposite of divine timing. Why couldn't they have crossed paths sooner? She wanted to trust that there was a reason, but that reason was not revealing itself. The truth was, he had tipped her whole world on end. When she did the math in her head—two men divided by one woman—it did not calculate well. If not Billy, then Clark. If not Clark, then what?

More than anything, she wanted to gather him in her arms and squeeze some life back into him. To tell him how she felt. Now was not the time, she knew that, but what if tomorrow was too late? An awful taste filled her mouth and she fought back tears.

Billy was another matter. How could she tell him?

Just before dawn, Eva laid out a musty army blanket on the floor next to his cot and curled up. Grace had dozed off in the hallway half an hour ago, and now she was back.

"I can't keep my eyes open one more minute," Eva said.

"I'll wake you up if anything important happens."

She was asleep in seconds.

At first she thought she was having a nightmare about Tommy Lemon again, in which he had gone blue but she had been unable to get Dr. Brown's attention. No one told her he had gone deaf, and she was screaming at the top of her lungs, but he remained hunched over the table, oblivious.

"He's blue. Get some oxygen on him."

Another voice. "He's not breathing!"

At some point, Eva realized this was no dream. She opened her eyes and saw a flurry of movement in the dim light. Someone had pulled the blankets off the windows and gray morning light shone in. *Who wasn't breathing?* She bolted upright and immediately looked at Clark, still sleeping and pale, but not blue. Judy was running out the door and Grace was leaning over Jack, performing chest compressions. Brandy sat on the foot of his bed staring him down. The dog's look reminded Eva of her own watchfulness over Clark, and how she'd been willing him to live.

"What happened?" she asked.

"I don't know. He was fine twenty minutes ago. I was

changing Sam's bandages, and when I turned around I saw him like this."

One glance and Eva knew he was done. Not even an intra-cardiac injection would help at this point. Against all odds, she had hoped he would pull through.

Dr. Newcastle came sweeping in with Judy at his heels.

"Is that a dog, or am I seeing things?" he said.

Eva scooped Brandy into her arms. "It came in with Jack, Doctor."

"Why is it still in here?"

Without waiting for an answer, he studied Jack for all of two seconds. "I'm sorry, but it's too late for this man."

There was still a faded *M* and *T* on Jack's forehead, offset by his blue skin. He looked so young and innocent, so boyish. *War does not care about age.* No one wants any of their patients to die on their watch, but Eva had developed a fondness for Jack. Something about the way he had pleaded for her to watch Brandy, as though Brandy was his own child, had touched her. And maybe also that he was in some way attached to Clark.

"I shouldn't have been sleeping," Eva said.

"Your eyes were closing of their own accord. You had to," Grace said, stepping away from the bed.

"But—"

"Stop there. We all slept at one point or another. What good are we to the boys if we can't keep our own eyes open?" Grace said with her arms crossed.

Dr. Newcastle seemed unfazed. "Ladies, I have rounds to make. This dog needs to be removed from the hospital at once, or do I have to toss it out the window?"

Eva pressed her lips together. She was already on his bad side. "We'll handle it," she said.

Once he was out, Grace sat down in the middle of the floor and burst into tears. Eva knelt down and hugged her.

"He reminded me of my little brother, and he was such a kind soul," Grace said, crying into Eva's shoulder. "I was rooting for him."

"We all were," Eva said.

Men had died in droves here, and men were going to keep on dying. The key was to try not to get attached, but that was as easy as it would be to swim back to America. And then there were always those patients that pulled you in, no matter how hard you tried to keep a wall up. The ones that had the same eyes as your uncle, or your brother's laugh, and they struck a chord that vibrated higher than the rest.

Eva was stroking Grace's silky hair when she noticed Clark watching them. His expression was unreadable but he spoke with conviction. "If that doctor so much as touches Brandy, he'll have me to contend with," he said.

Eva smiled, not wanting to point out the obvious—he was in no shape to stand up for anyone, let alone a stray dog. "You and the rest of the men in this room, I imagine," she said.

"I'll second that," Samuel said.

Brandy had gone and made herself indispensable in less than twenty-four hours. If only someone would tell that to Dr. Newcastle.

"Noted," Eva said.

At least she should take Brandy outside to do her business. Maybe she could leave her in their room in the nurses' barracks. But the men wanted her. They *needed* her. Could Eva risk it?

"Come on, girl, let's get you outside," Eva said.

Brandy retreated under Jack's bed and stood her ground, requiring Eva to get down on all fours.

"Maybe some food would help," Grace said.

"I don't have any food."

Grace pulled a few crackers out of her pocket and they held

them out for the dog, who hunkered down against the wall. It wasn't until two men came from the morgue to collect Jack that Brandy came out with her tail between her legs again and her head lowered. Eva attached a string around her neck and followed the men downstairs.

Outside, sunlight cracked through the clouds and the ground was damp. On any other day, she would have been gawking at the flowers and mist-filled valleys that the hospital backed up to. Now all she could think about was getting back inside.

Instead of going to the morgue, the men wheeling Jack's body continued down the street to an auditorium, where they'd set up a makeshift one. Brandy tried to follow them through the red wooden door. When it shut in her face, she sat down and began a soul-splitting groan that turned into a howl.

"This is where we say goodbye," Eva said to Brandy, rubbing her neck.

The dog's nose twitched and her ears stood straight. Eva wanted to turn and run the other way but Brandy planted herself on the sidewalk and refused to budge again. Given a choice, she probably would have sat there her whole lifetime.

"I'm sorry, Brandy. We have to go," Eva said gently.

Sorry. Such a useless word.

When Eva arrived back in the room, two of the prostitutes were handing out coffee and sugary blobs of dough. Lehua had changed into a gray Red Cross dress and now looked like a perfectly respectable woman.

"May I have two cups, please?" Eva said.

Lehua smiled. "Take three if it helps. And these *malasadas* will stick in your gut all day long."

Eva looked at Grace, whose lips were coated in sugar and cheeks packed full. Eva took two.

"What did you do with the dog?" Grace asked once she had swallowed the *malasada*.

Eva walked to the back window and looked down. "I tied her to the big tree out there with a bucket of water. That way I can keep an eye on her."

Brandy had not been pleased with the arrangement, at once wrapping the rope around the trunk six times and allowing herself only one foot of slack. Eva unwound her and left her sulking with her head resting on her paws and a long look on her face. At least she had stopped howling.

Judy had found a radio and set it up on a card table. She moved around like a woman on a mission, and Eva worried about what would happen when the initial shock of losing Sid wore off. The big news was that FDR was going to address the country at any minute. When his voice came on all crackly through the speaker, you could have heard a feather fall. Eva looked around at all the faces. Every man was glued to his words.

"Yesterday, December 7, 1941—a date which will live in infamy—the United States of America was suddenly and deliberately attacked by naval and air forces of the Empire of Japan....

"But always will our whole nation remember the character of the onslaught against us.

"No matter how long it may take us to overcome this pre-meditated invasion, the American people in their righteous might will win through to absolute victory.

"I believe I interpret the will of the Congress and of the people when I assert that we will not only defend ourselves to the uttermost, but will make it very certain that this form of treachery shall never again endanger us.

"Hostilities exist. There is no blinking at the fact that our people, our territory and our interests are in grave danger.

"With confidence in our armed forces, with the unbounding determination of our people, we will gain the inevitable triumph— so help us God. I ask that the Congress declare that since the unprovoked and dastardly attack by Japan on Sunday, December 7, 1941, a state of war has existed between the United States and the Japanese empire."

Cheers erupted. And just like that, the United States had entered the war. Eva glanced at Clark, who happened to be watching her.

"Nurse, can you come over here for a moment?" he said.

She was by his side in a second. "What is it?"

"Sit."

Eva sat. Being this close to him, she noticed a strange smell, like vinegar. Was it Clark? Maybe it was time to get him changed. In all the haste and turmoil, most of the soldiers hadn't been thoroughly bathed and cleaned and many still wore their clothes from yesterday. Burnt, oiled, bloodied.

Grace gave her a wink and headed out. "I'm going to see if they need help in Burns."

Clark stared at her as though memorizing the lines of her face. His eyes searching. She touched her hair self-consciously and focused on the fleck in his eye. There was so much she had wanted to say, and now she was voiceless.

"This wasn't supposed to happen," he finally muttered.

"Did you turn in the report? Tell anyone?" she asked.

"Straight off the boat. But I was instructed to keep quiet." Dried spit had formed in the corners of his mouth and she was tempted to wipe it away. "Not even tell my boss. It seemed unusual, and I had made up my mind to tell him on Sunday afternoon."

He paused to catch his breath.

"Not one person in charge I've spoken to has mentioned knowing the attack was coming. What do you think is going on?" she asked.

The two men next to them were asleep, but Eva noticed Samuel across the room, straining to listen in. She held her finger to her lips.

He whispered, "For whatever reason, someone wanted this under wraps. And these people mean business, Eva."

She didn't like his tone. "What do you mean?"

"I mean we have *never* had this conversation. Not on the ship, not here. If anything happens to me, you hardly even knew me. Got that?"

"Are you saying they *knew* and did nothing about it?" she said.

His look told her everything she needed to know. *Good Lord!* Who would knowingly let an attack like this happen? An island in ruin and half the Pacific fleet underwater. The room suddenly felt colder.

"Promise me you'll let this go if I don't—" he said.

She cut him off before he could finish. "Not another word. We're going to patch you up today and you'll be well in no time."

Eva's hand rested on his limp arm. Their eyes locked. She hadn't known him long enough to feel so much, and yet her heart said otherwise. Clark dying was not a possibility. He opened his mouth to speak, then seemed to think the better of it. Nothing Eva could say would be enough, so she bent down and kissed him on the cheek. Her lips lingered and wanted to stay there until his wounds healed over and the seasons changed. He turned so his mouth was on hers. Soft lips. Hot breath. The space under her ribs hummed. Eva was careful not to lean on him or press into his chest, while at the same time channeling every last ounce of love into the kiss.

"Eva," he whispered.

The door creaked and she glanced over. It was cracked but no one had come in. Kissing gravely wounded patients was not standard medical protocol and she forced herself to pull away. At the same time, a black nose with whiskers poked out from under the bed.

"You little sneak," Eva said with a laugh.

Brandy hunkered down with her tail wagging. She knew she'd been naughty, but who wanted to sit outside under a tree when all the people needing love were inside? Eva patted the bed next to her thigh. Brandy stood and placed her front paws up. Her whole body wagged along with her tail.

Clark moved his hand so it was in reach. "Hey, little lady."

Eva looked out the window and saw a frayed rope tied to the tree. "I should have known she'd break free."

It was nice to have hospital rooms with such big windows, and yet word was they would be painted black sooner than later.

"At least you tried," he said.

"You heard the doctor—she can't stay."

There was that one-sided dimple. "Dumb rules are meant to be broken," he said.

"I like your thinking. In the meantime, get some sleep. Dr. Newcastle wants to get you into surgery again this morning and remove that shrapnel."

His eyes were closed before she could blink.

ROWBOAT TO CHINA

September 21, 1941

Life is nothing but a series of choices, so choose wisely. Those words from her father bellowed out in her mind. Earlier that morning, Evelyn had made a choice that had killed a man. If not directly to blame for his death, she had chosen to walk out when she should have stood her ground. That much had become clear. The world had blown up around her and she needed to try to set things right. Jed Lemon deserved to know the truth.

Before opening the door to the main hospital, she smoothed down her hair and attempted to compose herself. Her footsteps echoed off the cool linoleum. The hospital suddenly felt like a giant tomb. Halfway down the hallway, she heard a loud voice reverberating pain off the walls. Her first instinct was to duck into the bathroom, but that would only prolong the inevitable.

"I want immediate action. No one this incompetent should be able to practice in my hospital. Or anywhere for that matter."

Evelyn knew the voice. Jed Lemon. Her immediate reaction was a powerful wave of relief. Someone else had finally come to the realization that Dr. Brown's surgical skills had long since expired. That he was a man clinging to a practice he should have packed up years ago. Any of the younger doctors would be eager to step in and take his place, and she would be eager to have them.

As she approached the nurses' station, people scattered like marbles. Brown was nowhere to be seen and the expressions of several nurses as they passed by were grim. Dr. Oswald had gone so far as giving her a wide berth as though whatever she'd done was catching.

What on earth had Jed Lemon been told?

A cataclysmic realization dawned on her just as a red-faced Jed Lemon came barreling down the hallway in her direction.

"You!" he yelled. "Goddamn killer of my son. Tommy is dead because of you. I always knew that women were not fit to be anything other than bandage changers, but no one would listen to me. They'll listen now, won't they?" Spit sprayed from his mouth and his face contorted with every word. "It may be too late for Tommy, but you're done here."

Not only was Jed Lemon mayor, he was on the hospital board and about every other board in town. You could build a house from all the boards he was on.

Evelyn felt as though he'd hauled off and hit her in the stomach with a sledgehammer. "Sir, there's been a mistake here. I wasn't even in the room. Please—"

"Overdose him with sodium thiopental and then run out in the middle of surgery? I'd say that was more than a mistake, you dumb bitch."

Jed towered over her, spewing hate and foul-smelling breath. This was a man in the worst kind of pain, but he wasn't making sense. "Running out in the middle of surgery? What are you talking about?" she asked, flipping through her memory of that morning.

"You know exactly. Some nerve you have coming in here. I were you, I'd be in a rowboat to China." He grabbed her arm, fingers digging into her flesh. "I hope you have some other skill besides nursing, because you're going to need it wherever you go."

Evelyn tried to wiggle free, but his grip was like shackles. "But I told Dr. Brown not to use the sodium thiopental!"

Something like a laugh. "Blaming it on the doc, huh?"

"I've had training—"

"I would have expected more from the daughter of Dr. Olson, but you clearly don't take after him."

"Sir, please hear me out."

"I've heard enough, now get away from me before I have you arrested."

Was that even a possibility?

"You have it all wrong," Evelyn said, backing away when she saw him raising an arm, tears streaming down her face. "Please."

"Go!" he snarled.

Evelyn went. Someone needed to talk some sense into this man, but Milly was right. She was not the person. Now was not the time. No matter which way you sliced it, it was Dr. Brown's word against hers.

ANOTHER DAY IN PARADISE

December 8

Dear Ruby,

By now, you surely know all about the attack at Pearl Harbor. A place that up until three days ago, no one outside these islands had ever heard of. I assure you that I am currently fine in health, in body if not in spirit. I wish I could say the same for the boys. The air still smells like burnt oil and smoke, and everyone is walking around with blank faces in a state of shock. There are things I wish I could tell you, but they are not things anyone wants to hear. About the soldiers we've been treating and the unspeakable things they have endured—the entire harbor was a burning field of oil with people swimming through it. I will spare you, though I'm sure you have seen photographs in the papers. Everyone on this island is walking on pins and needles and hiding out in the dark, terrified about an invasion on our shores. A fellow nurse carries a gun wherever she goes, ready to shoot herself rather than be taken alive by the Japanese.

And all the while, I am half-mad wondering if I could have turned the Day of Infamy on its side. I know it sounds crazy, *but it's true. When things settle, if they settle, I will attempt to call you and explain.*

Sending love, and asking for heaps and heaps of prayers. Take good care.

Your friend,
Eva

At half past one, Dr. Newcastle came in and checked on Clark, announcing he was up next for surgery. Eva was torn between wanting to assist and wanting to hide out in the closet and hold her breath throughout the procedure. Unfortunately, this was not her choice to make.

"You are to stay out, you hear me?" he said.

Despite his wounds, Clark had stabilized with all the fluids and the rest. There was always the danger of operating so close to the heart, and of infection, which she had been carefully monitoring, but she would have to give it up to God.

"Promise me no sodium thiopental," she said.

Something like a smile crossed Dr. Newcastle's face and he shook his head. "In all my years, I've never met a nurse like you."

"Please?" she said.

He nodded and walked out.

While Dr. Newcastle was cutting open Clark, Eva walked Brandy around the room to greet everyone and then headed down the hallway into the next room. It was certainly better than sitting around pulling out her hair, strand by strand. From the window, she had seen two of the other doctors outside smoking, so it was as good a time as any.

Sasha was in there, still in her tennis dress, checking bandages. "Here's something you don't see every day," she said.

"Will you look who the nurse dragged in!" cried a young man with two broken arms.

Brandy pranced across the floor with her head held high and made a beeline for him, standing at his bedside and wagging her tail.

"I've been worried sick if she made it or not," he said to Eva. "Come here, girl," he called. "This dog used to swim with us every morning. At first she hated the water, but we got her in there and she would swim around us, herding in any stragglers. Best dog in the world." Brandy swiped her tongue up his face. "Between Jack and me and a couple of others, we took care of her."

No sooner had he spoken the words than he broke down in tears. He leaned his face into Brandy's fur while his back shook with sobs. Brandy gave Eva a look that said, *I've got this covered*, so Eva let them be.

"Have they operated on Clark yet?" Sasha asked.

"He's in there now."

"Did you say anything?"

"There was no time," Eva said.

Sasha squeezed her hand. "He'll come out soaring, just you watch. But don't wait too long because you never know what's around the corner."

Eva didn't want to think about that. It was far easier to focus on the work at hand than what might happen in the next few hours or days. Sasha's dress had gone from white to rust colored overnight. Her dirty hair was pulled into a tight bun, but she still looked radiant.

"I'm glad you two are here. For my sake, at least. Though that sounds selfish, doesn't it?" Eva said.

"Funny how things work out, isn't it? Bree and I were fixing to head off to war, and then war finds us here. And it's not what I expected," Sasha said quietly.

"What did you expect?"

"It just feels so—so mind-numbing. I keep having to re-mind myself that this is real and I'm in the middle of it and the whole world has changed overnight. I may look fine on the outside, but I think my ability to feel has up and left," she said.

Eva wrapped her arm around Sasha's shoulders. "That's what shock looks like."

"There's no preparing for this kind of thing, is there?"

"Nope, but for what it's worth, we're in this together," Eva told her.

The man with Brandy said, "Say, did Jack make it out alive?"

One look at Eva's face and he got his answer.

"Damn, I loved that kid," he said, blinking rapidly and leaning into Brandy with more force.

If Eva had had a dime for every time she'd broken the news about one man or another in the past day, she'd have enough for another trip on the *Lurline*. It never got easier.

Back in recovery, two patients had been released to make room for recent post-ops, and each time someone came in the door, Eva jumped to the moon.

This time, it was only Grace with a can of tuna for Brandy. "Quick, give her some of this."

Brandy gobbled it up in three seconds flat.

"You realize you're aiding and abetting," Eva said.

"Let them arrest me. See if I care."

"I owe you," Eva said, looking at her watch.

Grace sat on an empty bed. "If you look at that watch one more time, you're liable to lose your arm."

Eva groaned. "Here I am supposed to be with Billy and all I can think about is Clark. I feel like a double-crossing scoundrel."

"Are you going to do something about it?"

Eva glanced around the room. None of the men were paying them any mind. "Billy proposed to me."

Grace's eyes grew wide. "Why didn't you tell me?"

"I wasn't sure what to do. After five days with Clark, I had fallen for him badly, which is obvious now, but I was so confused at the time. I had been pining away for Billy for so long, and I promised my father that I would marry him. This was all so unexpected. Clark, I mean."

"Did you say yes?"

Eva shook her head. "I blamed it on the army and that we can't marry. He caught me so off guard."

"Well, if nothing else, at least this war bought you some time. No one is going to be getting married anytime soon, I can promise you that," Grace said.

"I'm not marrying Billy. Ever."

"I guess that's settled, then."

Clark had always been the one, from the moment he set foot on that ship. She saw that now. Letting him walk down the gangplank without her had been the most foolish decision of her life.

From across the room, Samuel piped up. "I would marry either one of you right this minute if I wasn't already spoken for. Could one of you Janes help me write her a letter?"

Eva laughed. "What's her name?"

He got a funny look and scratched his head. "That's the thing. I can't remember," he finally said.

Good Lord, she hoped poor Sam was just shell-shocked and his memory would return in a couple of days. He had remembered his dog's name, but she kept her mouth shut on that.

"How about we write the letter and you can call her honey or sweetheart for now?" Grace suggested.

A goofy smile spread across his face. "I knew I wanted to

marry you for a reason. You're not just pretty, you're smart, too."

Grace's cheeks reddened.

Twenty seconds later, the door burst open and Bree and Dr. Newcastle wheeled Clark in. He was as limp as a dead body.

"Tell me he's alive," she said.

"We had to leave the shrapnel by his heart in place. It was lodged in the fifth rib and if I slipped while prying it loose, it would have killed him. We got the bullet out of his shoulder and the rest out, but he'll be hurting when he wakes," Newcastle said.

Grace rushed for the door. "I'll go get more morphine."

Eva was stuck on the words *shrapnel by his heart*. But he was alive.

Two cups of coffee and Eva still felt exhausted and drained and hollowed out like a reed. Now, instead of checking her watch every thirty seconds, she recited little prayers for everyone involved in this mess.

Please keep that shrapnel from moving. Sweet God, keep us all free from suffering. No more attacks and no more killing. Fears heaped upon fears were taking their toll. A sudden urge of homesickness and missing Ruby rose up. If things had once seemed bad at home, now they seemed downright peachy. It was one thing to have your own life fall apart, another to see the whole world fall apart.

With fewer new injuries coming in, the nurses busied themselves cleaning up the place in between surgeries and tending the wounded. You could hardly see the linoleum under mud, soot and blood. Beds and sheets were soiled, and so were the men. Now that they had time to undress them, the oddest things had turned up.

Bree had found a pocket full of maraschino cherries on

one sailor, and Grace a whole block of cheese in the pocket of another. On Clark, Eva discovered a smashed pickle was the cause of his vinegary smell. One grabbed what they could, she supposed.

The day moved along in a horizontal blur. Surgeries, scraping muck off the floor, holding the hands of terrified men and hearing how one had to leave his friend behind because he couldn't fit out the hatch and another because there was no room left on the dingy. They gave sponge baths with water that might have been poisoned by Japanese spies. The women took turns catnapping when they could.

On her way back from assisting Dr. Wallace with a surgery, Eva glanced out the window to catch the sun dropping into the ocean behind twisted battleships and smoking wreckage. *This did not have to happen.* The degree of her fury rattled her, and yet there was no other way to feel. All she wanted to do at that moment was collapse on the nearest mattress, but movement on the curb below caught her eye. Two men in suits hurried away from the hospital. One big as a moose. The other in a hat. They seemed out of place, but Eva didn't give it another thought until she returned to the room.

There was an empty bed where Clark had been.

"Where is he?" Eva asked Grace, who was listening to a young man's chest with a stethoscope.

"Who?"

"Clark!"

Grace spun around. "Well, I'll be damned. He was there a few minutes ago."

"Did anyone come into the room?" Eva asked.

"I ran out for a bit to get more gauze and saline bags so I'm not sure, but Clark was here when I returned."

"Are you sure?"

Grace wrinkled her forehead. "Well, I can't swear on a

stack of bibles. But I think he was. I was concentrating on not dropping my tray."

Eva looked around to see if anyone else was awake. Samuel was watching them with those sweet pale eyes.

"Did you see where Clark went?" Eva asked.

"Nope. I was busy writing my letter, but no one's gonna be able to read it." He looked to Grace. "Jane, can you help me rewrite it?"

"My name is Grace," she said, not adding *for the tenth time* as Eva would have been tempted to.

Keeping a cool head under pressure was what her father always stressed. *Some people have it, some don't.* Grace was in possession of an extra helping, and Eva was impressed by her once again.

Eva bolted out the door and checked the bathroom and all the other rooms on the floor. Could they have taken him back to surgery? That would make no sense. Nevertheless, she peered into all the operating rooms. There was no sign of him. She should never have agreed to help Wallace, but she couldn't just sit by Clark's bedside all day.

On her way downstairs, she ran into Bree. "Have you seen Clark?" she said, failing sorely at sounding calm.

Bree gave her an odd look. "He's sleeping upstairs, love."

"Not anymore he's not."

"Well, he can't have gone far," Bree said.

"Help me look, will you?"

Bree grabbed her arm. "Eva, he's probably just gone to the loo or something. Look at you, all forgetting to breathe. Let me hear you inhale." Bree drew in a long breath. "And exhale—"

Eva yanked her arm away and started off down the hallway. "He wasn't in any loo or anywhere else upstairs, I checked."

Bree set down a box she was carrying. "Come on, you take the right side, I'll take the left."

Eva opened every door, every broom closet, every cupboard without any sign of Clark. Bree turned up the same, and no one they asked claimed to have seen him.

"How can he have up and vanished?" Eva said.

"It does seem odd since he was stonkered last I saw," Bree said.

"Stonkered?"

"Knocked out, sorry."

"There's only one place in this hospital I haven't checked," Eva said.

Bree knew exactly what she meant. "Nope, not possible."

"I want to believe that." But there was no other explanation, was there? "Grace would have known if anything happened to him. But she did leave the room for a bit."

It made no sense.

"Could he have been transferred?" Bree asked.

"Where to? And why?"

She flashed to the two men she'd seen on the sidewalk. Had they had a hand in this? Clark had mentioned something about acting as though she didn't know him if questioned. When she thought about it, how well *did* she know him? Only a week ago, the name Clark Spencer meant nothing to her. The more she thought about it, the more she blamed the men. He was in some sort of trouble. It would have been easy to slip in and put something in his IV fluid and slip back out. And if anyone asked, they could have said they were just looking for someone.

"I saw two suspicious men outside earlier, what if they took him, or worse?" Eva said, feeling weak behind the knees.

"Oh, come on, love, now you're being dramatic. Why would anyone take him?"

Because he knows something, she wanted to say but held her tongue.

Eva slumped to the floor. She couldn't stop the fear from rippling through her body. "If he's dead, I need to know. Come to the morgue with me?"

"I will just to quiet you down."

Eva stood at the door to the morgue, unable to enter. She could *not* go in there. But if they had come for him, surely Grace or one of the other nurses would have known, wouldn't they? Maybe she was torturing herself unnecessarily. But where else could he be? Only hours out of surgery, he shouldn't have made it to the end of the block. Why was she suddenly so weak? She had survived losing both her parents, was handling the Ruby situation—if barely—but this…

This was something different.

"Will you look?" she asked Bree.

The door swung open and a man stepped out, his hand over his mouth and looking as though he might lose his last meal, if indeed he'd had a last meal. Cold, hard air blasted them. Bree took a big breath and stepped through the door. A squeaky gurney rolled down the hallway and Eva stepped aside as a man pushed past her. The shape under the sheet was big. She fought back a sob.

"Can I see his face?" Eva asked.

He gave her a funny look. "Ma'am?"

"One of our patients is missing, I need to be sure."

He pulled back the sheet to reveal the white face of an unknown man, mouth frozen open. Turning away, she said, "It's not him. Bless his soul."

Why was it that one minute of waiting seemed longer than an hour of going about your business? Eva paced back and forth in front of the heavy doors, and the way she was gnawing on her fingernails, you would have thought someone had taken a sander to her hands. She watched a brown spotted lizard following a roach and listened for the sound of footsteps. She forced herself to breathe.

At last, the door swung open again and Bree staggered out. "He's not in there."

Eva moaned and hugged her. "Are you all right?"

Bree shuddered. "I swear to you, that morgue right there is enough to turn anyone against a war. Even the most hardened general. You ask me, it ought to be required visiting for those folks."

Eva kept her arm around Bree as they walked back up toward the building. Army blankets had been hung in place again and were doing a good job of holding in the light. Only a few thin blue lines escaped.

"Clark?" Eva called out into the night. "Are you out here, Clark?"

Bree let her.

Back in the room, there was a body in Clark's bed and she rushed forward, but saw that it was only Judy, sound asleep and twitching.

"Any luck?" Grace asked.

Grace was sitting on the edge of Samuel's bed looking awfully chummy.

"I have a bad feeling," Eva said.

Brandy came over and sat at her feet, panting. "I bet you know where he went, don't you, girl?"

Brandy's ears perked up.

"If only you could talk."

The helplessness was crushing. Patients did not just up and vanish without someone knowing something. And if he had left on his own accord, why hadn't he said goodbye? Maybe he'd been transferred and did not even have the decency to leave a note or tell anyone. The bastard.

He owes you nothing, Eva.

WAR BLINDNESS

Just before midnight, Willa instructed Eva to go home, get cleaned up, sleep a little and return at six o'clock sharp in the morning.

"What about curfew?" Eva asked, imagining the hordes of trigger-happy soldiers in the area.

"It's only two blocks, and you're in uniform. You'll be fine."

Eva waffled about what to do with Brandy, but in the end, decided to bring her. Dr. Newcastle could not be trusted. Brandy had put up a good resistance to leaving her little spot under the bed, and Eva had to drag her out by the armpits.

Sasha handed her a used towel. "Cover her in this and get some sleep."

"What about you guys?" Eva asked.

"There's an extra room out back that Dr. Newcastle said we could sleep in. Later, though."

Once Eva and Brandy were outside, Eva let Brandy down but kept her on a thin rope that she'd coiled up. Brandy went straight to a clump of bushes and squatted for a good thirty seconds. As soon as she was done, she stuck her nose in the bush next door and wagged her tail.

Eva tugged. "Come on, little fella."

Oil must still have been burning on the water, because there were patches of glowing clouds here and there. The silence and darkness of the streets was unsettling. This gnawing feeling that at any moment another attack would happen, that this was it, the moment you wonder about all your life, death staring you in the face. And yet the disappearance of Clark seemed more important than the drone of Japanese Zeroes.

Where were her priorities?

Eva crept along, hugging a tall hedge, but fortunately the blackouts were doing their job and despite the fiery clouds, the streets were empty and dark. And warm. Back home she would have been in danger of freezing her nose off wandering around outside like this, while now she could have lain down in the grass and been perfectly fine without even a blanket. But there were far worse dangers here. She quickened her steps, but Brandy kept trying to pull her out into the street.

"You need obedience training," Eva muttered as she yanked the rope.

A block before her barracks, while Eva was imagining a steamy shower, Brandy came to an abrupt stop and growled. Eva thought she heard the slap of footsteps on pavement. A rustle in the bush. She was tempted to call out hello, but instead ducked behind a tree, heart skipping along at high speed.

She looked both ways up and down the street but there was nothing but shadow. Brandy continued on, sounding like an idling engine. As though worrying about the Japanese and Clark weren't enough, now she was afraid of the dark and those two mysterious men at the hospital. On the edge of all-out panic, Eva scooped Brandy into her arms and broke into a run. She half expected someone to tackle her from behind, but she made it to the front door without any fuss. Why hadn't she just slept in the hospital hallway with Grace? Or gone to the room with the twins?

If it had been dark outside, it was a complete blackout inside. Eva ran her hand along the grooved wooden walls to help locate her room. Brandy stayed almost underfoot and Eva nearly tripped over her twice. There would be no switching on the lights, and instead of going for a shower, she pulled off her smelly dress, splashed water on her face, brushed her teeth and laid a towel on the floor for Brandy. Eva heard Brandy sniffing around the towel, and then lay on the bare wooden floor.

Eva felt for the towel and patted it. "This is your bed, Brandy. Lie down." Brandy didn't budge. With not one ounce of energy left to negotiate sleeping arrangements, Eva gave in. "You're a stubborn thing, aren't you? Fine, have it your way."

Eva was asleep before her lashes hit her cheek. She dreamed of fires and explosions. A torpedo had ripped into the *Lurline* and they were going under. All the patients in the hospital were suddenly speaking Japanese. Clark and Billy had been roommates all along and she had to pick which one to get on a surfboard with. At some point in the night, Brandy nudged her awake. Horsefeathers, why was there a dog in her bed?

And then the stab of remembering. *Pearl Harbor.* She squeezed her eyes shut and tried to fall back to sleep but her heart was racing and there were too many thoughts swimming around in her head. She flipped over at least a hundred times. If only she could gather all her loved ones and have them with her at this very moment.

It wasn't until early morning, when she rolled toward the edge of the bed to avoid Brandy's extended legs, that she felt the piece of paper. It crinkled under her shoulder. She hadn't noticed it when she went to sleep, but then it would have been hard to notice in the dark.

Where was the stinking flashlight when you needed it? Stumbling around in the dark, Eva finally found it in the back of the desk drawer. Yesterday morning when she'd left, there had been no reason to have a flashlight handy. She returned to bed and pulled the blanket over her head. Brandy was still on her back with her legs stretched out like she was flying. The sudden light burned her eyes, but the words were what sent her entire being into a nosedive.

DEAR MISS OLSON,

WE KNOW YOUR IDENTITY. WE KNOW YOU WERE ON THE *LURLINE*. WE KNOW WHAT YOU KNOW. KEEP YOUR MOUTH SHUT AND YOUR SECRET STAYS SAFE. TELL A SOUL, AND NOT ONLY WILL YOU BE OUT OF A JOB, BUT YOU AND YOUR LIEUTENANT FRIEND WILL FIND OUT VERY QUICKLY WHAT THE US GOVERNMENT DOES TO SPIES. DID YOU KNOW THAT ABOUT HIM? WE DIDN'T THINK SO. WE ARE WATCHING YOU.

SAYONARA

Pricks of heat traveled across her skin. She couldn't swallow. Her eyes traced the words over and over again. *Miss Olson. Lurline. We know what you know. Lieutenant friend. Spies.* Who would write such a thing? And who would know all this? Even more frightening was the implication that Clark was a spy. Her mind raced through every conversation, every detail he'd told her. About Japan. About his work. Nothing stood out.

Surely it was just a scare tactic. They were out to rattle her. Whoever *they* were—those two men in suits. Her instincts had been correct and it had been obvious they were up to no good. But now they'd gone and broken into her room and threatened her. Her blood pressure rose. If they thought she was going to sit back and forget about it all, they were sorely mistaken. But who could she go to for help? And what if these men already had Clark and were planning to make him a fall guy? Kidnapping a man in his state reeked of desperation. Eva's mind was a tangle of questions.

Coffee. She needed coffee and fast. But first she showered, letting the steam loosen her coiled muscles and wash away layers of smoke and death and pain. If it had been up to her, she would have stayed in that shower all day, but it was twenty minutes to six and there was no time to dillydally. Brandy still needed washing and the dog revolted as soon as she saw where Eva was bringing her. But Eva won out. From the color of the water, it might have been her first bath ever. As soon as they were finished, Brandy ran tight circles around the room, leaping from the bed to the floor, skidding on the bare wood and burrowing her head into the rug. With her shiny, mostly white coat restored, she looked like a brand-new dog.

"Silly thing, you. Come on, we have work to do."

On the way to the hospital in her own fresh uniform, Eva tried to make sense of the note. Billy would know what to do. But telling Billy would cause him to wonder about Clark. Telling Billy about Clark right now was almost too much to bear, but he deserved to know. Her mind went back to the spy comment. Word on the radio was that several Japanese diplomats had been arrested soon after the attack, and a Kraut, of all things, but no Americans that she had heard of. Japanese and Germans she could understand, but there was no good reason an American would want to sell out his country unless it was for spite or money, and she couldn't picture Clark doing any of that. Not to mention the fact that he was almost blown to pieces by the Japanese. No, whoever had written the letter was banking on confusing her. And they had done a fine job.

After sneaking up the back stairs and depositing Brandy in her spot beneath the bed, Eva got to work. Every chance she could, she inquired about Clark. Nurses, doctors, anyone. *Did you see him leaving? Being carried out? Did you see the two men in suits?*

"Oh, I noticed those two guys, all right. Trying to blend in but they had G-man written all over them," said one nurse.

Eva perked up. "Did you see them with Clark? Or hear them say anything?"

"I don't know what Clark looks like, but they were alone when I saw them. Stone-faced and on a mission."

Why hadn't Grace stayed in the room? Why hadn't Eva? Frustrated at the lack of new information, Eva threw herself into helping those she could. Infections had started in, and they were going through sulfa by the truckload. They cleaned and scrubbed and wrapped limb after limb. She wanted to aid in surgery, but was afraid to go anywhere near Dr. Newcastle. At some point, she knew she'd have to face him, but right now she had even bigger things to worry about.

"Did you find your friend?" Samuel asked when he woke up.

"Nope. He's up and vanished. Are you sure you didn't see anything?" With that head injury, Samuel was about as unreliable as they came, but she had to ask.

He stuck a cigarette in his mouth. "Let me think on that. Can I have a light?"

"What's there to think on? Either you saw something or you didn't," she said, her patience wearing thin.

A slow smile spread across his face. "You sure are pretty when you're mad, Miss Emma."

"This is serious, Sam."

Sam's face pinched up. "You're telling me? My buddies are all dead they tell me, half of 'em stuck in a boat on the bottom of the ocean and the other half burnt to a crisp. But you know what? I don't even remember them. How's that for serious?" he said.

"Oh, Sam, I'm sorry for pressing you. I can't even imagine what you're going through," Eva said, sitting on the edge of his bed.

"Thing is, I don't remember any of them, so it's like I never knew 'em at all. I don't know if that's a good thing or not but right now it makes it easier. You reckon I'm ever going to remember?" he said.

"Oftentimes memory comes back, but sometimes it doesn't, so I'd be lying if I said yes."

He leaned his head back and stared up at the ceiling. "Damn it, how were they able to catch us with our pants down like that?"

"Good question."

Eva debated lighting his cigarette, but in her mind smoke and lungs did not go well together. The problem was, with catchy slogans like "More doctors smoke Camels than any other cigarette," and photographs of nurses in uniform with a cigarette in hand plastered across newspapers, who was going to listen to her?

"Smoking is bad for you," she said.

"Ah, come on, this cigarette in my mouth is the only thing keeping me going." He grinned. "This and your pretty friend Gina."

"You mean Grace?"

"Yep, her."

"You have a one-track mind, don't you?" Eva said.

Sam lit up as though something important just occurred to him. "You know, I did notice your friend propped up on the pillows. He was looking out the window like he was watching a ball game. A real focused face. I wanted to be able to see what he was seeing, but I only see the top of that palm tree from here."

This was news. "Lieutenant Spencer?" she asked.

"Yep."

"And then what?"

"And then I got mixed up in trying to write my letter and, to tell the truth, I might have dozed off."

Eva wanted to shake him to see if any new memories spilled out. "If you do remember anything else, please let me know, okay?"

He saluted. "Roger."

She tried to make sense of it. Clark had probably seen the suits, and either they somehow took him, or... Could he have left on his own? If it weren't for that damn piece of shrapnel. Clark had never talked about where he lived, or where the Dungeon was, but Eva supposed she could find out. But how would she find the time? And with all the suspicion going around, she wasn't likely to get very far. But she had to know.

Grace burst in and announced, "Men around the hospital are asking for Brandy. Did you bring her in today?"

"Against better judgment," Eva said.

"Sometimes you have to go with what your heart tells you to do. And my heart says these boys need her more than they need food and water."

"Do you know where Newcastle is?" Eva asked.

"In surgery. Take her to see John Turner first, the guy with the broken arm."

They made the rounds again, but this time, Eva cut up a piece of sheet, drew a red cross on it and tied it around Brandy's neck. They hadn't been back in the recovery room more than twenty seconds when the door swung open and Dr. Newcastle swept in. "There you are, Cassidy. Come with me."

She could have sworn he drew out *Cassidy* like he wanted to emphasize it. Her pulse bumped up. Head tingled. This was it. She glanced under the bed at Brandy and held her hand up in a stay command. Eva pleaded with her eyes.

Newcastle led her into the operating room without a word. When they arrived, there was a slight man on the table. A blanket lay over him, but he was still shivering. Black hair, tan skin. Pale. His eyes were closed, but from what Eva could tell, he was Japanese.

Newcastle said to the other nurse in the room, "You can go."

"Is he enemy?" Eva asked.

"Does it matter?"

The question floated there between them. *You are in dangerous waters, Eva.* She remembered the interaction with Dr. Izumi on Sunday and how Dr. Newcastle sent him off to the morgue.

For Eva, there was only one answer. "I'm a nurse, not a judge, Doctor. I took an oath to save lives. And skin color was never a concern."

His face gave nothing away. "He's Hawaii National Guard from what I understand. Alan Sakamaki. Shot near Schofield on patrol. Some trigger-happy soldier shot first, asked questions later."

Eva caught her gasp with a hand over her mouth.

"A sorry case of being in the wrong place at the wrong time. I want you with me on this one. This guy needs to live. Bullet to the neck and abdomen, neither exited. Lost a lot of blood," he said matter-of-factly.

Every once in a while, life hands you a big surprise. Dr. Newcastle had gone and done the unexpected, and Eva felt a flush of pride. Or maybe he was testing her? *Think about it later,* she ordered herself.

As Eva prepared the ether, she spoke softly to Alan. "This should not have happened to you, you hear me? We need you to hang in there."

No response.

Something inside her felt as if it might break. "Look at me if you can hear me."

His eyes fluttered open, short lashes, black with fear. It was a look she would never forget. "My wife. She's due any day now," he managed to say before his head rolled to the side and he was out again.

Eva said a special prayer for this one. She was furious at the injustice that his own men had done this to him. And determined that one more woman would not lose a husband today.

She touched him gently on the arm. "You may miss the birth, but you will see it grow up. And that's an order."

With such severe shock, anesthesia was dosed differently. And heaven forbid, no sodium thiopental. They also added another line of plasma. The bullet to the neck had lodged in Alan's rib, but Dr. Newcastle managed to extract it. The abdomen was another story. "His large intestine is perforated. I'm going to have to remove part of it."

Eva stayed on the vitals. Blood pressure dropped dangerously low. A coolness came over her despite the mounting pressure. "You'll need to work faster," she said as evenly as she could.

Dr. Newcastle's jaw clenched and beads of sweat turned his forehead into a glistening dome. He looked up at her, almost said something, then stopped himself. He switched out his scalpel and went back to snipping and sewing. She had to force herself to stay focused.

When it was all over, Newcastle said, "He just may make it."

"I have a feeling he will," Eva said.

Dr. Newcastle pulled off his surgical mask. "Is there something you haven't told me?"

THE TALK

At half past one, a Gray Lady with bright red lips brought around a tray of egg salad sandwiches and lemonade. Eva wondered who had time for lipstick in a place like this, but she was happy to take two sandwiches off her hands. One for herself, one for Brandy. She and Grace and Judy sat around the desk at the nurses' station and swallowed them down.

"Do any of you know where the Dungeon is?" Eva asked.

"What on earth?" Judy said.

Eva explained. "It's what Clark called the room they worked in. I need to see if any of them know where he is."

Grace waited until she was done chewing before answering. "We can ask around."

"If it has to do with his code-breaking business, it may be secret," Judy said.

"I have to try."

Grace assured her, "With all these men in here, someone is bound to know something."

"It terrifies me thinking that he's out there somewhere so weak and vulnerable. And what's even worse is I don't even know if he's still alive," she said.

Picturing Clark out there somewhere, dangerously wounded, made her bones ache.

Judy grabbed her hand. "Until you know for sure he's dead, be thankful. At least there's a chance. And right now, I would give anything for a chance."

Eva squeezed her hand. There were so many degrees of pain in the world, but it seemed like whichever one was yours at that moment, was the absolute worst there was. Until you were around someone like Judy. "I know you would, sweetie," Eva said.

Grace piped up. "I feel responsible. I should have stayed in the room."

Eva set down her lemonade. "Heavens, this is not your fault. None of us could have guessed."

If anyone were to blame, it was Eva herself. Not just for Clark, but for the whole smoky mess. Even if it had meant calling up the newspaper and making an anonymous report. Anything would have been better than sitting quietly with the information that might have changed everything.

"You want someone to blame? Blame those bloody Japanese pilots," Judy said with enough hate to sink a battleship.

That ended the conversation quickly.

After lunch, Eva ran Brandy out back to do her business. Standing in the sun was like standing in a furnace on full blast. Standing in the shade wasn't much better. Brandy decided she wanted to roll in a pile of leaves and dirt, which only seemed natural given she had just been bathed.

"As if I don't have enough dirt on my hands," Eva muttered.

Brandy cocked her head as if saying, *Who, me?*

"Yes, you!"

Nevertheless, it was hard to stay mad at her when she looked at you with those chocolate eyes.

"Evelyn, darling!"

Billy was walking toward her. He looked as though he'd aged ten years overnight. He opened his arms wide, and Eva was at a loss for what to do. As his arms closed around her, she felt her body tense up, cold and stony.

"I would have come back sooner but as you can imagine, we've been working around the clock. How are you?" he said.

Her voice was flat. "Exhausted, but hanging in there. What about you?"

"I've been better. Stayed up all night trying to get a handle on what comes next. Meetings in smoky rooms with a lot of angry men," he said with a forced laugh.

He was squeezing her a little too hard and the realization slammed into her that there was a good chance this would be their last hug.

Eva wiggled free. She was done pretending. "I need your help."

"They haven't found out about you, have they?" he asked.

"No, but I've been threatened," she said in a hushed voice.

He looked concerned. "By who?"

Words spilled out as she found herself feeling more desperate. "That's the thing. I don't know. I saw two men in here and I think they had something to do with Lieutenant Spencer disappearing, and then there was a note on my pillow saying they know who I am and that if I tell anyone about knowing what I know, that they will expose me and set up Clark as a spy."

Billy clutched her shoulders. "Slow down, Eva. What is it you know?"

"Remember when I told you about overhearing talk on the ship about the Japanese fleet? Well, Clark actually told me. We became friendly because we were some of the only ones not seasick. But that's all he told me, that he and the radio fella had picked up signals several nights in a row. He seemed very bothered by it, and I know he turned in a report when we docked, but then nothing happened."

Getting it out caused her to feel so much better.

"How do you know he turned in a report?" Billy asked.

"He told me."

A vein in his neck pulsed. "Christ, Eva, were you seeing him once you landed?"

"No! Nothing like that, but he was here at Tripler full of shrapnel and nearly dead, and then yesterday he up and vanished. I'm just trying to understand what's going on."

In that moment, he felt like a stranger in a uniform. Maybe he was.

Billy bit his lower lip, said nothing for a time, then, "So you have no idea where he went?"

"No one here does."

"Not a lot you can do at this point," he said.

That revved her up. "Someone has to do something. My friend is missing. He had information that could have prevented the so-called *surprise attack*, and you want me to do nothing?"

"Nothing you say can turn back the clock and save our men. And what about you and your career? Doesn't that mean anything? If the army finds out that you lied, you're done here. And Ruby…" He left the thought hanging between them.

They stood face-to-face. Billy looking angrier than he ought to be, and Eva feeling more anxious than ever.

"Please, can you help me find Clark?" she pleaded.

His face hardened. "Sounds to me like *Clark* was more than just your *friend*."

She looked over at Brandy, who was sitting under the tree watching them. One paw was crossed over the other, one ear bent. Either way, Eva was a liar.

"Nothing happened between us, if that's what you mean.

I care about him, period. If Grace or Judy went missing, I'd be concerned, too."

His eyes bored into her. "Tell me he has nothing to do with you turning down my proposal," he said, spitting onto the dirt next to Brandy.

Eva didn't like where this was headed. "I told you the army has rules. No married nurses."

"A *yes* doesn't have to mean immediately," he said.

"This is not the time nor the place for this conversation, Billy."

"A guy like Clark wouldn't tell just *anyone* about sensitive information. So with all those people on the ship, why would he single you out with the radio intel? I'm not buying it," he said.

Eva stood up straighter. "Because we had developed a friendship, that's why."

"Men and women don't have friendships for fuck's sake."

He kicked a fallen coconut and instead of going straight, it shot past Brandy. She leaped up and scooted off under a bush.

"Settle down, will you?" Eva said.

"You may as well just come clean," he said.

"Stop," she pleaded.

"What do you expect me to do? Smile and say 'Sure, Evelyn, let me help you find your lover boy and the three of us can live happily ever after.' I had a bad feeling about him from the beginning."

Brandy peered out from under a fern, panting. Her eyes fixed on Billy.

Eva said, "Whatever you're thinking, it's wrong. But I don't have another ounce of energy to argue or explain things right now. How about we both get back to work and talk this weekend?"

He smacked his own forehead and sweat flew everywhere. "Brilliant idea! Put me off a little longer. That's just swell."

"It's not my intention."

"Lying seems to be your strong suit, so how do I know you're not lying to me now?" He grabbed her upper arm and twisted it, pinching the skin.

Eva tried to shake herself away, but his grip was iron. "Ouch, let go!"

The half-cocked look on his face made her wonder what had gotten into him. America was now at war, she was in danger of losing her new job, Clark was missing and now Billy seemed to be coming apart at the seams. Her head felt like it wasn't screwed on straight.

After a few seconds, he released her. "Fine, but if you do find Lieutenant Spencer, you let me know, okay?"

The way he said it caused a shiver to run down her spine. *"Billy—"*

"If I were you, I'd take those threats seriously," he said and turned and stomped off through the grass.

Instead of going back to work, Eva waited until Billy was long gone and then took Brandy toward the administration building down the street. Someone there had to know about the Dungeon. Armed men patrolled the streets, soot covered everything and birds shone iridescent with oil. Every so often a gunshot rang out in the air. War had made its mark and there would be no turning back. On Billy, too. He felt like a different person from the cocksure officer she'd known back home.

When they reached the building, a guard who looked no older than sixteen held up his rifle and pointed it right at her. "Stop there, ma'am."

"I'm a nurse. Would you mind lowering that, please?" she said.

He dipped his gun and nodded back toward Tripler. "Hospital's back that way."

"I'm here on business. One of our patients disappeared and they sent me to see if he reported back for work. He has shrapnel near his heart and if he moves around he could die, but he doesn't know that. I have to find him."

"Sorry, but this area is off-limits."

Eva took a step closer. "Do I look Japanese to you? You think I might be a spy, is that it?"

"No, ma'am, just following orders."

"Can I make a suggestion?" she said.

He gave her a curious look. "Sure."

"Following orders is important, but every now and then you have to think for yourself. Lieutenant Spencer may die if I don't find him. Do you want that on your conscience?"

The young man blinked. "You got ID?"

Eva held up her badge. He studied it as though it were an impossible riddle, long enough that Eva began tapping her foot. Finally, he said, "Follow this walkway until you see a door, then go down the stairs. Give a knock on the steel vault below and wait until someone comes for you. Never been in there but I know they don't like visitors."

Eva started around.

"You can't take that dog."

Why was everyone so against dogs?

"Will you watch her, then?"

"No, ma'am."

She looked at his name tag. "Look, Private Knox, I am on your side, Brandy here is a mascot for the boys at Hickam, half of whom were blown to pieces. Can you please help me out?"

He glanced at Brandy, who seemed to be smiling up at him.

"Fine, but make it fast."

Around the side of the building, Eva saw an unmarked door.

It looked like it might open to a furnace room or trash area, but she tried it anyway. A set of stairs littered with stuffed bags descended downward. She entered. With each step down, the temperature plummeted. She wasn't even sure she was in the right place, but at the bottom, there was a vault-like door that belonged in a bank. She knocked, half expecting Clark to open up, pull her in and tell her it had all been a big mistake. The ships really had been trawlers—airplanes had checked—and the shrapnel had come out just fine and he was back at work cracking important codes. *If only.*

The space was silent as a tomb. No noise from the inside, no sounds creeping in from the outside. When it seemed as though no one was coming, she pounded again, harder. Thirty seconds later, the door swung open. A bulldog of a man took one look at her and said, "You must be lost."

"I'm looking for Lieutenant Clark Spencer," she said.

His eyes passed over her. "You a friend or is this business?"

"Both."

"Sorry to break it to you, but he's in the hospital, took some hits on Sunday."

"Yes, I know. I was his nurse, but he's gone missing."

His forehead wrinkled. "Missing?"

"No one saw him leave, nor was he taken to the morgue as far as we know. We thought he may have come back here, or maybe contacted one of you."

"What's your name, ma'am?"

"Eva Cassidy. I met Clark coming over on the *Lurline* and we became friends," she said, watching his face closely. Neither her name nor *Lurline* caused a reaction.

He motioned her in. "I tell you what, Eva, I'll ask the other guys if anyone has heard from him. Have a seat over here at my desk. I'm Chief Petty Officer Cory."

Smoke filled every nook in the cavernous room and by

the looks of it, they didn't believe in trash cans. Paper was strewed everywhere, maps and charts wallpapered the walls, and men crouched over desks, scribbling furiously. Eva sat on her hands to keep them warm. Cory went over and consulted with a man in an orange smoking jacket and house slippers.

The man came over. "I'm Ford. You say Lieutenant Spencer is missing?"

Ford was almost as tall as Clark, but half his mass. With wavy brown hair neatly trimmed, he was the classic idea of what an officer should look like, except for the smoking jacket over his uniform and the bags under his eyes.

"I don't know if *missing* is the exact word for it, but he left the hospital and we don't know where he went," she said.

"Two things I know about Clark. One is he's sharp as hell and two is he loves his job over most things. If he were out of the hospital, he would get in here as soon as he could. He must have been transferred, or…" he said.

The implication stood there between them like a silent scream.

"You think he's dead, is that it?" Eva said.

His face clouded over. "I haven't been inside Tripler, but I saw the mayhem outside there on Sunday. With that amount of casualties, bodies are bound to get lost."

Eva was tempted to gush on about the radio signals, the two men lurking and the threats. If Ford was Clark's boss, he probably already knew. "He survived two surgeries and as of yesterday seemed like he was going to make it. Not in any kind of shape to be walking around town, mind you, but alive. Perhaps he went home?" she said.

The chances of that were about zero, but she had to ask.

Cory jumped in. "He's not."

"How do you know?" Eva asked.

"Because I live next door."

"Would you at least check? Maybe he went in while you weren't there."

Ford nodded to Cory. "Go check."

Cory grabbed his keys from the desk drawer and left without a word. Now that Eva was alone with Ford, she decided to feel him out. "Did Clark say much to you about the trip home on the *Lurline*?"

"I hardly saw him, and we talked about the latest goings-on here. Why?" Ford said, meeting her gaze and holding steady.

"Just wondering."

"Is there something I should know?" he pressed.

Eva stood. Not knowing who to trust meant she couldn't trust anyone. "Nothing at all. I need to be getting back to the hospital. Please send word as soon as you know if he's at home."

"I will. And likewise if you find him."

THE SMELL OF LIES

September 22, 1941

The day after Tommy Lemon died, Evelyn showed up for work at Hollowcreek as she would any other morning. No one had told her to do otherwise and she was ready to stand up for herself against these awful accusations. Dressed in starched whites, hair pulled into a tight knot at the base of her neck, hat pinned on tightly. No one could accuse her of missing a shift or calling in sick out of fear or guilt. And, anyway, wasn't it *innocent until proven guilty*?

Coming up the pathway, she had been so wrapped up reciting her defense that she failed to notice a gang of men lurking around the front door, leaning on the railing smoking cigarettes. The smell was what caught her attention. As she approached, one of them pointed and they all jumped to attention.

"You're Evelyn Olson, aren't you?" a jowly man said.

Another man held up a camera and started clicking. All at once they descended on her like a pack of wild dogs. *Tell us in your own words, how did you kill Tommy Lemon? Did you really run out of the room? Rumor has it you got your drugs mixed up, care to comment? Everyone knows women are not meant to be doctors, what makes you think you're any different?*

The ground swayed under her feet and a flash went off in

her face. She held her forearm across her eyes and tried to push through them. "This is all a big mistake," she said.

"Tell that to Jed Lemon," one said.

A man with a twirled and waxed mustache was suddenly in her face. "You're Lon Olson's daughter, aren't you? Probably a good thing he ain't around to see this."

Up until this moment, Evelyn's life had been tame enough to never attract extra attention, especially from reporters. There had been the time when her father delivered Mrs. Finley's quadruplets on a sheet in the library, or when John Lockerbie climbed into the church tower naked and her dad had been the only one able to talk him down. Reporters had visited their house then, but to see Evelyn's father, not Evelyn.

"If my father were here, he would know exactly what went wrong and why," she said.

"Tell us, Miss Olson. What went wrong?"

The men all held their pens to paper. Oh, she was tempted to blurt out the truth. But until she knew what she was dealing with, and the accusations made against her, she would hold her tongue. "No comment."

"Are you prepared for a trial?" one asked.

"A trial?" she asked.

"Negligent homicide."

This was outrageous. Evelyn waved them off and stormed into the hospital, heading directly for Dr. Brown's office. She had no idea what she was going to say to him, other than she had to look him in the eye and demand an answer. People steered clear as she passed, and at the nurses' station, all conversations ceased.

"Where's Dr. Brown?" Evelyn asked the bunch of them.

She had that "nothing left to lose" feeling, which seemed to be a case of recklessness and courage and freedom all wrapped into one big brave package. The nurses scurried around, pretending to look for files or medicine or anything to avoid having to look her in the eye.

Joyce Hunter said, "In his office, but I wouldn't go in there."

Evelyn ignored her and continued on. She was beyond caring what anyone said. This was her lifeblood and reputation they were talking about, and someone had gone and trampled on it. The door was closed. She knocked.

"I'm busy," he grumbled.

She opened the door anyway. "It's me, Doctor."

He was crouched over his desk, scribbling notes. When he saw who it was, he scowled. "I have nothing to say to you. Go away."

Anyone could tell that he had hit the bottle last night, again. Shaky hands, patchwork skin that howled with redness and eyelids like piles of rope. What little gray hair he had left was matted to his head. And to think that this was acceptable from the head physician at the hospital. No one had ever challenged him.

That was about to change.

Evelyn took a deep breath. "Dr. Brown, I just had to fight off a crowd of reporters asking how I killed Tommy Lemon and talking about a trial and negligent homicide. My question to you is, *Why me?*"

He kept writing and didn't answer, so she continued.

"I wasn't even in that room when he died. And you and I both know I said not to use the sodium thiopental. The other nurse heard, too. How could you do this?"

Without looking up, he said, "Are you a doctor?"

"No, but I'm an anesthetist."

"Like I've said to you a hundred times before, you don't tell me what to do."

Her palms pressed into her thighs. "Even if what you're doing will kill someone? Sorry, Doctor, but your God complex—or maybe it's your alcoholism—has made you blind."

She felt a giddy surge as the words spilled out. Words that had been there all along, locked away but aching to be free. From this day forth, so help her God, she would speak her mind if it meant saving a life. So many doctors held to the notion that because they had been doing something for thirty years, they knew best. That kind of thinking stifled progress and led to dangerous mistakes.

A dark shade of red spread from his ears to his nose. "Why, you disrespectful little whore."

"At least I'm not a liar. We both know the truth, and I'm going to make sure it gets told," she said.

An ugly smile seeped across his face. "You think anyone will believe you?"

More than ever, Evelyn wished that her father were still alive. He would have gone head-to-head with Brown *and* he was on good terms with Jed Lemon. But Dr. Brown had already pointed the finger, and now it was frozen in her direction. The whole room had blurred but Dr. Brown came into sharp focus, a lifetime of bitterness etched into his face. The wrong priorities would do that to a person.

"They won't have a choice," she said.

As it turned out, they did have a choice. Dr. Brown stuck hard to his story, the nurse in the room refused to come forward, or even speak with Evelyn, and the townsfolk kept on believing that their doctor was infallible. The only consolation was that Jed Lemon agreed to drop charges if Evelyn was fired and stripped of her credentials.

There went her entire life, in a matter of days.

MISSION IMPOSSIBLE

December 9 & 10

Exhaustion and fear and worry were constant companions for the rest of the afternoon. Eva found it impossible to concentrate for longer than ten seconds at a time. She'd be changing a bandage and suddenly seeing the fleck in Clark's eye, or smell that Old Spice on his neck. The next moment, words from the letter haunted her. *We are watching you.* Had anyone seen her go to the Dungeon? And people all around her in the hospital were tense as telephone wires, worried about the next wave of attacks. The Japanese wouldn't have traveled this far across the ocean, bombed the hell out of the island and sailed home. Would they?

Her conversation with the girls about running off into the hills behind Waimea Bay gave her an idea. Clark's words had burned into her memory. *You'll see two gun turrets on each side of the beach, but you want to go back into the valley, not stay near the beach. Follow the stream back about a mile and you'll come to a concrete bunker built into the hillside. Two miles back is another one.* What if he had gone there? It was a silly notion, especially considering the shape he was in, and she swept the idea out of her mind.

At half past four, Grace waltzed in and said, "Sweetie, you look wiped. Maybe you should take a rest."

"How are you holding up so well? I need a dose of whatever you're taking," Eva said.

It was true. Grace looked better than ever. A new color was shining through on her face. An undeniable bounce in her step. While everyone around her had sleep-deprived eye bags and greasy hair, Grace seemed to have more color than ever. Instead of answering, she went over and sat with Samuel. He picked up her hand. She didn't pull away.

What the devil?

"Say, did you ever get that letter written? Or remember your girlfriend's name?" Eva asked Samuel, while glancing between the two of them.

Grace gave her an annoyed look. "Bits and pieces of his memory are coming back. It turns out Dottie was his *ex*-girlfriend."

That was awfully convenient for Samuel, and Eva could only hope it was the case. "Ah. I see." It wouldn't be the first time a patient had fallen for his nurse.

As much as she wanted to sleep, there was still too much to be done. New issues were arising constantly. Infections and shell shock now ran rampant. Fortunately, in their little room, Samuel was fine on the outside, Alex Wozniak's shrapnel had all been removed, Denny Washington had a pneumothorax but was recovering well, and the other boys had all been cleaned and dressed by Grace, a stickler for sterile conditions. Alex and Denny were making full use of their pastime kits, brought in by students from Punahou School, playing checkers and cribbage to pass the time. Eva had grown more relaxed about Brandy, who now lay at the foot of Samuel's bed, half-buried in sheets.

Eva's back was to the door when Dr. Newcastle arrived. "What is this, a kennel?" he yelled the minute he saw Brandy.

Grace, who was closer, swept Brandy off the bed and into

her arms. Eva spun. Dr. Newcastle wasn't looking at Grace and Brandy; he was eyeing her.

"Someone told me you've been parading that dog around the hospital. Is that true?" he said.

"The men were asking to see her," Eva said, trying to keep her voice under control.

"You disobeyed direct orders."

Eva held her ground. "No disrespect, Doctor, but in these desperate circumstances, the dog is a blessing. Have you taken the time to notice how their faces change when she walks into the room?"

You could have heard a feather drop.

"As if we don't have enough on our plates, now throw in fleas and ticks and rabies," Newcastle said.

"But she's bathed and healthy."

Apparently, that was not the right thing to say, because Dr. Newcastle lit up like a steam engine. "The dog goes or you go."

Samuel decided to join in the fight. "Lighten up, Doc. These ladies know what they're doing. You might be able to stitch people's bodies back together, but have you taken a good look around? It's our souls that need tending."

Eva couldn't have put it better herself. "He's right, and you know we had one back at—" She stopped a second before blurting out *Hollowcreek General*.

"Back where?"

"At a hospital I once visited," she said.

"And which one was that?"

"Greenwood."

He looked dubious. "We stick to the rules here at Tripler," Dr. Newcastle said.

"Sir, if she's kept clean and let out to use the bathroom,

why not keep her around? She can be our morale booster," Grace said.

Dr. Newcastle's nostrils flared. "Goddamn it, I said *no*. You're dismissed, Miss Olson, and when you come back— without that mongrel—you and I are going to have that talk."

It took a moment to register. *Olson.* The blood drained from her head. Had he really just said that? Eva looked to Grace, whose eyes were huge with surprise.

He knew.

There was nothing to do but leave. Eva called Brandy, who jumped down with her tail between her legs as if she knew what had been said.

"Come on, girl, let's go."

Grace came home three hours later, setting down her purse and a brown bag stained with grease. Eva had fallen asleep in her uniform, spooning Brandy on the bed. Her eyes felt gritty, like someone had thrown a handful of sand into them, and her body was a bag of lead. She rolled onto her back and propped her head on the pillow.

"I suppose I should pack my bags," she said.

Grace plopped down on the bed next to her, smelling of sulfa powder and fried chicken. "He did say 'When you come back.'"

"Did you not hear him? He called me Miss Olson, Grace. I'm done here."

"I heard. But with Dr. Newcastle, you never know. He'd have to be a numskull to fire you right now."

"From the minute I got here, I've been a thorn in his side," Eva said.

"A talented and smart thorn in his side. He's not blind."

On the whole walk home, Eva had replayed the interaction. She could tell he'd been furious for being publicly disobeyed, and then ganged up on. Why tell her to come back? Maybe he just needed time to write her up, report her, have her arrested. Who knew what the penalty was for lying to the military.

Eva sighed, rubbing her temples. "I just want a hot shower and a beer and then to sleep and never wake up. It keeps getting worse."

"No alcohol allowed, but go take a shower. I have food for us."

"No alcohol?"

"They've banned liquor sales," Grace said.

"Goodness. I suppose it's for the best."

The last thing they needed were angry drunken sailors in the streets, hunting down innocent local Japanese. She'd heard enough to know how many of the boys felt. Just by being Japanese, American or not, one was guilty as all get-out.

Once Eva and Grace cleaned up, they sat on the rug and gorged on fried chicken and rice. The chicken was soggy and the rice had hunks of black stuff mixed into it that Grace said was seaweed, but Eva swore food had never tasted so delicious. Brandy had manners, too, not one of those dogs that bites your hand off when you feed it. Eva made a mental note to find some kibble tomorrow and get her properly fed.

Through all this Grace seemed more bubbly and upbeat than she had since Eva had arrived. It certainly wasn't due to their current circumstances.

"Tell me right this minute what's going on with you and Samuel Matthews," Eva said.

"He's handsome, isn't he?"

"Handsome, yes. Available, who knows."

Grace had *goner* written all over her face. "He told me as soon as he gets out of here, he's going to take me to the Royal Hawaiian and wine and dine me."

"I just hope that when he remembers things, there's not a

wife and kids back home. You're walking on shaky ground, sweets," Eva said.

Brandy rolled onto her back and stretched to full capacity and exposed her stomach for rubs.

Grace wilted slightly. "You think that's the case?"

"We'll ask around. Probably not, but it would help to know before you go falling in love or anything silly like that."

Grace mumbled something under her breath.

"What?" Eva asked.

"Oh, nothing. Listen, you have enough to worry about, and speaking of falling in love—have you thought any more about Clark and where he might be?"

Every other minute.

"I have an idea, but it's far-fetched."

"Tell me anyway."

Eva told her she was going to try to find Clark's hideout, but left out all details regarding the G-men and the note. No sense in involving her and putting her at risk. "It would also mean taking off the morning and borrowing a car to go search for him."

"If it were Samuel out there, I'd follow any lead I had. You can use my car," Grace said.

"You think he could have made it there in his condition?"

"Stranger things have happened."

The following morning Eva rose before the sun. The old Buick took a few turnovers before its engine sputtered to life. Never mind the dull gray paint and rusted fender, Eva was grateful to have a set of wheels. Brandy had been hesitant to climb inside, but once the car started rolling, she stuck her head out the window and nose in the air.

Strands of sun lit up the water of Pearl Harbor. From their vantage point, it looked like an iridescent mess. Debris from all the explosions could be seen floating everywhere and for the first time, Eva wondered about the fish and sea creatures that had lived here. Turtles, rays, dolphins and even whales. What had become of them? Surely no animal could still be alive in that nasty water, and she felt a whole other layer of sadness settle in.

"Watch out, Brandy," Eva said as they careened around a corner. The car might have been old, but it had horsepower. Every time she lightly pressed the gas pedal, they burst forward and Brandy lost her footing. That didn't stop her from climbing right back up again. She could have sworn the little dog was smiling, and Eva was happy for the company.

Once out of the gates and Pearl Harbor, they headed toward the middle of the island, a high plateau between two long ranges. The mountains here were straight out of a dream. Tall and craggy and buried in dense foliage draped in mist. Eva looked in the rearview mirror every now and then to make sure no one was following. Setting out alone into the sugarcane fields and remote part of the island might not have been a smart idea, but until she exhausted all leads in finding Clark, she couldn't rest.

With each mile they claimed, the air cooled and the sky grew darker. At first she thought it was just because they were moving away from the sun, but once they reached the top of the plateau—where pineapple fields stretched out in all directions—she realized the road disappeared into a wall of gray clouds. Just her luck. She had packed food and water, but no raincoat. Eva pulled over near a grove of eucalyptus trees and rolled up Brandy's window. The scented trees reminded her of the lemon balm in their garden, and Ruby and all that was once good in her life. When the future had seemed so clear that she could have reached out and touched

it. A bright career, a healthy, thriving sister and a future husband all neatly wrapped.

All gone.

Before starting up the car again, Eva heard the hum of a
motor in the distance. She decided to stay put until the car
passed, curious and a tad apprehensive about who it might be.
When leaving her barracks earlier, she had scoured the area
for any signs of surveillance. Nothing had jumped out at her.
Now Brandy cocked her ears, tipped her head and watched
Eva with a look that said, *What are we waiting for?*

A shiny, black Model A came into view. For a moment,
Eva thought it was slowing and felt the stirrings of fear, but
the driver didn't glance her way and gassed it as he went by.
The man probably had a perfectly good explanation for being
on the road this early. Schofield Barracks, a small city unto itself, Wheeler Air Force Base and several minuscule plantation
towns were all out this way. Grace had told Eva she'd once
taken a sightseeing train to Haleiwa, and been sorely disappointed that the long, white sand beaches out front were reserved for servicemen. A common theme that seemed to crop
up in conversation. Officers Only, Army Only, Soldiers Only.
What of the local residents?

Allowing some distance between herself and the Model A,
Eva started up again. They drove right into the cloud as it
dumped bucketloads of rain onto the windshield. Eva couldn't
see as far as she could throw. She slowed the vehicle to a crawl,
wary of the deep gulches that crisscrossed the area.

Splashing through mud puddles the size of bathtubs, Eva
began to fret about Grace's car. Each bump sounded like it
was shaking something loose. A rattle here, a bang there. She
looked to the *Star-Bulletin* newspaper on the floor. Beneath
it was the gun. She felt silly for bringing it, and a little reckless, but if anyone stopped her, she would have no trouble

convincing them it was for protection in case of a Japanese invasion. Nevertheless, this felt like a clandestine operation, one which she was woefully unprepared for.

The rain continued to pelt down as she drove by Schofield and Wheeler. In the whiteout, Eva saw nothing but their signs and a muddy river about to overflow its banks. If the stream near Clark's hideaway was anything like this one, it would be swollen and dangerous and impossible to cross. Nevertheless, she kept going. And then the darnedest thing happened. The clouds thinned, strands of light filled the car and a minute later she popped out into blue sky and sunshine. Just like that. The land sloped toward the ocean like a lime-and-evergreen patchwork quilt, dark with pineapples and pale with sugarcane. The breeze carried a sweet burning smell, causing her mouth to pucker. Below, a white line of sand snaked along the coast, dipping into bays and coves as far as the eye could see. This was the Hawaii of postcards and dreams.

Not Pearl Harbor.

Not even Waikiki.

Haleiwa could scarcely be called a town. A one-lane road with lazy storefronts, a lava-rock church with a sign announcing that God was coming to town next week, and a dozen brown-skinned boys leaping from the bridge. They all waved as she drove past. One of them held out a stalk of sugarcane. "Twenty-five cents," he yelled. A smile warmed her insides. Kids would be kids, war or no war. As far as they were concerned, school was canceled and that was something to celebrate.

On the other side of the river, her mood dropped when she caught sight of something black parked under a tangle of bush. A Ford Model A. The same exact one that had passed her earlier. Her heart took off running, mind spinning with possibilities. *He's following you. No, he's just out for a drive. Don't* be ridiculous, no one would be out for a drive today, everyone's been urged to stay at home. He could be out here for a million reasons. Relax. Eva floored the jalopy, leaving a whirlwind of red dust in the air as she sped off.

The road went from bad to worse, but she didn't care. They careened around a sharp turn and onto the coastline. Poor Brandy fell from her perch and was pinned to the door.

"Hang on there, girl," Eva said.

A long straightaway paralleled an airstrip. She pushed the gas pedal until her foot hit the floor. This time, Brandy kept her head in the window. The boys back home used to drag race down by the old quarry, and Eva and her friends would watch for kicks. Right now, she was going fast enough to drag race an airplane and felt ready to liftoff. Thankfully, there were no other cars in the road, and Eva slowed it down when she felt she'd put some ground between her and the mystery man.

Between having to change her name and leave Michigan, keeping her guard up at Tripler, and now being watched by goons, Eva was exhausted. And in all honesty, all she cared about at this very moment was finding Clark.

After that, perhaps it was time to tell people the truth. About herself, about what she knew. Her father used to say that lies had no future, that they might take care of the present, but in the end, they always unraveled. Boy, was he right.

Beyond the airstrip, there was nothing but brush and spindly trees on one side, ocean on the other. Salt fogged up the air. On any other day, she would have pulled over and run down to the shore to feel the water on her feet and comb the beach for shells. Today, she barely gave it a glance. The only person around was a man with a fishing pole walking a goat. He rubbernecked as she flew by.

Fortunately, there was a slight hill leading to the bluff, or she might have missed the turn and ended up parking the car in the ocean. The sight stole her breath. Looking down over the turquoise water, you could see right through it to the pillows of coral below. Rocks the size of school buses stuck up here and there.

I dare you not to jump in, it seemed to say.

Set farther back, the beach was nestled between two sheer valley walls with green thickets crawling around on them. There were no signs announcing that this was Waimea Bay, but Eva knew without a doubt. Clark had described it tree for tree.

On the other side of the stream, a jeep road followed the base of an overhanging cliff. A landslide had taken down part of the mountain a little ways in. Eva looked up and saw giant boulders ready to topple down at any moment. The vibration of the Buick's engine might have been enough to dislodge them. Behind the beach, there was a clearing to park, but darned if she was going to leave the car in plain sight.

"What do you think?" Eva asked Brandy, as if the dog might tell her what to do.

Brandy whined.

"I guess we don't have a choice, do we?"

Eva turned up the road. The rockfall had taken out the old route, but someone had cut a path around it. *Just dandy.* Though the sun was shining, the high walls kept them in shadows. Mud caked onto the wheels, bogging them down. It was just the kind of adventure Ruby loved. Exploration with a hint of danger. Eva wanted nothing to do with it right now.

Ten minutes in, the valley split into two. There was little sign of human activity but for a trampled-down grassy area on the left where someone might have parked, which could have also been bedding for wild pigs. To the right, the stream ran swift and wide. Had Clark mentioned the split? She couldn't recall.

There was no road, only an overgrown trail. They hopped out of the car and followed the trail up a ways, batting at mosquito clouds and ducking under vines the size of her forearms, only to find that it dead-ended at the water's edge. They'd have to cross if they wanted to go any farther. Getting to a bunker surely would require an easier route. Brandy drank happily, careful not to get her feet wet.

"Let's try the other way," Eva said, turning around.

Back where they started, Eva gathered her pack, slipped in the gun for good measure and moved the car behind a bush. Anyone looking would see it, but they would have to drive all the way in there. What had once been a road had been mostly reclaimed by the jungle. It was so dense you could scarcely see the blue sky above. A narrower stream cut through. She'd expected a clearly marked road, signs, soldiers, while this had the feel of an abandoned mine.

Chirps and tweets and trills sailed around them. A gray blur here, a red flash there. The forest was a symphony of birds. As they trudged deeper in, Eva kept reminding herself that Hawaii had no snakes or poisonous creatures, no crocodiles or alligators, and no man-eating mammals. Anywhere else in the world, this would be the kind of place the forest swallowed people whole.

Brandy pressed her nose to the ground, darting ahead and into the bushes, but always coming back. Her white paws were now caked brown. Eva scanned for signs of recent footprints, but the mud had been trampled by pigs, and where there was grass, it was impossible to tell. At some point, it seemed a vehicle had come through, but it was hard to know when. She got the distinct feeling this was a wild-goose chase. No one in their right mind would think to come here unless an invasion happened. Or they were mad with fever.

If the beach was hot, the jungle was sweltering. Though

there was no sun, there was also no wind. The cliffs took care of that. Eva's blouse was drenched in no time. The smell of rotting fruit and decaying leaves simmered in the heat. With every snap of a twig or creaking branch, she jumped, nerves working double time. But as far as she could see, no one was following. Hopefully, she'd given Mr. Model A the slip, if indeed he had been after her.

Every now and then Eva called out, "Hello, anybody out here?"

Only the birds answered.

They finally reached a clearing along the stream. This time, tracks were more visible. Off toward the bottom of the cliff, next to the stream, a concrete bunker hid beneath a mass of vines. Pinpricks of sun lit the leaves. No one had been tending this place, that much was clear.

"Hello?" Eva said, louder this time.

Silence.

Disappointment slammed into her. If Clark wasn't here, where on earth would he be? Not his house, not any other hospitals—Grace had checked. The only alternative was that he had been kidnapped. She hopped from grass patch to grass patch, avoiding the mud as much as possible, though her shoes and ankles were already layered with it. Halfway to the bunker, Brandy began sniffing and snorting all over the ground.

"Stay with me, Brandy."

It wasn't until Eva reached the entrance that she spotted the jeep. She froze. Her hair stood on end. Someone was here and not answering. Maybe he was out. Or hiding. Or dead. She felt for the gun in her pocket, cool and heavy and reassuring. That she was in the jungle carrying a gun, running from bad men, running toward trouble, seemed as unlikely as walking on the moon. Yet here she was.

"Is that you in there, Lieutenant Spencer?" she said.

Still no answer.

This so-called bunker had a screen door and was more like a concrete box with a window, also screened in. Without them, a person would be one big mosquito bite. Eva pressed her face to the door and saw an empty cot with a crumpled army blanket. She stepped inside and Brandy darted past her, nose down, tail wagging. A backpack leaned against the wall, its contents scattered on a small table. Pills, bandages, alcohol. Eva bent down to have a better look. Next to the pills was a watch. She blinked in the dim light. The letters *CS* were engraved on the inside.

Eva shot up. "Where is he, Brandy? We have to find him," she said, now having no qualms about regularly consulting the dog. It was keeping her sane.

Outside, Brandy took off down a narrow path between tall, shaggy bushes laden with red berries. Eva followed. The rush of water moving on rocks grew louder until it was almost a roar. When they reached the stream, a shaft of sunlight shone down so brightly it hurt her eyes. And she couldn't believe what she was seeing. Eva crouched down behind a boulder.

A man.

Prone on the riverbank.

Naked.

No mistaking: *Clark.*

THE McCOLLUM MEMO
EIGHT-ACTION PLAN

7 OCTOBER 1940

9. It is not believed that in the present state of
political opinion the United States government is
capable of declaring war against Japan without more
ado; and it is barely possible that vigorous action
on our part might lead the Japanese to modify their
attitude. Therefore, the following course of action is
suggested:

    A. Make an arrangement with Britain for the
use of British bases in the Pacific, particularly
Singapore.

    B. Make an arrangement with Holland for the use
of base facilities and acquisition of supplies in
the Dutch East Indies.

    C. Give all possible aid to the Chinese
Government of Chiang-Kai-Shek.

    D. Send a division of long range heavy cruisers
to the Orient, Philippines, or Singapore.

E. Send two divisions of submarines to the
Orient.

F. Keep the main strength of the US fleet now in
the Pacific in the vicinity of the Hawaiian Islands.

G. Insist that the Dutch refuse to grant
Japanese demands for undue economic concessions,
particularly oil.

H. Completely embargo all US trade with Japan,
in collaboration with a similar embargo imposed by
the British Empire.

10. If by these means Japan could be led to commit an
overt act of war, so much the better. At all events we
must be fully prepared to accept the threat of war.

—*From a six-page memo to President Roosevelt from Lieutenant*
Commander Arthur H. McCollum.

UNTIMELY

December 10

Clark lay with his arms stretched out as though trying to make snow angels, only he was on hard black rock, not snow. One foot floated in the clear water. If she hadn't known better, Eva might have thought he'd slipped and fallen from the cliffs above. When Brandy saw him, the fur on her back ridged up and her leg lifted in a point.

"Stay," Eva whispered.

It was hard to tell if he was breathing from this distance. Eva squinted into the blinding sun. A fly buzzed around his head. Her pulse sped up as she mustered the courage to go to him.

She cleared her throat. "Lieutenant Spencer?"

No reaction. She stepped toward him, careful to skip the mossy rocks. This was the part where he was supposed to sit up, call her over and kiss her under the waterfall. "Damn you, Clark, wake up!" she said.

Once by his side, she squatted down and placed her hand right over his heart. The sunlight had warmed his skin. Either that or he was hot with fever.

"Oh, Clark," she sighed, voice drowned out by water pounding on rocks.

One of his hands came up fast and grabbed her wrist, burning into her skin. His eyes blinked open and he squinted to make out her face. At first she thought he didn't recognize her, but then he said incredulously, "Eva, what are you doing here?"

She was suddenly furious with him. "I could ask you the same question."

"How did you know to find me?"

"A lucky guess."

Eva forced her eyes to remain on his face.

"Damn, it's good to see you. But you shouldn't have come," he said.

Her voice went up an octave. "Me? What about you? You think it was smart for you to come traipsing out into the jungle in your state? If that shrapnel comes loose, you're—"

"Did anyone follow you?" he interrupted.

Anger seared through her. "Let me finish. I had no idea if you were dead or alive. Did you ever think about that? You could have told one of us nurses, or even left me a note. I've been half-mad with worry over you."

He gave her an amused look. "You're even prettier when you're angry, has anyone ever told you that? Your eyes fire up."

Part of her wanted to splash him in the face, the other wanted to lean down and bury her face in his neck. "Stick to the matter at hand, please," she said, trying to remain level-headed. One of them had to be.

He must have suddenly realized he was naked, because his hand moved to cover his privates, though he made no move to sit up. "The two guys came to Tripler for me. I saw them from the window," he said.

"Which two guys?" she asked.

"Feds. They stopped me a couple of days before the attack and threatened to put me underground if I talked about the radio signals. I could tell they meant business. Them snooping around the hospital could have only meant one thing," he said.

"You really think?" she asked.

"I know."

"But they're part of our government, they can't do that."

He sneered. "They're above the law, Eva. Anything can be justified in the name of national security. It's all part of the deal."

A branch snapped nearby. Eva spun around but only saw layers of trees and a mess of branches. Her spine tingled as she thought about the man in the Model A. "There was a note on my pillow, it must have been from the same folks."

Clark sat up faster than he should have. "What did it say?"

"They told me you were a spy and they knew what I knew, and that if I told anyone, we would both be dealt with as spies and…" She let her voice trail off. Clark didn't know about Tommy Lemon or the name change, and she hated to get into that now.

"And what?"

She turned the focus back on him. "Well, are you a spy?"

"Do you really need to ask?" he said.

They sat there with eyes locked. No one had ever made her feel this way—all stirred up and yet firmly rooted at the same time.

He swatted at a mosquito. "I'm not a spy, Eva. These are bad people, trying to cover up a big secret or mistake or whatever mess they made."

She fought back a sob. "I know you're not. I'm sorry, it's just that the world is unraveling around us and I'm scared."

"You're brave for coming out here," he said.

"Or stupid. I left with only you in mind, but a man in a black Model A passed me on the way out and then I passed him later outside of Haleiwa town."

In the distance, thunder rumbled.

Clark craned his neck skyward. "We should get back to the bunker."

A drop of rain landed on her shoulder. Eva turned away as he dressed, if you could call wrapping a dingy towel around your waist dressing. She hollered for Brandy, who, from the sound of it, was splashing her way downstream. Despite his wounds, Clark moved lightly along the trail. The rain picked up in earnest and blotted out the sun. They were both soaked by the time they made it back, but the warmth of the rain was more refreshing than anything.

Clark handed her a shred of cloth to dry off with. "Did you get a look at the man in the Model A?" he asked.

"Nope, and I sped off so he didn't see me turn in here. I'm sure of that."

He stepped closer, and his presence was like a hot wall of fire brushing at her edges. The room fell away. Eva stood transfixed as Clark bent down slowly and kissed her. The dark curves of his face met hers. Soft lips, hard body. She gave way against him. The way he touched her face, as though she was the world's most fragile piece of glass, caused a beautiful ache swirling downward.

"Billy and I are done," she whispered between breaths.

Her words switched on something inside him and the kiss grew fierce. One hand clutched at her waist, the other held her face. He was so tall that Eva had to tippy toe with her neck craned up, but she didn't mind. She could have stood there forever tasting river water and peppermint and man. His lips opened and closed, tongue brushing her lips, neck, collarbone. Heat coiled around them. Eva felt herself panting with longing.

When they finally pulled apart, he wiped his lips and said, "That was twelve days and a whole ocean of wanting you all built up inside. Sorry if I was out of line."

"Did I seem bothered?" she asked with a smile.

Something wet bumped against her leg. Eva looked down to see Brandy sitting patiently, wagging her tail and dripping water all over the concrete floor.

Clark reached down and scratched behind her ear. "Looks like someone is feeling left out."

Eva wasn't in the mood to share him right now. "Go lie down, girl."

At the tone in Eva's voice, Brandy's ears drooped and her body wilted. Eva immediately felt awful and scratched behind her other ear. "Now you have both of us, are you satisfied?"

After a minute or so of undivided attention, Brandy had apparently had enough and meandered around the room, finally settling in the far corner on a woven mat. Clark pulled Eva with him as though he couldn't bear to let her go for even one second and they sat on the cot with their backs against the wall, shoulders and hips and legs touching. Her feet came to his ankles.

"I suppose I should tell you my real name is not Eva Cassidy, it's Evelyn Olson, but I'm not an outlaw or anything like that," she said.

He rested his hand on her thigh. "Just tell me it doesn't have to do with a man."

"Well, it does and it doesn't," Eva said, as she began to tell him the whole ugly story. She kept her eyes on a lizard on the wall as the words poured out. Clark listened without interrupting and his warm palm was reassuring on her skin.

Reliving Tommy Lemon's death is a true nightmare.

When she finished, he squeezed her leg and said, "Dr. Brown sounds like a top-notch jerk, not to mention a liar. You did the right thing, coming out here. Look how many lives you've already saved, knowing what you know about anesthesia. Mine included."

A warmth swelled in her chest. "You think?"

"One hundred percent, Eva—Evelyn."

"You can call me Eva. I don't mind."

He shifted so he was facing her. "If it weren't for Brown, you wouldn't be sitting here next to me in this bunker, so in a roundabout way, I'm grateful."

It was hard to argue with that, but for Ruby. "I just worry about my little sis. I wanted her here so badly, but now that won't happen."

"Ruby is going to be fine. I'll go get her myself if I have to," he said with such confidence that she had no choice but to believe him. "And while I'm at it, Dr. Brown and I will have a talk."

Clark wouldn't be going anywhere for a while, but she held her tongue. Just the thought of someone sticking up for her was enough. Especially a man like Clark. They sat in silence and Eva contemplated the peculiar nature of life and all its twists and turns. How one event could spiral out into the future in unimaginable ways, branching down pathways you never even knew were there. Strangely, it gave her a small measure of hope. The familiarity she had felt that first day when she saw him on the gangplank, that had been no accident. That was her heart already recognizing him.

"You know what?" she said.

"What?"

"My father used to say that important encounters were planned out by heaven and if you were observant enough, you could see them plain as day. Just before we set sail, I saw you stepping onto the *Lurline* and you seemed so familiar to me. Now I know why."

He twisted a lock of her hair around his finger. "Our meeting wasn't chance, that was clear from the minute I walked into the dining hall. You stood out like a neon sign."

She laughed. "Most of the ship was in bed that night."

"If every soul had been in there, nothing would have been different."

Wind blew down the valley, shaking trees and swirling rain in through the screen. The jungle felt wild and alive. Doing its best to weave a spell around them. She wanted to get him out of here, back to hospital safety, and yet she wanted to savor the moment.

"You should lie down," she said, unable to tell if the sweat on his brow was from illness or the humid and sticky air.

"I'm not going to break, Eva."

She refused to lose him just because he was as stubborn as an old mule. "You're in a precarious position with that shrapnel, Lieutenant. You had better listen to your nurse."

"I made it out here all right."

Eva threw up her hands. "You lost blood, there's metal lodged in your chest and you think you can just waltz around as though nothing happened?"

"Okay, okay." He lay down and pulled her with him. Propped up on one elbow, Eva looked down into those endless blue eyes. The dimple was there, too. "Is this better?" he asked.

"Better."

He traced her lips with one finger, and the ache started up again. "That last day on the *Lurline*, I put on a good face, but I was broken at the thought I might never see you again."

"You weren't the only one," she said.

"Things sure went south, but I gotta say that I'm not complaining at this very moment," he said, shifting around on the cot and bringing her leg over his.

This time, she kissed him. All of her worry and fear wrapped into it somehow made it more real. Fire beneath her skin. She had wanted him all the way across the Pacific, too, and now here they were, a tangle of love and limbs.

Then, from the corner, Brandy growled. Clark immediately went rigid. His hand covered her mouth. Eva looked to Brandy, who was sitting up with her fur in a high ridge along her back.

"A wild boar," he whispered.

With all the wind and rain and thrashing of branches, sounds all blended together. If there was something out there, or someone, they wouldn't know. If the man in the Model A had indeed followed her, she would never forgive herself.

A shadow emerged at the screen door. "I'll shoot the dog," a voice said flatly.

The world froze.

Eva cracked.

That voice.

"No!" she cried.

"Hold the dog or it's dead, I mean it," said the voice at the door.

Eva was beside Brandy in less than a second while at the same time trying to make sense of what was happening.

"What are you doing here, Billy?" Eva gasped.

This was a man she had spent the past two years pining for. His letters had sustained her across space and time and an empty heart. The screen creaked open and Billy stepped inside. His gun was pointed at Clark.

She had the sudden, horror-filled thought that he was going to kill them right then and there, and she and Clark would simply never be heard from again. Just another statistic of missing in action.

"So, you're behind this," Clark said.

Her eyes bounced between the two men. What was he talking about? Billy leaned against the concrete wall and put a cigarette between his lips, gun hand never wavering. With his free hand, he lit it. The look on his face was twisted and ugly.

"We were going to let you be and just keep an eye on you, but then you had to go and put your dick where it doesn't belong," Billy said.

Clark was sitting up now, looking pale but collected.

Eva felt the blood rush to her head. "You have it wrong."

Billy waved the gun around. "Oh yeah? You two half-naked, don't bullshit me."

Smoke poured from his nose and formed a hazy wall between them. Eva was torn between wanting to march up to him and slap him in the face, and staying alive.

"Too late, Irving, I already told Ford about the signals," Clark said.

Had he?

Eva paused. "Wait, how do you two know each other?"

"He's the guy I handed the report in to after we docked. The one who made sure our admirals never saw it. Lieutenant William Irving," Clark said.

Shock waves rippled through her. *Billy knew!* The radio signals, the advancing Japanese fleet. He knew and he kept the information from getting out. *Lord have mercy.* This was not a breakdown in communication, it was an all-out conspiracy.

"Just following orders," Billy said.

"Orders from who?"

"That's on a need-to-know basis, and you don't need to know."

Eva was still in disbelief. "But why?"

"This isn't a social visit. Get up, Spencer. We have somewhere to go," Billy said.

Over his uniform he was wearing a thick black raincoat, like a gangster. The look on his face was somewhere in between loathing and fear, and he had the air of a man who was coming to pieces. He stomped his boots to shake off the mud. This was a stranger, not the Billy she once thought she loved, and her mind tried to call up signs that she'd missed. Driven and focused had morphed into fanatic and desperate.

Brandy still rumbled, but Eva held her tight. "People already know," she said, close to all-out panic.

"No one else knows, besides Wilson, and he won't be talking. If Ford knew, I would have heard by now."

Clark was sitting up, with his elbows on his knees. "We could have gone out there and bombed the hell out of that fleet and their surprise attack on Pearl Harbor would never have happened. Why?"

"People like you are too dumb to understand."

Her pulse nearly stopped. The face of every sailor, every casualty that she had treated played in her mind. The sound of their fear and the smell of their agony. Each man facing his own personal nightmare. *Avoidable.* Eva wanted to reach out and claw at Billy, but all she could think was, *Keep him talking.* In the most polite voice she could muster, she said, "You always were the smart one, perhaps you can explain it to us so we're on your side."

"War with Japan was inevitable. We just orchestrated it on our terms, lured them in like fish to bread. I don't see anything wrong with that," Billy said.

Clark opened his mouth to speak, but Eva shot him a silencing look. "How'd you manage that?" she asked gently.

"Once Germany and Italy signed the Tripartite Pact with Japan, it was blindingly clear that was our ticket into the war. And they were so easy to provoke, they're not as smart as you think. Japan is only a pawn, Germany is the king and we are the queen that will take him down," Billy said.

The gun was still leveled at Clark, but his eyes hopped back and forth to her. He was gloating.

Clark jumped in. "But we backed Japan into a corner."

"It had to be done."

"Who did the orchestrating?" Eva said.

"Washington."

Eva swallowed hard. "The president?"

"Wouldn't you like to know," Billy snarled.

The air in the bunker was too thick. Eva trying to talk Billy out of whatever he had in store, Clark sitting pale faced and motionless. If ever there was a time to send a prayer up to Heaven, it was now. A prayer for themselves, a prayer for all the people killed in the attack, a prayer for their country.

"Why are you here, Lieutenant Irving?" Clark asked in a tired voice.

"You two are my garbage to deal with."

As if on cue, the rain pounded the roof and the branches outside in a deafening rush. Eva had to yell to be heard. "Leave us alone, Billy. Your little plan worked. We're at war. Let it go."

Billy waved the gun at Clark. "Get up, Spencer. We're going."

At least outside, they could break off and run, but Billy was a crack shot, and he was certain to hit at least one of them. Her mind went off in a hundred and one directions trying to think of anything she could say to sway him.

"What would your dad think if he could see you now?" she asked.

"Shut up. Move."

Clark stood.

Eva stood. "Where are we going?"

Billy backed into the downpour and let the screen slam shut behind him. "Somewhere with a view."

She stole a look at Clark, who seemed to want to go for his

backpack but thought better of it. Billy meant business. You could tell by his cool demeanor.

"We have to bring the dog," Eva said.

"Enough with the dog. It stays or I shoot it, your choice."

Eva kissed Brandy on the top of the head, told her to stay and followed Clark out the door.

Billy pointed toward the valley wall, where a thin path switchbacked up. "Follow that trail and keep your hands where I can see them."

Clark paused so Eva could go first, but Billy wouldn't have it.

"Nope, she goes between us," he said.

By the time they reached the base of the cliff, they were soaked. Neither she nor Clark were wearing shoes, and mud squished between her toes and rocks tore at her flesh. As they climbed higher and higher, Eva got the notion of what Billy's plan was.

Clark must have, too. "Think about what you're doing, man. If we disappear, people are going to start nosing around."

"As far as anyone knows, you died from your injuries at Pearl Harbor, and Evelyn only has a half-dead sister, so no one's going to notice her gone," Billy shouted from the rear.

His words caused a boil in her blood. "Ruby is not half-dead, and why don't you just get it over with, then? Be a man."

Oh Lord, what was she doing? *Keep your mouth shut, Evelyn!*

"Easier if you do it yourselves," Billy muttered.

Had they been anywhere other than on a switchback trail with a steep drop on one side and a rock face on the other, they might have had a chance to escape, to bolt off into the trees. It would have been worth the risk.

At a bend, Clark stopped and bent over to catch his breath. Beads of rain covered his entire body like tiny crystals.

"Keep on going," Billy said.

"Heavens, let him rest for a second, will you?"

When Clark glanced back, his face was pale. His breath came in short bursts. They'd be lucky if he even made it to the top, which was now hidden in clouds.

Eva turned to say something to Billy, but he shouted, "Keep your eyes ahead, I don't want to see your traitor face."

They trudged on until the ground leveled out. Rain stopped falling. The silence of clouds surrounded them in a milky, eerie whiteout. Ahead, trees emerged one at a time from the mist. Now would be as good a time as any to run, but she couldn't leave Clark behind. He muttered something, not quite loud enough for her to hear, but it sounded like Japanese. Again, he spoke, this time a little louder. *"Gomen, Utsukushīi kimi ni boku no kimochi wo tsutaeru koto ga dekinakatta."*

All she understood was "beautiful."

"Quiet up there, Jap lover." Billy prodded them forward a bit farther, then stopped them. "Here's good."

Out of breath herself, Eva felt her heart spin out at two hundred beats per minute. Now was their only chance.

Clouds lifted.

A sheer drop twenty feet to the left.

The gun in her pocket.

"Billy, please," she said.

"It's not my fault that you two wandered off the trail in the fog. Happens all the time. Go on," he said, nodding toward the edge.

The whole way up, Eva had been asking herself if she could shoot Billy when the time came. The best answer she could come up with was *maybe*.

"You want to live with this on your conscience?" she said.

"Sometimes we do what we have to."

She glanced over at Clark, who stood poised to do something foolish. If he even so much as leaned toward Billy, he'd be shot. That much was clear. Eva turned so she was sideways to Billy, one hand slipping into her pocket, unlocking the safety. He stood about ten feet behind them, wide-eyed and fidgety.

"Let's talk this out. There's got to be another way," she said.

He waved the gun around carelessly. "Give it up, there's nothing you can say. Now get to the edge."

"How about this, Billy?" She paused for a moment to catch her breath, which was hitched and shallow. "Clark is a far better kisser than you."

His face flashed red. "What the——"

At the same moment, Clark made his move and lunged, torpedoing his body at Billy's lower legs. Eva watched in horror. The distance between them was simply too great, especially in Clark's weakened state. Billy stepped back and raised his arm to shoot.

In one motion, Eva whipped out her gun and fired, gripping it tight with both hands. A split second after her shot, another one rang out. Her focus was locked onto the barrel, and she swore she saw the bullet leave it, spin through the air and collide with Billy's shoulder. He staggered back, unsure of what had just hit him. Pain twisted his features. His gun fell and then he did, but when she turned her attention to Clark, he was also lying facedown in the dirt.

"Clark!" she cried. Another injury would do him in for sure. "Are you hit?"

No sign of any holes. He rolled onto his side and pushed himself up, eyes on Billy. "Missed me by an inch. Looks like you're the better shot."

Billy groaned as blood seeped out beneath him. "Evelyn, why?" he gasped.

A numbness washed over her, as though she was watching this on a movie screen. Someone else had done this, not her, yet there Billy lay crumpled on his side, turning white before her eyes. Her stomach went sour and she fought back the urge to vomit.

"This was your doing," she said softly.

Clark slid over and picked up Billy's gun. "Irving, this never had to happen."

Eva was afraid to get any closer, and yet she felt a responsibility to save him. That was her job—nurses saved people. "What do we do?" she asked Clark.

"Judging from the amount of blood, you hit him in the heart or an artery. Not much we can do."

Eva knelt next to Billy with one hand on his back and one on his chest. He was hot and trembling and wheezing. Clark was right, he was beyond help. Eva sat with him. She prayed for him. And in the end she cried for him, big heaving sobs. She had to steady herself on a spindly tree. Her lungs seemed void of air, and no matter how hard she tried, she couldn't suck in a breath. The bullet meant for Clark must have somehow hit her and she hadn't even realized it.

"Am I shot?" she suddenly asked.

Clark came over and wrapped her in his arms, kissing the top of her head. "Sweetheart, you're in shock."

The clouds returned and they stood that way for a long time, clinging to each other and blind with tears. It might have been a minute, or an hour, she wasn't counting.

A LONG WAY DOWN

That she had killed a man—Billy, no less—played in her mind like a silent film on repeat. She tried to block it out, but with no success. On the walk down to the bunker, Clark had pointed out the obvious, that it was either Billy or them, but she still felt like a cold-blooded killer. All those women back home had been right, after all.

Murderer.

They had no idea who or what would be waiting for them when they got back to Pearl Harbor. Eva insisted on driving, and forced Clark to lie down in the reclined passenger seat, to which he reluctantly agreed. Brandy must have sensed something had happened, and refused to get in the backseat, so they let her curl up on the floor beneath his legs.

Eva's teeth chattered the whole way back. Here she was, on the run again. She could scarcely think straight, but they managed to agree that they should tell Ford the full story and go from there. It was time to let someone else in on what they knew, and what that had resulted in. Not everyone could be involved in the cover-up, and Clark trusted Ford with his life.

Clark dropped off Eva at his house and left to track down Ford. She passed the hours languishing in his bed like a dying fish, flipping and flopping and sobbing in between fits of sleep. Her mind was spent, and yet it refused to rest. Everything in the room was an ugly shade of reddish purple, like blood, that even after several showers, she still couldn't wash away.

There was also the matter of Billy's associates. Every slamming door or creak in the hallway sent her nerves scattering. If she had been jumpy after Pearl Harbor, now she was a shaky, jittery mess. For all she knew, they might be storming in at any moment to haul her away for murder and lock up Clark for working for the Japanese.

This new nightmare, the one that would follow her to her last breath, was deep enough to drown in. Facing Dr. Newcastle would be nothing compared to this. So what if he knew who she was? Time to come clean on the small stuff. She would find a way to pay for Ruby, as long as they didn't arrest her and have her court-martialed.

When Clark returned late in the night, he looked gray in the face and ready to drop. He lay on the bed next to Eva and pulled her in, kissing her as though she were a tragic, broken thing.

"How did it go?" she asked.

"As good as could be expected. A lot of unanswered questions. The radio signals were news to him. Which means, when I dropped that report to Irving, who knows what he did with it after that. I don't know if we're dealing with a small group of conspirators, or a whole secret branch of intelligence that I'm not privy to."

"Billy would have wanted to be in control. A piece of information like this he would have kept close," she said.

Clark coiled her hair around his finger. "I should have told Ford right away."

"You thought you were doing the right thing."

"Irving demanded that I not tell a soul. I should have seen that he was manipulating me."

His head rested in his hands and he stared up at the ceiling. Eva felt the guilt, too, haunting her. To have known and not done anything about it. This was the bitter truth they would have to live with.

"There was no way you could have guessed how he was going to handle that report," she said.

"The intoxication of power," Clark said.

"Billy was always driven, but somehow I missed the faulty wiring that led him to this point," Eva said.

"He took a wrong turn, maybe starting off thinking he was doing something important for his country. That's where people get dangerous. When they begin to believe the end justifies the means," he said.

Eva sighed. "What next?"

"Ford said he would handle the situation with Billy. But I'm sure they'll want to talk to us. Until then, we wait, and we do our darnedest to right the wrongs that have been done here. You have patients to heal, and I still have codes to break."

"Will they believe us? That's what I'm worried about."

"I guess we'll find out. There are already rumblings and fingers being pointed. Army blaming navy, navy blaming army, that kind of thing. It seems like the powers that be have bigger things to worry about right now. Ford is going to talk to Wilson and find out if he wrote a backup report," Clark said.

"What'll that do?"

"It's a crucial piece of history," he said.

Eva sat up so she could see his face. "From what Billy said, it sounds like this whole cover-up went far beyond those radio signals. Washington knew this was coming long before we crossed the Pacific."

"But the public should know."

People did have a right to know, and yet if those men who worked for Billy got a whiff that she was making trouble, they might make good on their threats.

"Wait until things settle. The damage has been done," Eva said.

He frowned. She thought he was going to argue, but instead he pulled her down and buried his face in her hair. The warmth of his body against hers, his spicy smell and all that love seeping into her gave her a warm feeling in the center of her chest. They had survived another day. They were together. They were breathing. This was what mattered above all.

But those boys at Pearl Harbor would never get this chance. *Death is never fair. Life is never fair.*

"We'll lie low for now and let Ford take over, but I won't forget," he said.

"Never."

A hollow knocking woke Eva, who saw that Clark was already slipping into a robe and shuffling toward the door. In the predawn hours, the room was still dim. For a split second she debated climbing out the back window, but that was not the answer. They both had slept fitfully and Clark had broken out in several cold sweats, but was adamant about not returning to Tripler. Eva had made sure to clean his wounds well.

A man's voice cut through the thick morning air followed by the heavy clunk of boots on the wooden floor. Ford had said he would handle it, and Eva had been attempting to delude herself that with his senior position he might somehow be able to pull some strings and sweep the whole thing under the rug. It was wishful thinking, she knew.

She had killed a man.

"Is Miss Cassidy here with you? We need to speak with her," the voice said.

Clark answered, "Have a seat, I'll go get her."

When he opened the door to the room, she was already sitting up and pulling on her dress.

She was terrified on so many levels and yet ready to come clean.

One look in her direction and his pinched face broke into a small smile. "You look pretty harmless to me, but they need to speak to you. Just tell them what happened," he said quietly.

She just hoped these men weren't in cahoots with Billy's thugs and once they got her out of the house, they would drag her out to the cane fields. Eva splashed some cool water on her face, smoothed back her hair and walked into the kitchen. She was beyond caring whether she looked presentable or not.

Two men in uniform stood by the door. Navy from the looks of it. "Miss Cassidy?" the smaller of the two said.

"That's me," she said, relieved to the bone that he had not said *Olson*.

"As you can probably guess, we need you to come with us for questioning in the death of Lieutenant William Irving," he said.

The other one stood as straight as a beanpole and just as expressionless. Clark handed her a banana. "Can you bring her back here when you're finished?" he asked the men.

"Depends on what transpires," the speaker said.

Eva felt her knees go weak. Clark gave her a look that said, *You can do this*, and saw them all to the door. If only she had the same kind of confidence as he did. On the way to wherever they were taking her, she sank back into the cracked leather seat and looked out the window. Coconut trees next to blown-up buildings, shredded jeeps and the smoking ruins of battleships sitting across the glassy waters.

She thought about Billy and that first day down by the stream, each trying to shoot a smaller target, at a farther distance, and

impress their respective fathers. He had turned on the charm
full force and she had fallen for it. But had she really ever loved
him? Or known him, for that matter? She had loved the *idea*
of him to be sure, but looking back, she came to understand
that the Billy she knew had been a flimsy impostor of a much
darker man. She forced herself to put him out of her mind, instead watching a pair of black, kite-shaped seabirds hovering
over the shore.

After ten minutes of driving, Eva finally asked, "Where
are we going?"

Neither man answered.

"Excuse me, but don't I have a right to know?" she said.

"Patience, ma'am."

When they pulled up to a gray concrete building on the far
side of Pearl Harbor with no signs out front, Eva grew jumpy.
Her heart was racing and skipping and threatening to give out.
They ushered her down a long hallway with gray doors on
both sides, and into a room with a table, chairs and a mirror.

The beanpole man offered her coffee, which she gladly
accepted, and the three of them had a seat on hard wooden
chairs.

"My apologies for not introducing ourselves earlier. I'm
Sergeant Perry. Captain Billings and I were briefed by Ford
about what went down yesterday with Irving, and we need
to take your statement."

Captain Billings lit a cigarette with a bandaged hand. He
had the look of a bad boy who had turned over a new leaf,
with a blotchy tattoo peeking out from his shirtsleeve and a
disinterested look on his face.

"Fine," Eva said, shivering even though the air in the room
was stale and warm.

"Why don't you just start from the beginning? Tell us who
Irving was to you, and what led up to the events yesterday."

It felt like an inquisition and reminded her of being questioned about Tommy Lemon. Only this time she was guilty and everyone knew it. Clark had instructed her repeatedly to stick to the facts. *The less you say the better.* Still, the whole story poured out of her, and with each word that came, she felt lighter.

We had a long-distance love affair. He proposed, but I wasn't ready. He knew I had met Clark on the Lurline. *He followed us and tried to kill us.*

"Why were you two in Waimea Valley, Miss Cassidy?" Perry asked.

She felt herself tense.

"Clark had told me that in case the Japanese invaded Oahu, it would be a good place for us nurses to hide out. He was showing me where to go," she said as naturally as her voice would allow.

Billings ashed his cigarette and took a sip of coffee. "Isn't Lieutenant Spencer badly wounded?"

"He is, but he was worried about us, especially after seeing firsthand what the Japanese are capable of. He took the risk." Her voice sounded small and unconvincing.

The two men exchanged glances, and then Perry said, "Slow down and tell us what led to you shooting Lieutenant Irving."

Eva went over how he forced them up the foggy trail with the gun pointed at their backs, and what happened at the edge of the cliff. "He lifted his gun to shoot Clark, but I'm a better shot. He left me no choice."

"You got anyone that can corroborate that?" Perry asked.

Sure, back in Michigan, where everyone knows me as Evelyn Olson. "Of course."

"We can collect names and numbers later."

"Certainly," she said with a forced smile.

"And it was Irving's gun that he had given you at the hospital, correct?" Billings said.

She nodded. "Correct."

"Why did he give you a gun?"

"Again, in case the Japanese came ashore."

"So you had two men looking out for you. Sounds like it could have been complicated…" Billings said, letting his voice trail off.

Perry leaned back and folded his arms. "Yes, sirree."

She didn't bite. "I told you everything."

The two men continued at her from various angles, but since her story was true for the most part, they didn't seem to be able to find any holes in it. After an hour or so of questioning, they loaded her back up in the car and delivered her to Clark's doorstep. They told her they would be in touch if they had any more questions. And not to leave the island.

As if leaving were possible.

Eva watched them drive away and for the first time in days, had a feeling of reluctant hope. Life was moving forward, one way or another.

Clark had left a note saying he was at the Dungeon, which was foolish of him in his state. It was still early, and Eva cleaned up and went straight to the hospital on the off chance that she would find Dr. Newcastle in his office. Beams of morning sun painted the hospital walls honey colored and gave the place a warm and almost cozy feel.

So many souls lost here, but so many souls saved, too. Men with grit. Men with heart. No matter what happened with Newcastle, this place and its people would live on tucked inside her until her dying days. But she also came to realize how desperately she wanted to stay and finish what she'd started. It was as essential as air.

Eva was *meant* to be here.

The hallways were silent but for the click of her heels. Dr. Newcastle's office was in the back of the first floor; his door was closed. She sucked in a deep breath. Knocked. Half of her wanted him to answer, the other hoped he was out doing rounds. A moment later the door swung open and they stood face-to-face. As usual, he looked fresh and rested. Did the man ever sleep?

"I take it you've come to have that talk," he said.

"I have."

He stepped back and ushered her in, pointing not at the bent metal chair in front of his desk, but toward a cracked leather love seat. Eva sat, worried her voice would fail her, and chewed her lip while considering where to begin. Several old photographs lined the walls, along with diplomas and certificates. She scanned them, and her gaze skidded on one that nailed her to the couch.

Dr. Newcastle started in. "From the first time I saw you, I thought you looked familiar, but I couldn't quite pinpoint where I'd seen you…" He let the words fall away and stared at her, waiting.

Eva coughed, cleared her throat and swallowed a big wad of dread. "I see that you completed orthopedic training at Hollowcreek General. You must know Dr. Brown," she said.

Of all the places for him to end up.

He flattened his lips together. "You could say that."

"Look, Dr. Newcastle, I think we both know why I'm here. My real name is not Eva Cassidy, it's Evelyn Olson. I really am a nurse, but I got into a situation at Hollowcreek, which I'm guessing you know about, that left me unhireable, so I changed my name and fudged my papers. Is that what you want to hear?"

Newcastle rose and went for the pot on his desk. "Coffee?"

This was not going as expected.

"Sure. Thank you."

He took his time pouring, adding cubes of sugar and a generous pouring of cream, and stirring. Meanwhile, Eva felt her courage leaking away. She wanted this to be over with, and he seemed to be enjoying dragging it on.

"You lied," he said, handing her the coffee and joining her.

She nodded. "Yes, but I had no choice. Tommy Lemon's death was not my fault. In fact, had the doctor listened to me, he never would have died. Nursing is my life, and Dr. Brown unrightfully took it away from me."

"Tell me your side of the story," Dr. Newcastle said.

Eva told him. Every word, every drop of medicine, every last vital sign. When she finished, he glanced up at the wall, eyes resting on the certificates.

"Dr. Brown was my teacher. He knew his stuff, but he had a flaw," he said.

Eva was beyond caring about propriety. "I'll say."

"To lose sight of the fact that you're capable of error is fatal in a doctor, and he never had that sight in the first place," Newcastle said.

"He's not the only one," Eva argued, not wanting to point out that Newcastle had leanings toward being that way, too.

His knee bumped up against hers and she wasn't sure if it was by accident or on purpose. "Doctors are a tough breed, but we aren't all the same. I think of Brown when I want to remind myself how *not* to be."

Had she heard correctly? "Excuse me?"

"He used to have a saying that he used residents to wipe his ass. What kind of man says that?"

"An arrogant one."

Hope twitched in her chest.

Dr. Newcastle continued, "When I read the story about

Tommy Lemon's death in the paper, I knew Brown was to blame. No doubt in my mind."

The sweetest words she could have ever heard, but too late to change anything.

"That lie ruined my life," she said.

"You can see it like that. Or you can believe that it brought you here to Pearl Harbor, to Tripler, where you've saved a hell of a lot more lives than you would've back home in Michigan."

Her father would have said the same thing. *Life is full of reasons, most which will only reveal themselves miles down the road.*

"So I'm not fired?" she dared to ask.

"Far from it, Miss Olson."

ARMY, NAVY CHIEFS OUSTED OVER PEARL HARBOR UNPREPAREDNESS!

—*Headline of the* Los Angeles Examiner, War Extra, *December 18, 1941.*

SISTER LOVE

December 25, 1941

Dearest Eva,

Merry Christmas! Though I know it is far from merry and I am
worried sick about you, I'm trying to keep a positive mind about
things. Every last inch of ground is covered in powdery snow, and
it truly is a winter wonderland, but I miss you and I miss Dad.
Being in the hospital is no place to be for the holidays, as you
know, but the staff has done their best at adding trees and lights
and cheer to the place. Say, do I ever have news for you. Are you
sitting down? I hope so, because I'm not—I'm standing! It's true, my
legs are growing stronger and I'm able to stand for periods of time.
I'm working on lifting my legs and my feet, and I've been following
your words of wisdom. All this movement is helping me so much
that the doctors and nurses are stunned. Walking is next. I can feel
it. It's not easy, but I've stuck with it, mainly so I can get out of the
cold and come visit you. They say that warmth would be good for
me and even though there's a war going on, I'd rather be with you
in the middle of a war zone than without you altogether.

But here's some other big news. It turns out my new nurse,
Samantha, was in the room with you that fateful day—she'd gone in
to get sheets. Not only that, but we've become close and she confided

in me that Dr. Brown almost left a pair of forceps in a patient, until she convinced him to open the man back up. Sure enough, they were lodged against the man's innards. Can you believe that? Brown told her she'd be fired if she told anyone. I've convinced her to go to the board and tell, along with a few other nurses. She's also agreed to come forward on Tommy Lemon. You heard me right. I will keep you posted on what transpires, but I have a good feeling.

Anyway, these are the two most wonderful Christmas gifts a girl could ask for. As far as I'm concerned, Santa Claus can fly right on past. I keep one ear glued to the radio and pray that you will be kept safe and sound. Stay out of trouble.

Love from home,
Ruby

A FEW GOOD MEN

May 1942

While Clark walked down to the Dungeon, he counted his blessings with each step. In hindsight, he found it ludicrous to imagine himself ever questioning whether to pursue Eva or not. Love didn't give a damn about wars or lost wives and cracked hearts. Love was more an unruly guest that showed up knocking when you least expected it. The big test was always whether or not to open the door and invite it in.

Clark thought back to that first night on the *Lurline*, when dinner had ended and Eva left the table and slipped out the door. The feeling that someone had wrapped a leash around his neck and was yanking him after her was inexplicable, and yet he had followed along blindly. He had excused himself just in time to see her slip into the bar. Outside the bar, he had stood for a full five minutes debating whether to go in after her. In fact, he had turned to leave, but literally could not walk away. Now he knew why.

Eva was the answer to a question he didn't even known he was asking.

When the heavy metal door clicked behind him, he moved across the smoky room to Ford's desk. The Dungeon had been a hotbed of all-nighters and frenetic activity for months now, but ever since mid–May, the pace had doubled. JN–25, the Japanese code, was all but cracked, and the Imperial Japanese Navy was gearing up for another big offensive. A lucky intercept sent to a Japanese supply ship, the *Goshū Maru*, had revealed the location. The ship was to "load its base equipment and ground crews and advance to Affirm Fox ground crews. Parts and munitions will be loaded on the *Goshū Maru*…everything in the way of base equipment and military supplies which will be needed in the K campaign will be included."

Clark and the boys had been tearing their hair out trying to convince Washington that Midway Atoll was the target. They knew that the *A* in AF stood for *American*, in fact Station HYPO had confirmed more than fifty sites—AH being Hawaii, for example—and back in March had made the connection that AF meant Midway. But some of the people at OP-20-G were unconvinced, even going so far as to say it was a trap. Such men of little faith, Clark hated that they held so much power over HYPO.

It was the morning of the nineteenth and Ford had asked Clark and a few other analysts in their tight inner circle to come in for a "golf" meeting, which meant *important*. In his customary orange smoking jacket, Ford pulled up a chair and said, "It's come down to this, fellas, Admiral Nimitz says he can't stake the entire Pacific Fleet on radio intelligence. No more guessing, we need to prove without a doubt that AF is Midway. So if any of you have an idea, I'm all ears."

"It's already plain as day," said Hammersmith.

Ford shrugged. "They need it plainer."

Clark glanced over at Huckleberry, who leaned against a tower of crushed file boxes and stared at a crack on the wall. In times like these, with all his years of experience, Huckleberry had a tendency to draw brilliant ideas from the atmosphere. He might need a little extra time to think, but then *bam*, problem solved.

"We need to bait them," Clark said, though how, he had no idea.

"What do we bait them with?" asked Hammersmith.

Ford said, "Any of you ever been to Midway?"

Heads shook. No one had.

A light went on in Huckleberry. "I haven't been there, but when I was at the university, we had to engineer a project using salt water and coral on Midway..." His voice trailed off.

"And?" Ford said.

Everyone perched on the edge of their seats, waiting for the answer they knew was brewing. You could have heard a knife slice through the air.

Huckleberry got up and began pacing, then said, "Fresh water is a premium, so if we have the folks at Midway radio us something about a failure in the water filtration system, the Japs will be on it like flies. Wake will pick it up and relay it to Tokyo."

As simple as that, they had a plan.

Twenty-six hours later, Clark was consulting Ford on his latest translations when Hal Dunn stormed over. As of late, his beard looked like it could house a few sparrows, but when you were one of the top navy cryptos, you got away with being a nonconformist. It went with the territory.

"Dangnabbit, those idiots on Midway, what are they thinking?" Hal fumed, whipping down a yellow notepad covered in chicken scratch.

"What happened?" Ford asked, raising an eyebrow to Clark.

Hal stabbed the paper with his ink-stained finger. "This

message was sent in plain language! The bastards didn't even encrypt it."

"You know none of us can read your writing. What does it say?" Ford said.

Hal's face was purple. "It says, 'At present time we have only enough water for two weeks. A mishap at the water distillation has left us critically short. Please supply immediately.' Of course, Wake immediately passed it on to Tokyo."

Clark realized that no one had mentioned their plan to Hal, who had been off yesterday. Ford pulled out a chair. "Sit down."

"Whoever sent this should be court-martialed," Hal said.

By now, everyone in the room had an ear in their direction.

Ford lowered his voice. "We set this up, buddy. It's a trap. Tell me word for word the transmission from Wake to Tokyo."

Hal looked as though he'd been slapped in the face. "Jesus, why didn't you tell me?"

"You weren't here."

"It would have been nice to know," Hal huffed.

"You know now."

From his notepad, Hal read. "Wake says, 'There appears to be an emergency at AF and that the water distillation broke down. AF asking Pearl to send water quickly.'"

AF. Midway. Indisputable.

Ford high-fived Clark. "Nice going, Lieutenant, you may have just won us the war."

Clark felt a swell of pride. "It was mostly Huckleberry."

"You planted the seed," Ford said, slapping him hard on the back, enough to knock the wind out of him.

"Genius," Hal said.

It was a moment he would never forget. All those damp, smoky hours poring over translations. Countless spotty nights'

sleep. And the nagging sensation that Pearl Harbor had somehow been his fault. All worth it. They might not have been
able to stop the Imperial Japanese Navy at Pearl Harbor, but
they damn well would now.

TALKING STORY

May 20, 1942

Eva arrived early to the auditorium. The whole island was now in bloom and fragrant trees lined the courtyard. Sunny plumeria, pink and red hibiscus, and vines of passionflower creeping along fences and attracting half the honeybees in the Western Hemisphere. War was still a sore reality, though the edges had softened some around here. The army and navy had come back swinging and now were hell-bent on throwing every ounce of force at the Imperial Japanese Navy. Still, fear lurked in everyone's minds.

It felt surreal to walk into the same lecture hall where she'd heard the first bombs fall five months ago and men had run in wide-eyed and hollering that Pearl Harbor was under attack. Just the thought caused a hitch in her heart and almost brought her to her knees. The drone of engines and taste of smoke in the back of her throat would always be there. Today, the building seemed even larger than it had back then, with enough room for an army. And indeed, the seats were filling up quickly. Sweat formed on the back of her neck. How had she let him talk her into this?

Eva sat in the front row, fidgeting with her hair and reviewing her notes. Public speaking never had been a strength, but now she would be addressing a room full of doctors. She'd be lucky if she didn't faint. The army had asked Newcastle, and Newcastle had all but forced her into accepting to speak on the dangers of general anesthesia in patients with severe shock.

I have faith in you, he had said.

In the months since Eva came clean with her secret, the two of them had become something resembling a team. Looking back, the other nurses had made him out to be worse than he was. Oh, he had his share of offenses, but the difference between him and Brown was an open mind and a willingness to change. If a nurse knew more than Newcastle, it might pain him to admit it, but given enough proof, he could be swayed. He was willing to listen, an ingredient entirely missing from Brown. In those first days after the attack, Eva had proven to him that in the area of anesthesia, she had a leg up on him. Not from any lack of training on his part, but from different experiences. And what are humans, but a culmination of their own experiences?

The doors closed and the lights went on. Brandy lay at Eva's feet looking very official in her newly sewn vest with a red cross stitched across the back. It had taken a petition organized by Grace, but they won Dr. Newcastle over in the end. Every man in the hospital had signed it, some with lipstick, some with blood. Eva reached down and scratched behind Brandy's ears. Doctors from around the islands, as well as army and navy surgeons on their way to the Pacific Theater, crammed together for the lecture.

Dr. Newcastle stood up and began his introduction. "Gentlemen, thank you for coming on this beautiful Hawaiian morning. Let me start with saying that it was Hippocrates who wrote, 'He who would become a surgeon should join an army and follow it.' For all the chaos and atrocities it brings, war has the potential to advance medicine at an accelerated pace.

In peacetime, none of you would ever see the same number of patients in a lifetime as you saw in a week during wartime. In those first few hours after the attack, we took in close to four hundred wounded at Tripler, and the naval hospital saw even more. A crash course in trauma medicine if there ever was one." That elicited a few chuckles in the audience, though none of this was a laughing matter. "Among the madness, one nurse stood out in particular. Not afraid to challenge me when needed, this woman turned out to be one of our greatest assets both in the operating room and at the bedside of the wounded. We are fortunate to have Miss Evelyn Olson sharing her expertise today on anesthesia and shock. Please give a round of applause."

One clap, then another, then a couple more. That was it. Winning over this crowd would be a rough go. But her job was not to win them over, it was to give them critical information to take with them into the jungles and beaches and field hospitals of faraway lands. Just then, the door at the back of the auditorium opened and a tall man dressed in uniform walked in and sat in the last row. His familiar, handsome face gave her the boost of courage that she needed. The butterflies settled a notch.

You can do this.

Eva stood at the podium feeling very small. She exhaled and said, "Let me tell you a short story before I begin. I learned the hard way about the lethal combination of sodium thiopental and severe shock, and I'm hoping that by sharing my story, it will prevent needless deaths on and off the battlefield…"

Murmurs rippled through the audience—some probably having heard of the scandal—when she got to the part of Dr. Brown being asked to leave Hollowcreek General. Two months after Ruby's Christmas letter, Eva had received another letter, this one a full apology from Jed Lemon. Nothing could have been sweeter than having her reputation restored and the knowledge that justice had won out in the end.

"Due to its depressant effects, sodium thiopental should never be used in patients with chest wounds or in a hypo-volemic state…"

As Eva continued, her voice steadied and she made it a point to make eye contact with her audience and pause long enough for her words to sink in. A man in the front row with bushy eyebrows and suspenders, the two Japanese doctors in the second row, a serious-faced navy man toward the back. They were all rapt. She might be a nurse, she might be a woman, but Lord did she know her facts. And no one could argue with science and firsthand knowledge.

When her speech finally came to an end, Dr. Newcastle and Clark both stood and clapped. Ten seconds later, the whole room was standing and the sound of applause hummed through Eva. Pride tore at her seams. If only her father could be here to see this. Or Ruby. But she had a feeling there would be more days like this, more opportunities to share what she knew and to save future lives.

It was just the beginning.

They held hands the whole drive out. By some fluke, Clark had managed to get the rest of the afternoon away from the Dungeon, and he seemed both giddy and preoccupied. Every so often Eva would catch him sneaking a glance at her. The rest of the time he was staring off into space with a smile on his face. Goodness, how she loved him.

Looking back, life had thrown her a whole wheelbarrowful of coconuts, and she had come out the other side a changed woman, not unscathed, but a stronger, better version of her previous self. Love, war and sticking to your truth would do that to a person.

The blossoms on every corner made the air heavy with fragrance. Eva admired the green-soaked mountains, the pineapple fields and the lightly rippling sugarcane as they traversed Oahu. In the backseat, Brandy hung half her body out the window. It always worried Eva, but Brandy seemed sure-footed as a goat. On the radio, Bing Crosby belted out "Hawaii Calls," and Clark sang along.

"Something's gotten into you," she said finally.

He squeezed her hand. "Today's a good day, what can I say?"

She sensed it was more than that, but kept quiet, enjoying the rest of the drive with idle small talk. Instead of turning right at Haleiwa, they went left, toward a beach with an unpronounceable name. "Moh-koo-lay-ee-ah," Clark repeated a few times slowly.

"I don't have the knack for languages that you do," Eva said.

"Come on, humor me."

Ten minutes down the road, across from Dillingham Airfield, they turned off onto a dirt lane hidden by towering ironwood trees. Had she blinked, Eva would have missed it. A heavy chain blocked the way.

"Hang on," Clark said, hopping out.

Thirty seconds later, he had the lock off and they bounced their way to a powdery beach that stretched down the coast like a white ribbon. There was no sign of life in either direction, only thick coils of barbed wire.

"I get the feeling we aren't supposed to be here," she said.

He winked. "We're on official business." From the back of the jeep, he pulled out a cardboard box and an army blanket. "Pretend this is a picnic basket and a red-and-white-checkered sheet, okay?" he said.

For the time being, Eva would pretend whatever he wanted. The war could go to hell for all she cared.

As soon as he spread it out, Brandy trampled sand all over the whole thing, then took off for the water.

"Aye, aye, Lieutenant."

On the blanket, he popped open two Coca-Colas and handed her one. "When I make a promise to show a lady around, I mean it. I apologize for not bringing you out here sooner."

Eva laughed. "As if you don't have a good excuse."

Clark held up his Coca-Cola. "Cheers, my *utsukushīin*. To a beautiful future without war and hate and shrapnel."

The metal hunk was still lodged near his heart, but Dr. Jensen, a top-notch cardiologist, would be arriving in Honolulu in two weeks' time and had agreed to assist Dr. Newcastle in removing it. Eva would rest better once that was handled.

Their bottles clinked. This stolen moment, she would take.

"Something happened in the Dungeon today, didn't it?" Eva said.

He smiled. "I can't talk about it."

His dimpled smile was enough of an answer as he leaned in to kiss her. Eva had all the faith in the world that this time around, the Americans would come out ahead. No one had more heart than these boys. She'd seen it firsthand. The way they carried each other into the hospital, bleeding and damaged, shell-shocked. How some of them never stopped asking after their buddies only seconds away from taking their last breath. *So much love.* She would put money on them, stake her life on it and then some.

★ ★ ★ ★ ★

Author's Note

While this book is a work of fiction, the passages in between the chapters are real communications, messages, advertisements, headlines and memos, or are written based on real events. Everyone knows about Pearl Harbor, but what I found intriguing as I delved deeper into my research was how many disparate pieces of information, intelligence, personal accounts and stories are relatively unknown to the general public. Pearl Harbor might have seemed like a surprise attack, but was it? There are numerous opinions on the matter, none of which are definitive.

One tidbit of information that I found particularly interesting and ended up basing part of the book upon was the story of Leslie Grogan, second radio officer aboard the Matson Steamship and Navigation Company's SS *Lurline*, and how over several nights he picked up a series of "repeat-back" radio signals from Tokyo that led him to believe a fleet of ships was headed northwest of Honolulu. I began to wonder what happened to his report after it was handed in to a lieutenant commander of the Fourteenth Naval District, as well as what was in the ship's logs, which were confiscated by a USN boarding party upon arrival of the *Lurline* back in San Francisco. Grogan had written his own "Record for Posterity," which later went missing from the naval archives in San Bruno. This made me curious and became the jumping-off point for my story, and a case of what-if concocted purely by my own imagination.

Other real-life players that inspired characters in my book include Dr. John Moorhead, an emergency medicine surgeon from New York who traveled to Hawaii to give a series of lectures at Queen's Hospital on traumatic injury. His lecture on the morning of December 7 was interrupted by the bombing of Pearl Harbor, and Dr. Moorhead and fellow doctors ended up rushing to Tripler to take part in the massive job of tending the wounded. Commander Joe Rochefort, who is best known for his cryptanalysis and intelligence work at Station HYPO that enabled the victory at Midway, also played a less known but equally important role at Pearl Harbor. And my grandmother Helen Iverson Larsgaard, who was not a nurse, but sailed to Hawaii aboard the *Lurline* to meet my grandfather Herman, whom she hardly knew at the time. On the journey, she fell for a navy officer, but to her dismay my grandfather was waiting on the dock and dropped down on his knee and proposed to her as soon as she disembarked. My grandmother said yes, but she never forgot about that officer and talked about him throughout the years, and I've often wished I knew his name and could go back in time and find out more.

As one does in a work of fiction, I have taken liberties with historical record to suit the story. I owe much to the following works for offering up so much information. I could not have written this story without them and encourage anyone who would like a better understanding of Pearl Harbor to read them:

Borch, Fred, and Daniel Martinez. *Kimmel, Short, and Pearl Harbor: The Final Report Revealed*. Annapolis: Naval Institute Press, 2004.

Carlson, Elliot. *Joe Rochefort's War: The Odyssey of the Codebreaker Who Outwitted Yamamoto at Midway.* Reprint edition. Annapolis: Naval Institute Press, 2011.

Fessler, Diane Burke. *No Time for Fear.* East Lansing: Michigan State University Press, 1996.

Helling, Thomas. *Desperate Surgery in the Pacific War: Doctors and Damage Control for American Wounded, 1941–1945.* Jefferson: McFarland, 2017.

Krantz, Lynn Blocker, Nick Krantz, and Thiele Fobian. *To Honolulu in Five Days: Cruising Aboard Matson's SS* Lurline. Berkley: Ten Speed Press, 2001.

Nelson, Craig. *Pearl Harbor: From Infamy to Greatness.* New York: Scribner, 2016.

Villa, Brian, and Timothy Wilford, "Warning at Pearl Harbor: Leslie Grogan and the Tracking of the *Kido Butai*," *Northern Mariner*, Volume XI. Ottawa: The Canadian Nautical Research Society, 2001.

Acknowledgments

I am forever grateful to the following people for helping to bring *The Lieutenant's Nurse* to life. Elaine Spencer, my wonderful agent, editor and champion. Without Elaine, none of this would be possible. Margot Mallinson, my editor, who has an incredible knack for zeroing in on brilliant solutions and is always there to answer my thousands of questions. She does such an amazing job of steering the whole ship. Also, to Meredith Barnes, Mary Sheldon and all the wonderful people at MIRA who believe in my books. As always, to my mother, Diane McFaull, and my second mother, Marilyn Carlsmith, who help shine a light on what it was like to be kids in Hawaii during the war as well as always being there for me. And last but not least, for my boyfriend, Todd Clark, the best man in the world.

Love and aloha to you all,
Sara

THE
LIEUTENANT'S
NURSE

SARA ACKERMAN

Reader's Guide

1. If you had the chance to sail off to Hawaii in 1941, do you think you would have gone? What part of the voyage appeals to you most?

2. Do you think Eva made the right choice to leave Michigan? Was concealing what happened at the hospital justified?

3. Do you think it was right to keep Brandy at Tripler Hospital to keep up the morale of the wounded? Do you believe in therapy dogs/pets? Have you had personal experience with one?

4. Eva had to stand up to some powerful men who didn't necessarily respect her or her expertise. Do you think she handled it well? Would you have been able to speak up?

5. How did you feel about Eva's loyalty or disloyalty to Billy? Do you think she acted appropriately? Should she have followed her heart with Clark sooner? Or not at all?

6. Do you have any relatives or know anyone who was at Pearl Harbor during the attack? During the war? If so, what were their experiences?

7. Unless one has been through an event such as this, it's hard to imagine the terror and fear that was experienced. If you put yourself in the shoes of the nurses, how do you think you would have held up?

8. The nurses got each other through the days after the attack. Have you ever been in a situation where you needed to rely on the support of a group of friends or colleagues? What is the effect of shared trauma on a group?

9. What are your thoughts on the advance knowledge theory about Pearl Harbor—that some people knew the Japanese attack was coming beforehand?

10. What did you learn about Pearl Harbor that you didn't already know?